REBELLION

THE LAZARUS ALLIANCE, BOOK 3

BLAZE WARD

KNOTTED ROAD PRESS

Rebellion
The Lazarus Alliance: Book Three
Blaze Ward
Copyright © 2021 Blaze Ward
All rights reserved
Published by Knotted Road Press
www.KnottedRoadPress.com

ISBN: 978-1-64470-199-7

Quotes from *The Prophet*
Original copyright 1923 by Kahlil Gibran
Copyright renewed 1951 by Administrators C.T.A. of Kahlil Gibran Estate
and Mary G. Gibran

Cover art:

ID 114928039 © Luca Oleastri | Dreamstime.com

Cover and interior design copyright © 2021 Knotted Road Press

Reviews
It's true. Reviews help. Even a short one, such as, "Loved it!" So please consider reviewing this book (and all of the ones you've read) on your favorite retailer site.

Never miss a release!
If you'd like to be notified of new releases, sign up for my newsletter.

http://www.blazeward.com/newsletter/

Buy More!
Did you know that you can buy directly from my website?

https://www.blazeward.com/shop/

ALSO BY BLAZE WARD

The Lazarus Alliance

Escape

Return

Rebellion

Revolution

The Jessica Keller Chronicles

Auberon

Queen of the Pirates

Last of the Immortals

Goddess of War

Flight of the Blackbird

The Red Admiral

St. Legier

Winterhome

Petron

CS-405

Queen Anne's Revenge

Packmule

Persephone

Additional Alexandria Station Stories

Siren

Two Bottles of Wine with a War God

The Story Road

The Science Officer Series Season One

The Science Officer

The Mind Field

The Gilded Cage

The Pleasure Dome

The Doomsday Vault

The Last Flagship

The Hammerfield Gambit

The Hammerfield Payoff

The Bryce Connection

The Science Officer Series Season Two

Alien Seas

The Handsome Rob Gigs

Can't Shoot Straight Gang

Can't Shoot Straight Gang Returns

Hunting Handsome Rob

Handsome Rob, Assassin

Shadow of the Dominion

Longshot Hypothesis

Hard Bargain

Outermost

Dominion-427

Phoenix

Princess Rualoh

ONE

LAZARUS

LAZARUS STUDIED the man seated across from him in his office. Well, coiled, actually.

Addison Wolcott was a Churquen, an alien from Innruld Space. Pure snake from the waist down, but more manlike above that. Scales instead of body hair. Spindly arms compared to a Human. Probably as intelligent as Lazarus was, and far cannier.

Today, Addison was dressed as a Commander in the Rio Alliance Navy. Sort of. Thadrakho the Necherle mechanic-turned-occasional-tailor had found a tan uniform jacket similar to the one Lazarus had on, but one that would fit Addison with a few tweaks. The sleeves were gone, as Churquen didn't have shoulders to speak of.

As Captain, Lazarus had approved modifications to add an X-framed bandoleer harness with pockets and pouches, as well as a sash tied around where Addison's hipbones would be if he were a biped.

"I still don't think rank tabs and unit insignia are the wisest course of action, Lazarus," Addison mused aloud into the silence, as though reading Lazarus's mind.

He might be. Addison had been a Director on his own vessel, the Innruld equivalent of a Captain, for a long time, of the cargo runner *Shiva Zephyr Glaive*. The man, the Churquen, understood command.

"On the contrary, my friend," Lazarus stopped his own wool-gathering to focus now on his First Officer, coiled in a compact loop on the other side of the desk. "The authority invested in a Rio Alliance Captain in wartime allows him to impress civilians into service voluntarily, and to promote them as a brevet, pending approval by the authorities back home. They might not let you keep that rank, but they will have to do all sorts of investigations into things before they can overrule me and take it away. At a minimum, everyone is drawing pay and benefits right now."

"What about Xiuying Bălan?" Addison asked. "I haven't pried, but I get the impression that he previously served in the same navy with you?"

"The man was a marine, Addison," Lazarus said, sobering. "That is a term for a combat specialist, rather than a sailor. Based on a few things he has told me, he held a fairly senior enlisted rank with an elite Services team, possibly similar to the ones I did when I was much younger, although I don't remember him."

"Would you?"

"The Services were elite, but they were still huge," Lazarus replied. "I knew the men on my two teams, but there were hundreds of such groups, scattered across Rio Alliance Space. But I'm not worried about him. He's taken well to returning to the tan uniform and is temporarily a Senior Chief, which works. Almost everyone else outranks him as an officer of some sort, except Thadrakho, but neither of them wanted to be officers anyway."

"So you continue to insist on the charade?" Addison harrumphed politely.

"It's that, or we turn fully pirate, Addison," Lazarus said. "I don't know who to trust in the senior ranks of the Navy or the government. Someone has to be a spy. Westphalia knew where to find me, at the one time they could defeat this ship. And knew to bring enough force to do it. That was not accidental."

"And if the Alliance just orders you to surrender the ship and turn over your crew of alien misfits?" Addison's voice grew just as serious.

"They are welcome to try," Lazarus said in a voice that didn't brook any more discussion.

He would not budge on that. Not until he had the truth.

And if he couldn't get satisfaction, he would flee back to Innruld Space where he had found his new friends and start a rebellion over there without any help.

This ship could go for another year or so before it started needing specialized replacement parts and techniques to maintain the experimental systems. Longer if he took the time to start building things from his various onboard stocks, which he intended.

Addison noted the chapter break and sat back on his coil for a moment, poised in thought.

"You have called *Ajax* a Light Starcruiser," Addison shifted directions. "That of course suggests such things as Heavy Starcruisers. Are we at risk from your folks when we get to Brasilia?"

Lazarus smiled. Chuckled even.

"A Heavy Starcruiser has nine Star Lances instead of our three," he replied. "And significant numbers of Star Spears as defensive weapons against small ships. If they get close enough to us, then yes, a Heavy is a viable threat. You can, however, outrun one easily, and Kirov's Lance has almost triple the range of a Star Lance, if you have to shoot someone with it. Stay back and snipe at him from a distance if it comes to that."

"And a Westphalian GunWall?" Addison asked.

"Sixteen Phalanx-Class Destroyers up front, with those silly shields they use," Lazarus said. "One Star Spear centered and eight Powerbolt Cannons around the rim of the shield. Protecting four Archer-Class Destroyers with the same Gunshield but a Star Lance and four Powerbolt Cannons. Plus one CommandWall, which is a modified Archer without the Star Lance and all of that space is dedicated to flag operations instead. Kill them in reverse order."

"Can *Ajax* fly backwards to do it?" Addison asked.

"Huh?"

"Retrograde motion," the Churquen leaned forward. "Humans and Churquen can both do it. This ship's engines are riding on gravity lines of force, rather than ejecting physical matter to produce thrust. If a GunWall shows up, can we entice them into chasing us with Kirov's Lance pointed at them the whole time?"

"Yes," Lazarus said in a smaller voice a moment later. "I've always thought of *Ajax* as an offensive tool, and designed it to swoop in and smash something with Kirov. Most likely that would have come up during training, but we never got that far. Let them chase you while backing away…"

"Not every battle requires me to wade in throwing punches, Lazarus." Addison smiled with the scales around his jaw and eyes. "Sometimes you have to outthink the eggless bastards."

"Which is exactly why you have and should continue to maintain the rank and position of First Officer, Addison," Lazarus smiled back. "One of these days we're going to go find a Westphalian GunWall and return the favor for what they did to me and this ship."

"And if Brasilia doesn't welcome us?" Addison asked.

"Maybe them, too," Lazarus said.

TWO

OLUCHI

AT LEAST THERE had been enough spare fabric in other colors lying around that Oluchi wasn't required to dress in the tan uniforms everyone else had taken to wearing. Not that he had anything against tan, but he worked so much better when he could use fashion and style as a social weapon.

And it wasn't that he had anyone here he needed to use them on, but one should never get out of practice, especially not today. Forty Years Standard old wasn't that far off. The prettiness of his youth had already given way to ruggedly handsome, thank the various gods, but eventually he was going to look like a responsible adult.

Best to be able to fool everyone when that time came around.

So he was wearing dark slacks today. Not black, but still far beyond just blue. The fabric was not cotton, not hemp, but close enough for him. Completely alien but the Necherle mechanic/tailor had a sewing machine. Recognizable, even, but physics was physics.

His original white shirt had been dismantled for patterns,

so he was probably never getting it back, but Thadrakho had made him a similar one in an egg cream just a little too light to be a faded mustard.

And the Navy insisted on jackets for their officers, so the ship was always kept cool enough that he could wear his opera cape most of the time. One must maintain image.

Sometimes, Oluchi even believed it. Convinced himself that he wasn't just a jumped-up gigolo running for his life from creditors and angry husbands.

Standing outside of the Captain's office door, pausing for a long breath, he wasn't so sure.

Yes, he had helped the man named Lazarus and two others invade the personal yacht of one of Yisan's finest, old-money plutocratic bastards. And killed the man and his crew in the process of rescuing Eha and Aileen before Strav Ardna managed to murder the two women.

Eduardo Martìnez, the true money on Yisan, had made sure that Oluchi Pryce was at the center of that operation, so he supposed that he had graduated from gigolo to fixer, at least in a few people's eyes. And a fixer was just a pimp with a wider and occasionally more reputable clientele, right?

But Captain Lazarus of Bethany had asked him to a meeting.

Oluchi wasn't wearing tan. Didn't even make a pretense of being under military authority. He didn't know of any outstanding warrants on Brasilia or the inner core of stars that made up the Rio Alliance, but he wasn't here to represent the ship.

Just the merchants of Yisan. Even a few basis points on contracts into Innruld Space would be more money than Oluchi ever needed. The power that his position would bring would do much for an aging Lothario like him, at that point where his smiling face didn't automatically guarantee a woman's attention.

That only opened the doors anyway. You still had to charm her. And Oluchi was always amazed how few men just listened to a woman when she wanted to vent. You didn't have to do anything. Just smile, nod, ask occasional questions to show that you were hearing and understanding her. Wine and chocolate were good, too.

Very few successful seductions began or ended in bed, after all.

Christo, get hold of yourself, man. You're acting like the Headmaster finally caught on to your games.

Oluchi shivered once, settled himself, and knocked.

The door opened immediately. As though Lazarus had a camera outside and had been watching. Hopefully the muttering had been too quiet to pick up.

"Come," Lazarus called.

Oluchi entered. Found the Captain behind his desk. Eha Dunham, the Churquen Ambassador to the Humans, was coiled on the open space to the left, so Oluchi took the only remaining chair.

When most of your crew had the wrong physiology, chairs must be an interesting choreography. He had heard stories of *Shiva Zephyr Glaive*, but not seen any pictures of the interior. The updated bridge of *Ajax*, however, told him all he really needed to know.

Oluchi turned to Eha and studied her for clues.

The woman had spent a week recovering from her trauma. Kidnapped. Threatened but not beaten. Aileen had been the one to suffer all the physical abuse, and it had taken four Humans, two with shock rods, to hold the angry Yithadreph woman down.

But Churquen didn't swim. And she'd had to escape from a yacht in the middle of a hurricane at sea, just before Lazarus and friends blew it up. Most of the bruises remaining on his legs had faded from where she had wrapped herself around him in a panic.

She smiled. It was good.

Lazarus was not smiling, but he rarely did. Oluchi understood that the man had the weight of the cosmos on his shoulders, Atlas-like.

"Nice cloak," Lazarus said as a beginning.

Oluchi smiled. Watched the other man relax a shade.

No, I won't join your navy and come under your orders, sir. Let's not even bother pretending.

But that was unsaid. He belonged, as much as the three newcomers did. The Humans. The others were a family, not just a crew.

Oluchi could aspire to join them, one of these days.

"How can I serve, Captain?" he asked in a vague, empty voice best suited to a poker table, rather than a boudoir.

"There is only one of me," Lazarus replied. "I cannot be in two places at once."

Oluchi nodded. He'd done the same math. He'd been waiting for the shoe to drop.

"While I respect all the risks you and the others took for my friend on Yisan, I have concerns," Lazarus said.

Oluchi nodded again. That math wasn't that hard, either.

Random stranger walks up and introduces himself. Invites everyone to a party. The women get kidnapped by a stranger. Oluchi has friends. Everyone goes out and kills the man purportedly responsible. The ship and crew flee before any truth might get out.

Neat with a bow, depending on how you wanted to interpret it.

Oluchi Pryce was a master of interpretation.

"Are you safer taking us all to Brasilia, or leaving us here?" Oluchi asked, turning to include Eha in the conversation.

"That was exactly the point of discussion," Eha replied with a nod.

"Bălan is pretty much exactly what he looks like," Lazarus continued. "I know the type, and all the subtle cues someone could not pick up any way other than serving. Grace Savidge is a killer. Period. Probably has all manner of other skills and is certainly beautiful and charming, but at her core she is one of the most lethal beings I've ever encountered in a lifetime of professional mayhem. Any species."

Oluchi nodded. That pretty much summed both of them up. Crude and a bit simplistic, but good enough to place a figure on the game board.

"And me?" he asked.

"You're the wild card, Pryce," Lazarus said. "Appropriate, as you appear to be a professional gambler, among other things."

Oluchi didn't think it was possible for a man like him to blush. He was wrong.

But hey, hopefully you learn something new about yourself every day, right?

"I want to get rich," Oluchi replied. "But more importantly, I want the power that comes with riches. The freedom. Those folks back on Yisan all had more money than they could possibly spend, so their only risk was boredom and ennui. That was why they needed folks like me."

"And now?" Lazarus asked.

"Today, I need to be a fixer," Oluchi said. "For you, for Eha, and for Eduardo. The man who gets things done because he has a cousin in the industry. That middleman who greases the wheels of commerce for a small percentage. Yisan is outside of Rio Alliance laws, so those folks will be expecting me to route things through them on the way to Innruld Space so they can get more fabulously rich. Eha and her folks will need civilian hulls as well as military surplus hardware to do their thing to the overlords of the galaxy. The Rio government might not want all that to be on the main screen of the new channel, so they'll need someone expert in just handling things quietly."

He paused and squelched that voice of *Doubt* that wanted to remind him he'd been nothing more than a jumped-up pretty boy two weeks ago, only good for keeping rich widows and wives entertained.

"I would like to also go with you to Brasilia," Oluchi said. "Start building up Eha's new network of spies and smugglers."

"Become rich and powerful?" Lazarus asked with a doubt not quite verging on derision in his eyes and voice.

"Become relevant on a grander scale, maybe," Oluchi countered, finding a heat he hadn't anticipated in his stomach when the word came out. "Nothing I've ever done until now has qualified. No, that's not true."

He tuned to smile at Eha.

"I can think of one time I've had a positive impact on the galaxy."

Lazarus studied him for a long time. Eha as well. Neither smiled all that much, but neither did they frown.

The Captain surprised him by turning to the Ambassador.

"Eha?" Lazarus asked.

"I think he'll do," she said, smiling finally. "We have to begin trusting someone, if we want to start a revolution."

THREE

AILEEN

AILEEN STEPPED onto the mat and studied the Human standing across from her.

"It doesn't work if you're not calm, Aileen," Xiuying said. "All of your training must begin with calm focus, so that the next time you get into a fight it becomes automatic."

"You assume a next time?" she asked.

Xiuying smiled.

"Gonna turn over a new leaf and become a master of Zen instead?" he laughed. "I mean, technically, you already are, according to the boss, but you've never turned it into an art form."

He meant packing boxes. Loadmaster aboard *Shiva Zephyr Glaive* for so many years. And now **Quartermaster** of *Ajax*.

She'd never considered it a thing, but Lazarus had pointed her at the right books, so she'd read some on Zen, but the Innruld/Interlac translations didn't impress her much.

"No," Aileen decided.

Might as well be honest with herself, as well as the Human training her to fight with their forms.

Yithadreph didn't have martial arts as Humans understood the term. The Innruld masters weren't about to allow a dangerous underclass to study close combat fighting techniques.

"So breathe," Xiuying said as he stood there. "Calm energy. We'll start with punch hands and then move on to Tai Chi."

The frighteningest thing to her was the raw number of ways Humans had perfected barehanded fighting. Aileen had done some research in *Ajax*'s computers, and been utterly appalled at the number of pages dedicated just to listing them, to say nothing of the chapters describing them all.

Lazarus had studied some. She knew that from the way he'd beaten up three Innruld in a tea shop.

Xiuying was a *bouncer*. What did it say about Human Space that they had tea rooms serving poisons and getting so rowdy that they had professionally violent persons on staff, on duty, in order to beat up other Humans who lost their manners due to drink?

But he was also teaching Wybert the ancient Human fighting style called Sōjutsu. *The Way of the Spear*. Aileen wasn't sure if it was a good idea or a bad one to have an Ilount like Wybert of Capantzina turn into a more dangerous warrior, especially with that powerspear he carried everywhere like a lucky charm.

"Hands," Xiuying said firmly. "Stance. Focus."

Right foot forward. Left hand up for blocking. Right fist back to punch. This art did it that way. Others had their own take.

The first punch came slowly. Deliberately. Softly.

She blocked with her left hand by just touching the back of the fist and directing it to one side, using that motion to cock her hips and right hand back in order to return the punch in the same slow motion. Her eyes and whiskers were focused on the hand as it approached, missed, went past, withdrew.

Xiuying blocked her fist the same way. Soft. Just enough deflection to make you miss, while conserving energy you needed later.

She fell into the rhythm.

After a time, his punch also included a kick, slow and steady. Aileen rocked her weight backwards and pulled her right foot off the ground. Just enough to be clear. She returned the kick with her own punch.

More rhythm.

She didn't notice time passing until the Human stepped back suddenly and grinned at her. Aileen could smell her sweat.

Xiuying threw a real punch at her. Badly for the Human, cocking his fist back on his hip and stepping forward like she'd seen that Innruld do in the bar.

Her hand came up and she felt her whole body rotate out of his way as he snapped a fist into her face at a speed where it should have been a blur.

But her body slowed it down. She touched the fist and it missed her. Her own fist came up and caught him right in the center of the chest with a loud thump that drove Xiuying backwards a step.

He laughed as she watched, open mouth hanging.

"See?" he said. "It becomes automatic after a while. You'll need years to get there, but we can fast forward you a considerable distance just working out for a few hours every day. Plus, it gets me back in shape, between you and Wybert."

"What about Grace?" Aileen asked innocently.

She saw the Human's face shadow.

"That one doesn't need my help," he said ambivalently. "Only thing I could do for her would be to provide a sparring dummy she could throw around the dojo floor when she wanted live practice."

"Is she really that good?" Aileen asked.

She'd heard both Xiuying and Lazarus say that, but she really hadn't had any context to rate deadliness among Humans. The many Species back home didn't do violence as a rule, beyond rare fist fights in bars or on docks.

"She really is, Aileen," Xiuying turned and took up a stance beside her now. "The men and women who trained me weren't even in that woman's league. Now, focus."

She flowed into the stance. Short form. Designed to be meditation in motion. Poetry of the body, as done by storks like this Humanwith impossibly long legs, even if Xiuying was half a head shorter than all the other Humans. He was still a foot taller than her.

She fell into the breathing pattern as her hands came up, held, and then flowed down, before moving outward. Blocks. Kicks. Punches. Stylized and elegant, but she'd just thrown a real block and stepped directly into a punch with Xiuying, so she was beginning to understand how such things happened.

Humans did violence like no other species in the galaxy that she was aware of. They'd beaten her badly at Yisan, although it eventually took four of them to subdue her.

Next time, she wanted to be better prepared.

FOUR

ADDISON

IN HIS WILDEST DREAMS, Addison Wolcott had never imagined commanding a ship like *Ajax*. *Shiva Zephyr Glaive* had been his pride and joy, but *Ajax* was huge. The bay wasn't big enough to have brought his cargo runner aboard, so they had left it behind inside the Phraettis Nebula, shut down and with all the water tanks completely drained for long-term storage.

He still looked forward to returning for his ship someday. Just looking around the bridge of *Ajax* left him unsettled. Lazarus had needed to design and build a ship long enough to hold all the hardware and generators for Kirov's Lance. The final design reminded Addison of a grappling hook, with a long body reaching back to three enormous fins, one hundred and twenty degrees apart. Nearly a mile long, with a permanent, eventual crew of five hundred Humans, plus space for another two hundred or so for whatever diplomatic or exploratory missions the Rio Alliance Navy planned, plus all their equipment.

And Addison was in command now.

The bridge space was a cathedral. The bow of the ship

had looked like a graceful goose's head from a distance, but the ceiling was vaulted nearly twenty feet above his head. A handful of stations sat inside an oval ring, with twenty more up a step on a slight catwalk, facing outward.

It felt empty, with only four of them in here. Cormac the NavCrawler was plugged into his station next to Kuei Akeley, Addison's pilot. Wybert was on the other side in his very serious role as Fusilier.

Human militaries had a person whose entire job involved shooting other ships with enormous beam weapons, up to and including something capable of possibly annihilating Zhoonarrim Station with a single shot.

Addison wasn't sure if he was more appalled or frightened to have Wybert in command of that firepower, but he didn't have anybody on his original crew better suited, temperamentally, to the task.

"Flight deck, this is the bridge," Kuei said calmly, drawing Addison's eyes back to the present from the various daydreams a middle-aged Director might have on a warship more dangerous than anything he'd ever imagined possible. "The bay is cleared for departure. Good luck and Godspeed."

What a strange phrase, but it was apparently a traditional send-off in the Rio Alliance Navy, and the Vaadwig woman had been assiduously studying training videos in all her spare time.

Like him, she'd spent years on *Shiva*, flying port to port with the occasional mission off the scanners to meet up with other smugglers. Now, she was flying *Ajax*. Like him, she wore a modified tan uniform, in her case a jumpsuit like she normally wore in the old days, with holes for arms, legs, and tail, plus the pouch she stored things in.

Wybert had a tan tunic and Thadrakho had even managed a thing a biped might have called shorts, if they had ten legs and a pair of spinnerets to deal with.

Hells, even Cormac had asked for someone to paint his top hull tan with a Lieutenant's pips, so he fit in as crew.

What was the galaxy coming to?

That was a trick question. Like before, Lazarus, Eha, and Aileen were going off in one of the pinckes to visit Brasilia, home world of the Rio Alliance and hopefully a place where they could finally get help to fly this mighty beast of a starship.

Unlike Yisan, they had taken a larger crew along this time, the other three Humans who had joined them after their first adventure.

That left an entirely alien crew in command of a Human warship. Again. But this time they were in the middle of Human Space. Hiding, true, but places none of them had ever been.

Addison watched the screen as the shuttle craft Lazarus called a pincke emerged and began moving away from *Ajax* at an accelerating clip.

Now Addison was on his own. Ereshkiki Nisab, Kuei, Wybert, Khyaa'sha, Remahle, and Thadrakho, plus the two Crawlers: Cormac and Lenox remained with him, but that was it.

"Redshifting shortly," Aileen announced from the pincke.

And then it was gone.

Addison studied the screens.

Alone. Possessed of enough firepower at his fingertips to overthrow the Innruld, perhaps. But his mate had gone on, along with his Loadmaster and his Director.

His friends.

Like before, he and Lazarus had made plans to move *Ajax* around regularly to various systems, with a schedule of where they would meet later, when it was safe, along with passwords to indicate status when he arrived.

"Helm, come about to port and nose down," Addison announced after a long moment of contemplation.

He had all the maps and information available to a secret, experimental warship of the Rio Alliance, so he knew every star on any future colonizing list. Those he would avoid. Nobody needed to even suspect that *Ajax* had survived.

But he had a second mission. Something he and Eha had come up with in their spare time, when they weren't acting like teenage kids in love.

Even if the war between the Humans and the Innruld stretched on, the Churquen and other Species needed a place where they could be free. They hadn't explicitly discussed this with Lazarus, but after this long, Addison had a pretty good idea about how the man's mind worked. He would be in favor, regardless of what his superiors might think.

After all, while the Humans dominated this region of space, there were other species. The Human supremacists of Westphalia didn't recognize them as having any rights, but the Rio Alliance also included Moah, Gnashiiley, and Atomarsk as founding members.

The whole point of bringing all of the Species Underground to Rio attention was to get help to end Innruld dominance.

But they also needed a place to escape from all the wars.

And Addison was going to find it.

FIVE

LAZARUS

BLUESHIFT. The spark of light that signaled the arrival of an FTL vessel on star drives.

Lazarus smiled as he imagined what would happen next. There was no way to sneak into a system easily, unless you came out of jump clear at the edge of a solar system and then perhaps spent weeks sailing slowly down into the heat and light. Anything faster and scanners would pick you up anyway.

Here, they had just gone ahead and leapt to a middle distance in one of Brasilia's inbound lanes. You were supposed to come out at a slow speed, in case anyone else was close enough that you needed to maneuver. It also put you under the guns of a couple of watchtowers that were more rescue and customs stations than armed fortresses designed to repel a Westphalian invasion.

The real strength was sailing around him in the darkness right now, watching like sharks that could pounce on an invading force.

Lazarus knew. He'd been one of them a few times.

"Brasilia Inbound Operations, this is vessel 17930235 in

the Inbound Lane, holding for flight instructions," Lazarus announced on a radio band, while also transmitting the pincke's identification information, minus the fact that the vessel originated aboard *Ajax*.

If you didn't already know that, you weren't cleared to know anything else.

He turned to Aileen, in the co-pilot's seat, and smiled.

The crew with him were an interesting mix of fashion. He'd gone ahead and put on one of his good uniforms for this. Aileen wore a Yithadreph version, as produced by Thadrakho, complete with Commander's pips on the collar, however brevet they might be.

He had still inducted her with the rest and given her a temporary promotion to the same rank as the last Quartermaster he'd had. Ernesto da Silva had made it to the escape pods when *Ajax* was about to be scuttled, but Lazarus had no idea if the man had been interned or traded home. He didn't know enough to spill anything useful, but Westphalia might not have been feeling nice.

Xiuying had also worn tan. In his case, the excuse had been that they'd probably just reactivate his enlistment anyway at this point, so he might as well have a uniform that fit when they did.

Grace and Oluchi were dressed as civilians. Nothing he could say would convince them otherwise.

Eha was dressed like a Churquen Ambassador to the Humans. Tunic in a light blue that showed off both the emerald dominating her scales and the honey-striped accents along her length. Black leather harness with pouches, modeled after one of Addison's.

Bright golden eyes focused on him. She didn't say anything now, partly because they had hashed it out so much on the flight here, and partly because she understood that

Lazarus still didn't necessarily trust the other three Humans along with them.

The Human saying involved gift horses, but the Churquen had something that translated just as well.

"17930235, this is Inbound Control," a woman's voice came back on the channel after a long enough time that Lazarus assumed she had looked up the number, panicked just a little, and called her boss. Her voice sounded a little tight and breathless. "Please confirm the last date you were in-system."

"May Eleventh, Inbound Control," Lazarus said with regret in his mind. "Outbound."

Headed out on a shakedown cruise to make sure that everything on *Ajax* worked well enough to start getting serious.

Right before landing in a Westphalian GunWall's killing zone.

"17930235, your docking transmission shows six aboard," she said now. "One known and five not listed in our records."

"That is correct, Inbound Control," Lazarus said calmly, wondering how long it would take for a warship to land in his lap to take control of things. Obviously, they hadn't caught the Xiuying was a former marine when they ran the records.

Or would they route this ship to the station itself to answer questions. He couldn't see the military wanting any civilians to know what was going on. How much secrecy did they invoke right now?

He had given them names. Only Francisco Luiz Oliveira would mean anything to their computers. And it had probably ignited a bureaucratic tizzy.

"Do you have any medical or quarantine needs,

17930235?" she asked now, obviously working her way quickly down a checklist.

"Negative, Inbound Control," he replied. "Just a place to dock so I can talk to the people who'll be along."

"Understood, 17930235," she finally said. "Transmitting coordinates now. Please fly directly to this location and stand by for further communications."

Lazarus checked them. Up and to starboard across a quick sail. Out of the way of everyone coming in behind him. Off of the slidewalk, as it were.

He assumed that meant a warship was being rounded up and dispatched to take him aboard. Presumably an important one with an *Almirante* already aboard.

And one the Navy trusted to keep his mouth shut. Certainly someone had warned the woman on the other end of the line to keep things vague and as meaningless as possible.

"Now what?" Aileen asked.

"Now we wait," Lazarus replied tensely.

SIX

EHA

SHE HAD FINALLY MADE it to Human Space. Eha wasn't willing to necessarily count the pirate lords of Yisan, in spite of everything, mostly because they wouldn't be helpful to her long-term mission.

Human pirates in vessels far in advance of anything in Innruld Space would make things worse, not better. The Innruld would have to clamp down even harder on the Species Underground than they already had. People would get hurt.

But that star in the distance was Brasilia's. Lazarus's homeworld. Center of the Rio Alliance.

Hopefully a place where she could get help. As long as the spy that Lazarus expected could be discovered and eliminated. She didn't expect the hostility that Strav Ardna had evinced, but hopefully something more like Eduardo Martìnez, or the two Human women, Leena Hernández and Fernanda Flores.

Lazarus had left the communications channel open and loud enough that she heard the call, even stretched out in the cargo bay in a hammock while the other Humans sat strapped into uncomfortable jump seats.

"Vessel 17930235, this is Rio vessel *Recife*," a voice came over the line. "Hold in place for identification."

Eha had met enough Humans now to place it as male from the tone and timbre.

"Understood, *Recife*," Lazarus answered in a calm voice.

Eha assumed at this point that they were scanning the pincke with everything they had. And presumably swallowing their tongues.

"17930235, who is flying that vessel?" the man demanded.

"*Pancho* Oliveira," Lazarus said, using his Human name. The one from before he became Lazarus.

There was another pause.

"17930235, come about and prepare for docking," the man ordered. "The bay will be opening shortly."

"Acknowledged, *Recife*," Lazarus said.

Eha unwound herself from the hammock and hung down to the deck, expertly catching a jumpseat with her tail after so much practice and flipping it down. She coiled enough to hold it and then lowered, grabbing the second one and holding it. Oluchi stretched and flipped a third down, and she had a spot to sit when gravity came back on.

"We trust them?" Aileen asked in a louder than normal voice.

"As much as anyone," Lazarus replied. "The Director on that ship was someone I served with previously, at least a year ago."

"You owe him any money?" Aileen laughed.

"No," he laughed back. "Just you and Addison."

Eha watched the three Humans prepare. Xiuying would know what to expect, having served with the same military, but Grace and Oluchi were going to be outsiders. At least

Human, compared to her, but the locals would not trust them even as much as Lazarus did.

And she knew that Grace and Lazarus had never been intimate. Not yet, anyway. She suspected that would change at some point.

Out the front windshield, the immense size of the vessel *Recife* became obvious. But where *Ajax* was long and thin, this vessel looked more like a stone that had been polished into smooth lumpiness by a river. Not as asymmetric as things routinely were in Innruld Space, but not the clean, straight lines of *Ajax*, either.

They flew into a landing bay marked by an overabundance of lights. Or perhaps she was just used to the relative dimness of an Innruld station, where the cargo bays always seemed seedy.

The pincke was like a seed in a bucket, rattling around loosely. Lazarus landed them closer to the left rather than in the center, the magnets clunking loudly as they engaged and the gravity of the vessel gave them down again.

Lazarus locked everything down and spun his chair around.

"We're here," he announced unnecessarily. "Everyone leave all your weapons aboard the pincke, regardless of intent. That's a Rio Navy Heavy Starcruiser around us. They'll be nervous and assumedly uncooperative until they get the whole story out of me. And maybe even after that. Please don't do anything to provoke them until I can talk to my direct superiors?"

Heads nodded and everyone stood. The space was large, since this vessel was intended as a cargo transport, rather than a compact personnel vehicle.

Lazarus moved to the small airlock on the pilot's side. They had discussed just opening the cargo airlock, but decided that she and Aileen might really surprise them.

Better to let the Humans come around slowly.

On the hatch, a light finally turned green, showing that the bay was fully pressurized. On an Innruld station, a customs inspector would have come out and banged on the hull to let the people inside know that they were allowed to open up, but here things were different.

Lazarus opened both doors and stepped out as she watched. The others waited.

This was when it would get interesting.

SEVEN

LAZARUS

HE WAS HOME. Sort of. Aboard a Rio Alliance Heavy Starcruiser, which was the sort of place he'd been before *Ajax*.

The Almirante in command was obvious concerned, given the number of marines in armored suits that had piled into the bay just now. About half were arrayed in a tight semi-circle in front of Lazarus, with the rest stretching like horns around the sides and rear, in case anybody tried anything.

Lazarus was wearing his best Day Uniform, rather than anything dressy. He had exactly one good one with all the ribbons with him, back on *Ajax*, but had left it there. For what was coming, he wanted at least some level of comfort.

He doubted that they'd let him get much sleep, any time soon.

Lazarus came to rest about fifteen feet from the line of marines with their helmets closed up. All of them had guns, but none were *currently* pointed at him. At some unheard comment, the inner hatch of the bay's personnel airlock opened and a lieutenant in field armor stepped out. He had a helmet on, but the faceplate was open, showing bones and color suggesting a Chinese heritage. Similarly, he had gloves on and could presumably survive a short burst of vacuum, if they had to blow the bay for some reason.

The marines would just EVA home once they stopped tumbling.

Lazarus came to something approaching attention. He did outrank the man approaching by several steps, but he was here as a refugee, not a commanding officer.

Or something.

The lieutenant stepped to about halfway between Lazarus and the marines. Paused. Studied him closely enough that Lazarus assumed he was making a visual identification from file records.

"Captain Oliveira?" the man asked simply. "Commanding officer of the Rio Alliance Light Starcruiser *Ajax?*"

Lazarus nodded. "There have been *developments*, Lieutenant."

"Understood, sir," the man nodded. "There are five other life forms on the pincke, Captain."

"Indeed there are," Lazarus nodded, noting that the marines had all perked up another notch now. "Three of them are Humans who helped me get back. The other two are friends I met on the far side of beyond when I was marooned. All are currently unarmed. One of the aliens also has a field induction and brevet promotion to Commander, where she currently serves as my Quartermaster aboard *Ajax.*"

"And the other?"

"An Ambassador, Lieutenant," Lazarus stated clearly. "A representative from the aliens I met out there with credentials to come to the Rio government and negotiate. Could you let your troops know so we can all handle this calmly and rationally?"

The man studied his face for a long moment. A hand went out and gave a gesture that Lazarus recognized from his time, about this kid's age, doing similar things with crazy-ass marines.

The line of troops calmed back to what they had been before. High-strung, but relaxed. Presumably safeties were set, not that they couldn't get them clear fast enough.

"Go ahead, Captain," the lieutenant continued.

Lazarus turned in place, facing the shuttle.

"Xiuying, Grace, Oluchi, could you join us, please?" he called in a clear voice.

Xiuying Bălan was short, just tall enough for recruiters. And probably stronger than most of the men and women in this bay. Originally of North Asian stock, his skin was far more golden, compared to Lazarus's paleness. Close to the lieutenant's. And he wore the uniform of a Senior Chief marine, complete with a set of tags that would probably be exactly appropriate, if Lazarus had looked in his personnel file.

He walked close and came to attention with a knowing grin at the marines around him. Like Lazarus had expected.

Oluchi Pryce came next. Still dressed as something of a dandy, to make himself stand out. That opera cape was just a complete statement of purpose, on a starship without weather. Nobody that could be mistaken for anything but a civilian.

He came to rest close to Xiuying and nodded at some internal commentary.

Grace Savidge's ancestors had come from south central Africa. Fairly recently, as well, as her skin was on that fine dark line between ochre and onyx that hadn't been blended with any of the lighter-skinned folks from other parts of the original Earth population, on whatever colonies they might have been.

She moved like her name. Stealthy but sure. A panther who projected her dominance over everyone here like a scent.

Lazarus saw a few of the marines bristle, but he doubted that any of them could take her on a dojo floor, if they were dumb enough to offer. Even with friends.

Like Oluchi, dressed as a civilian, but on her that meant blacks and grays, where everyone else was in tan. Muted and quiet, as if she might need to disappear a second from now.

"Commander Enjehn?" Lazarus called, once everyone had a moment to settle.

Aileen emerged and all the marines he could see flinched.

Made sense. She was four foot six inches tall, and looked like an oversized otter wearing a Rio Alliance officer's uniform. Brown fur on all the parts visible. Highly expressive ears and whiskers, if you knew what to look for. Modified uniform and her old shoes, because her feet were so different from anything Human.

Lazarus knew that Aileen didn't like noise and people, but she was putting on a show today because he had asked. She even stepped right up next to him and came to something that would pass for parade rest, looking up at the Lieutenant's face with a smile.

Lazarus gave the man a moment to find himself and close his mouth from the surprise.

The next one was going to be even better.

"Ladies and gentlemen of the Rio Alliance vessel *Recife*, I present to you Eha Dunham, *Ambassador to the Humans*," Lazarus called in a voice loud enough that even the microphones piping all this to the bridge would be clear.

Eha emerged and the Lieutenant gasped. Probably most of the marines, too, but they all had their darkened faceshields closed right now, so he couldn't hear. The posture changed enough for Lazarus to smile.

And no rifles came up, which was good.

She slithered like a queen, even smoother than Grace had walked. Came to rest on the far side of him and coiled herself enough to study the Lieutenant.

"What is your name, Lieutenant?" she asked with a nod and a smile.

"Lam, ma'am," he stammered. "Lucas Lam."

"Very good, Lieutenant Lam," Eha said with a smile. "Please take me to your commanding officer?"

EIGHT

RODRIGO

BECAUSE NOTHING HAD PREPARED him for this, Rodrigo took a long breath as he studied the image on the screen. One of his comm officers had zoomed the camera close enough to confirm *Pancho* Oliveira was truly the man standing there.

A little worse for the wear. Lost some weight and the orange hair on the sides was starting to show gray threads, but still *Pancho*.

Recife had been the closest ship with an Admiral aboard when they'd identified his shuttle, so Command had vectored him in. One of *Ajax*'s shuttles, but the ship was nowhere to be seen.

Standing orders. Rodrigo had heard the outcome of the battle. Ambush and flight. Presumably *Ajax* had been destroyed before it could fall into Westphalian hands. The Captain was supposed to go down with his ship. Tradition and all that.

Something else had happened.

Something *big*.

"Admiral?" Captain Quispe asked from his space across the flag bridge.

Rodrigo sighed. Captain Paulo Quispe was already above his pay grade on this one. Hell, Rodrigo might be, but he was the man on the scene. The government down on the planet would eventually get involved, as would the Admiralty Staff.

Once he figured out what the hell to do next.

"Treat the snake just like an Ambassador, Captain," Rodrigo said. "And the other one as a senior officer on detached duty. But keep them all together for now, including *Pancho*."

"Understood, sir," Paulo said as he turned and started issuing orders.

This was not a rescue. Whatever the hell it was, *Pancho* had wanted it to be quiet, which was why he never said his name on an open line, and only identified himself by the tag number on that pincke, trusting that computers would flag it for review and others would react quietly, too.

And *Recife* had had the bad luck to be the ship on station.

Rodrigo slicked back his black hair and made sure all the buttons on his jacket were fastened. That snake had presumably recognized Lam from his uniform tabs, rather than *Pancho* saying anything.

That meant it was smart.

How smart?

What the hell had *Pancho* done this time?

NINE

LAZARUS

"WE'LL NEED to move at something of a sedate pace, Lam," Lazarus said loudly as everyone fell into a rough column.

Most of the marines were behind them, with only a pair forward, a bowsprit parting the storm waves, as it were.

"Sir?" Lam paused on his third step and looked back.

"Neither Aileen nor Eha move quickly under normal circumstances, Lieutenant," Lazarus smiled.

"Oh," the man said. "Right."

He set off again at a slower pace. More deliberate this time. Lazarus glanced back and caught the grins on the two women.

Interestingly, Grace was right behind the other women and the two men were at the tail, with a dozen marines trailing. It made a nice symmetry to have two men at either end and the important women in the middle. After all, he was just the rescued sailor being finally brought home. Aileen and Eha were the prize.

Now, to convince Command not to do anything stupid.

He'd spent nine months trying to get people to step

outside their immediate reactions and think long term. The Species Underground had been all set to kidnap him away from Addison's crew. Only the authorities coming to arrest *someone* had let him escape.

Lazarus still didn't know who they'd been after. Didn't matter now, though, as he was just as much a fugitive in Innruld Space as the others, after blasting his way out of Zhoonarrim Station.

And now the shoe was on the other foot. Or something. Whatever term a Churquen would use. Lazarus made a mental note to ask sometime. It was probably pretty rude, from some of Addison's off-color jokes.

Lazarus had to keep the Admiralty Staff from getting stupid with two new alien species.

The two they knew about.

And oh, there are seven more on the ship, currently hiding from you, but we won't talk about what I did to hide Ajax *yet, will we?*

The marines did their job, protecting the ship from potential invaders at the same time that they kept the crew at a safe distance. In a few of the longer corridors, there seemed to be more than the usual traffic, but everyone stepped into side corridors and just watched the parade of weirdness.

Eventually, they came to a door and the marines entered.

Lazarus found himself in a large conference room, looking at a couple of faces he was at least familiar with from other places.

He stepped up and came to attention, snapping off a crisp enough salute when he recognized Admiral da Silva standing there. Faces fell completely slack when Aileen did the exact same thing a moment later.

But then, she was technically a Commander now. Under military discipline and subordinate to the Admiral and a

Captain that Lazarus didn't know all that well. Quispe, he thought was the man's name, but that was only a guess.

First generation colonist, from the look of him. Inland South America on Earth itself. Looked more Ecuadorean than Brazilian. Lazarus was always the one that really stood out, the pale and freckled Anglo when the others were darker-skinned.

"Chairs," Admiral da Silva mused aloud, apparently realizing that everything in here was designed for Humans with long legs.

"A couple of books would be sufficient for me to sit on," Aileen turned to Lam and sounded like a Commander ordering a Lieutenant around.

Lazarus felt his face screw sideways in a partial grin.

Eha entered and the room fell silent.

Rodrigo da Silva had dyed his white hair black for as long as Lazarus had known the man, having gone gray at a young age. It was his one affectation. Otherwise, the man was solid.

"Ambassador Dunham," da Silva said, bowing his head and shoulders. "Welcome aboard the Heavy Starcruiser *Recife*."

"Thank you, Admiral," Eha replied, slithering off to her left as Lazarus watched the impact of the two women on everyone present.

It would have been nice to have a couple of female senior officers present, but the Rio Alliance Navy wasn't all that accommodating about certain things, so men tended to outnumber women about three to one at the rank of Commander and above.

Lazarus wondered if that was another revolution that needed to happen around here, after all the various ones he already had in mind.

Lazarus stepped around Eha's coil and pulled a chair away from the table, turning and handing it to the closest marine to stow. That put him on one side of Eha with Aileen on the other.

The rest of the team filed in and took seats, even though Xiuying looked like he wanted to be standing along the wall with the rest of his kind.

"Eha Dunham, this is Admiral Rodrigo da Silva," Lazarus introduced. "A former commander of mine from a while back."

He didn't say friend, although he didn't remember anything he might have done to piss da Silva off. And the man was smiling well enough now. Lazarus held on to hope.

"Captain Paulo Quispe," Rodrigo introduced the other man. Lazarus had guessed right, but had only seen the man at functions.

"Commander Aileen Enjehn, Quartermaster Corps," she introduced herself with all her whiskers forward, like this was a grand charade. It kind of was.

Everyone was settled.

Rodrigo studied the group as Lazarus waited.

Two and a half civilians, depending on how well they'd been paying attention earlier when he had said that they were all civilians that had helped him get home, even as Xiuying was wearing a uniform.

Two aliens.

And one Rio Alliance Captain, slightly worse for the wear.

"*Pancho*, what the hell happened?"

TEN

EHA

EHA FOUND IT INTERESTING, watching the interpersonal byplay around her.

She already knew Humans came in an impossible array of skin tones, from Grace's duskiness all the way to Lazarus's paleness. The two officers across the table were closer to Grace than Lazarus. The Lieutenant looked like a distant cousin of Xiuying's.

And all that was just one species.

She listened as Lazarus gave an abbreviated and sanitized account of his adventures, leaving out the parts where she was a spy but letting the Humans know that the Innruld as a people would be at least as bad as Westphalia.

Nobody mentioned that Humans had a distinct technological edge, though. Best not to tempt the Rio Alliance or Westphalia to try to conquer over there. Not when they had a war going on directly in front of them.

"And that got us here," Lazarus concluded his tale.

She liked the way the Admiral turned and studied all the twenty heavily armed men and women along the walls, as if he could see through the blank face plates to the souls beyond.

"The security classification around this entire event will be sufficient that all of you are now covered by various Official Secrets laws sufficient to put you in jail forever, *forever*, if you talk to anyone outside this room," the man announced in a hard, stern voice.

Several of the guards she could see winced at the tone. But Humans were a violent species.

Or were they just free to be violent? Eha had seen Moah and Gnashiiley at Yisan that looked larger and more robust than their distant cousins in Innruld Space. Did the Overlords of the Galaxy do something to keep all the other species in check?

Could Churquen turn out as fighters, like Humans, given a few generations of freedom from fear?

"Where is *Ajax*?" Admiral da Silva finally asked in a calm voice still cast in steel.

"My First Officer took the vessel and the remaining crew and moved into deep space," Lazarus replied in an equally heavy tone. "I have memorized a series of coordinates and timelines that can be used to rendezvous with them at a later date. After that first battle and then Yisan, I had my concerns about operational security, so I have chosen to exercise care."

"And you believe that a spy alerted Westphalia to your earlier mission?" da Silva asked.

"An entire GunWall, Admiral," Lazarus's voice got more emotional now as Eha listened. "Already primed, arrayed, and firing almost as fast as they recognized my blueshift. I should have been dead. *Ajax* should have been dead. Twenty-eight of my sailors are still out there in the freezer, while the rest were presumably taken prisoner. Do we have any news?"

"I do not, but will send my report in and see what they will tell me," the Human replied. "I am more concerned that you left an experimental warship in the hands of aliens, Oliveira."

"My friends and my crew, Admiral," Lazarus replied sharply, nodding to Eha. "Her mate is the commander right now. His former crew are my officers and staff."

"What will they do if you don't return?" da Silva asked.

"Presumably return to Innruld Space and become pirates, if I know Addison Wolcott," Lazarus said. "He would have burned Yisan to the ground, had anything happened to Eha. I'm hoping that the Rio Alliance government recognizes her as an Ambassador and doesn't do anything stupid."

"Would he attack Brasilia?" the other officer, Captain Quispe, spoke up now.

"I highly doubt it, gentlemen," Lazarus replied. "Yisan had no orbital defenses sufficient to defeat *Ajax*. Brasilia does. But I cannot speak of impossible hypotheticals. You'll transport us to the Admiralty Staff. They and the government will treat Ms. Dunham as she should be. Everyone will be happy and Oluchi Pryce will work on getting rich."

She watched both Humans turn to Oluchi now. Calculating stares. Weighing the man's soul, as it were.

"You are not an Alliance citizen," da Silva accused.

"That is correct," Oluchi nodded and smiled. "I represent various mercantile houses that currently maitain trade treaties into both Rio and Westphalia. Folks who have a vested interest in facilitating trade with the species of what we currently call Innruld Space."

"Currently?"

"They appear to me to be just another Westphalia, gentlemen," Oluchi's smile turned so cold that Eha had to look twice. "A single species intending and maintaining legal domination of all others, planning on subjugating them forever. With Human help, the other forty species might be liberated from the Innruld, in which case Innruld Space will need a new name."

"Forty?" da Silva gasped. Others did as well. Heads turned back to stare at her.

"Forty or so," Eha smiled. "Depending on how you wish to classify certain sub-species slowly separating. And Oluchi is essentially correct in his assessment. I have come seeking Human help to overthrow the Innruld. Your help."

"I am merely a military officer, Madam Dunham," da Silva said. "I can make no promises binding my government."

"That I understand, Admiral," she said. "But it will begin with you."

ELEVEN
RODRIGO

"THOUGHTS?" Rodrigo asked after everyone left. It was just him and Paulo now.

Captain Quispe grinned.

"So glad that this is your problem and not mine, Rod," he said. "I just have to fly you around."

"Very funny, Captain," Rodrigo lamented sarcastically. "You've got an Atomarsk engineering officer, right?"

"Lt. Commander Slani, yes," Paulo nodded.

"Detach him from duty and bring him up to date on everything," Rodrigo ordered.

"Her," Paulo corrected. "And she's an engineer, not a diplomat."

"She's a non-Human, Paulo," Rodrigo countered. "This is bigger than just the Navy now. Her people will want to know what's happening. Maybe they already do. She can use this as an opportunity to see if she wants to transfer out of engines. Not going to hold it against her if not, but I need some non-Human advice right now."

"What are we doing?" Paulo asked.

"We're going to sail down to orbit instead of short-hopping," Rodrigo decided. "That gives me a few days to send reports ahead and prep the 4-stars at home for what I'm about to unleash."

"Unleash?" Paulo asked.

"This is probably as big an event as that first Atomarsk ship encountering Human explorers way back when, Paulo," Rodrigo said. "That was the day Humanity really split into two pieces, Westphalia and what would become the Rio Alliance. Those who wanted to work with the aliens out there, and those that wanted to conquer them."

"And forty new species?" Paulo asked.

"Are they enough to conquer us?" Rodrigo replied. "Should we be making common cause with Westphalia against a huge block of other aliens nobody knew about?"

"Shit," Paulo whispered.

"Yes, my friend," Rodrigo nodded. "That's how ugly this might get."

TWELVE

ADDISON

"COMMANDER, I believe it would be in everyone's interest if you joined me on the bridge."

Addison rocketed out of his coil like it was a spring and moved as fast as his keel scales could grab onto the carpet beneath him.

Cormac had the bridge. Kuei was presumably asleep right now.

With a crew this small, everyone was stretched thin, but at least he had a friend like Cormac the NavCrawler, who didn't need sleep except for a good solid reboot every few months.

Addison had been doing something in his office. Lazarus's office. The place where the duty commander would do paperwork if he had a crew large enough to push paper around.

Mostly noodling and letting himself wander down burrows in Human encyclopedia data, tracing after whatever struck his fancy.

Cormac was plugged in and had a camera eye deployed

up and rotated back to stare at him as Addison got clear of the door.

"What happened?" he asked, breathless.

Cormac never got twitchy. That was the benefit of a NavCrawler in the first place. All the brains, very little of the emotional instability.

"*I have detected what might be construed through a Human lens as a space battle, Addison,*" Cormac said.

"Main screen," he replied automatically. "Wake Kuei. I can always apologize to her later if need be."

"*Initiating.*"

Addison coiled on his nest and brought the various screens and controls live. It always amazed him that a vessel this huge could be run with such a small crew. About the only thing that they couldn't do was fight their own pitched space battle.

"Background?" he asked aloud.

"*I have been tracking various signals, Commander. The current lag is two hours, following our slow sail into this system rather than invoking a visible blueshift by approaching too closely.*"

Blueshift. Like a supernova if you were close enough to see this warship come out of jump. So they had landed clear out at the edge of the system and ridden the gravity lines down quickly.

9087 Geminorum, according to the charts. Fourth world out looked like it might be relatively habitable, according to ancient records, but nobody lived there.

Nobody was supposed to live there. But someone had engaged in something in the last few hours.

Addison turned to the radio traffic as Cormac has transcribed it. Cultural idioms took some work to translate, even when everything was in a common, universal tongue he knew as Innruld and the locals called Interlac.

"Pirates, attacking a colony on the surface of the planet?" Addison asked.

"That is my interpretation, Addison. They arrived and immediately destroyed an orbital communications platform, then deployed small vessels roughly equivalent to our pinckes carrying what appear to be large numbers of security troops to the ground."

Addison nodded. Nobody was supposed to be living here. Said so right there in the records he had accessed. Obviously, those records were wrong. Or squatters had snuck in, but nobody had filed a legal claim to the planet itself as recently as a year ago.

Kuei entered the bridge now.

Everyone was used to the Vaadwig in ships built for others. Low ceilings and all that. They saw the tripod movement where she had to shift around awkwardly on feet and tail.

Everyone forgot that Vaadwig could *leap*.

She had opened the main hatch, shuffled forward a little, and then launched herself unerringly across the space, bounding twice and landing exactly next to her station.

"Pirates?" she asked as she brought her controls live. "Do we run?"

Of course we run. What kind of a silly question is that? Nobody knows we exist. Nobody should know, until Lazarus and Eha are ready to show us off.

Except that pirates were raiding someone's colony. Doing bad things to people merely because they had guns and presumably could overwhelm the folks on the ground.

And the Rio Alliance, of which he was a temporary but representative member, however strange that outcome had been, had prided themselves on being the good guys.

But he couldn't take prisoners. What would he do with

them, considering that they probably outnumbered him tens or more to one?

"Cormac, what do your scans show for ground population, given Human habitation norms?" Addison asked.

Cormac actually raised another camera to look at him. It was the NavCrawler equivalent of an exasperated tail flick.

"*Stand by. Approximating Human density models to low-technology agrarian societies. Estimated at four thousand Humans, ranging from newborn to elderly.*"

"And the vessel in orbit?"

"*A standard model available in my records. Retired military escort supposedly demilitarized of most beam weapons. Crew normally forty in Westphalian service.*"

Assuming that the pirates brought Kreeghal or the Human equivalent in a transport, then forty crew is probably two hundred troopers, depending on how far away they were from their base.

Too many decades as a smuggler and overall criminal, Addison could do that math in his own head.

"Kuei, can you land us right behind them at optimal range for the Star Lances?" Addison asked.

She turned to him and the look on her face wanted to scream *ARE YOU NUTS?* but she didn't say anything. Just did some math on her screen.

"Piece of cake from here," she finally said. "Assuming that they haven't moved from that geo-synched orbit in the last two hours."

"Unless they were in a hurry, the troops are only now about to land on the surface," Addison said.

"And we're going to stop them?" she asked with a sarcastic grumble.

"Cormac, wake Wybert and tell him to come to the bridge."

THIRTEEN
LAZARUS

LAZARUS HAD SEEN the others to bed before he even considered settling. *Recife* had a full ambassadorial suite aft, so everyone was together and had individual bedrooms off the same common room. If they were locked in, he couldn't fault Admiral da Silva's response. At least they had a kitchen back here and it had been stocked.

So he was in the main room. *Recife*'s day was later than *Ajax*'s, so it felt like the middle of the night to him, even though it was just a few hours after ship's dinner.

Still, he was exhausted. He was a scientist and engineer, not a diplomat. But Eha needed someone who could translate things that didn't hop cultures as she fenced with Rodrigo da Silva.

Lazarus had his shoes off and his feet up, turned sideways on a couch with a covered mug of decaffeinated coffee in his hand. The lights in the lounge area were low enough that he might fall asleep if he wasn't careful, but everyone else needed time to settle.

After all, he was the only true naval officer here. The rest had just been sucked along in his avalanche, trying not to be carried under.

A hatch opened behind him.

Lazarus craned his head up enough to look over the back of the couch, setting his coffee mug down on the deck next to him.

Grace.

He'd wondered if she would make a move. Or when.

Lazarus still doubted that Eduardo Martìnez had been able to read him well enough in that short of a period to know how many buttons a woman like that might push on poor *Pancho* Oliveira. More likely the merchant prince had picked the most effective tool for the job at hand, rescuing Eha, and then given Grace as much latitude as an expert like her felt she needed.

She saw him and her face brightened.

Instead of coming over to talk, however, he watched her move silently to an open space in the center of the suite, over by the main hatch. The sort of place where you would welcome guests and then direct them to the dining table or the salon where he was, with portholes showing stars in the distance.

She came to rest standing erect but facing away from him. One quick glance back at him showed her grin, and then she turned away. Her weight shifted and settled, and she began to move.

Lazarus had studied various martial arts early in his career. Japanese, Chinese, Brazilian, Viet, Central African. Anything that involved using the Human body as a weapon.

There were no original things left, after this long. Everyone just had a different way of assembling the motions into a harmonious whole.

He recognized this as an opening that originated from

Chinese forms, but he wasn't sure which form or lineage she was using.

But it was calming to watch her move. Step, pivot, block, move.

Slow and steady. Peaceful, but he could see what it would look like at full speed, surrounded by a half-dozen assailants intent on doing her harm.

Meditation in motion.

Somewhere in the middle of the form he fell asleep watching her.

FOURTEEN

GRACE

GRACE COMPLETED the long form a second time and came to rest, a little sweaty and utterly relaxed. She didn't need to do it every single day, as long as she worked through various katas and movements constantly. Muscle memory would carry her forward, but it needed to be reinforced.

She hadn't been expecting Lazarus to still be awake when she emerged, but had decided to go ahead and work out rather than talk to the man. From the look on his face, he'd been carrying the weight of this starship on his shoulders and needed the sleep.

So she danced.

At some point, he had even fallen asleep, possibly staring at her, but she'd been in another place.

Grace considered waking him. The couch didn't look all that comfortable, but he was snoring quietly now. Probably good to let him sleep for a while.

The suite they were being kept in was luxurious, but Grace had no preconceptions that it was anything other than a gilded cage. *Pancho* Oliveira had returned from the dead as

Lazarus of Bethany, and brought strangers and aliens with him. She was perhaps the least strange of the group, which brought a smile to her face as she settled on a chair to watch Lazarus breathe.

Time passed.

He started in his sleep. Opened his eyes. Focused on her, all of ten feet away.

"How long?" he asked.

"You've been napping for about twenty minutes, I think," Grace replied. "Considered getting Xiuying up to carry you to bed, but I decided you needed to rest more."

He shrugged.

"Long day, long week, long year," he offered. "Not done yet."

"What does done look like?" Grace asked, wondering if she was finally going to get a glimpse of the real man, hidden so carefully behind those walls since the moment she met him.

"*Ajax* leading a squadron of killers over into Innruld Space," he replied. "Maybe after I shatter a couple of Westphalian GunWalls first."

"Will they let you?" she asked, leaving the *they* part ambiguous for now.

Again, the shrug. Not a man who wore his emotions on his sleeves.

"They don't have much choice," Lazarus said. "The only question is whether I'm in command when it happens or Addison."

"You'd go without them?" Grace pressed, seeing something of the man now.

That unquenchable hunger that had driven him this far. The willingness to go beyond what was merely necessary in order to do what was *right*.

The man who had been Francisco Luiz Oliveira, once upon a time.

"If necessary," he replied simply. "Innruld Space is just another Westphalia, but *Ajax* can break the Innruld alone. My hope is that the Rio Alliance comes to its senses and sees the Species Underground as an ally, and not a threat."

"Threat?"

"Do the fools in charge panic and decide to make common cause with the rest of the Human species, regardless of politics, in order to merely displace the Innruld?" Lazarus asked. "We didn't tell them how easy it would be to annihilate an Innruld Security Barc, because that might inspire them to go do it."

"Rio?"

"Westphalia," Lazarus corrected her. "This news will get out soon enough. Sooner if there really is a spy at a high level feeding them information. What happens if a GunWall, or even just a couple of five-ship Patrols headed over there?"

"Mayhem, I presume," she nodded. "How do we stop it?"

We?

When had she joined his revolution?

She knew that Lazarus didn't fully trust her. Didn't understand her motives. Something kept him at a step of reserve, when she hadn't done anything.

She didn't think the man was married. He'd made no mention of any sort of family or home life, even when asked by the others.

Perhaps a social trauma over a woman? She understood that sort of history.

Wanting something so much that others grew distant when they couldn't be involved.

Couldn't challenge for the very best that they could be.

Settled for merely good.

Grace refused to settle.

He was studying her closer now. Perhaps Lazarus had caught the linguistic twist in her words.

"We strike hot and fast," he said. "In my perfect world, Eha is treated like a proper Ambassador and I'm freed up to grab Aileen and a couple hundred sailors and go meet *Ajax*, bringing Addison up to strength."

"And then going after the Innruld?" she asked, finding herself leaning forward in spite of herself.

"Wouldn't take much with *Ajax*," he smiled. "I suspect that all I have to do is blow up a couple of Security Barcs and I could force the rest to be abandoned. At that point, the chains come off everyone else and the question is whether or not any Innruld survive."

"You don't seem disappointed by that outcome," Grace probed.

"You'll have to meet a few, one of these days, in order to truly appreciate things," Lazarus said. "But if you weren't Human and landed on a Westphalian world, they would treat you in a manner similar to how the Innruld treat everyone. I'd like to stop that."

She leaned back and studied the man. Saw the fire that kept him warm at night. The anger at misdeeds by others.

Grace rose and gestured for him to move.

"Slide back," she said, resting on the edge of the couch and then laying sideways and pushing him the rest of the way back with her bottom.

Arms came up around hers and she could feel the man's heartbeat pound against her back.

He started to talk and she shushed him, pulling his hands and arms tighter around her.

Eduardo had sent her to make sure this man was successful in his mission. To bring an enormous new trade to

Yisan, after they had all come that close to watching the planet be destroyed by an angry Churquen warrior.

Lazarus still needed help. Needed her around.

And she wanted to see Innruld Space before it was destroyed.

Maybe help him break it.

FIFTEEN

LAZARUS

LAZARUS TRIED NOT to completely freak out as Grace joined him on the couch. He'd wondered if she would break the ice first, or if he'd finally manage to do it.

The depth of those scars still surprised him, decades later. But he supposed that he'd gone into the service instead of staying home and getting married. Instead of joining her father's company and working his way up to running it by now, more than likely.

He wondered who Maria had finally settled on after he'd left. A woman like her wouldn't take being scorned like that, especially if she had absolutely no understanding of what *Pancho* had really wanted out of his life.

Up and out. The Rio Alliance Navy, first as a special forces killer, later as a scientist, when they realized that he also had a brain.

Lazarus could feel Grace's heartbeat where their chests touched. And in his hands that were wrapped around her chest right now, although carefully not touching any place that relative strangers shouldn't.

Were they still strangers? He and Grace had packed an

awful lot of life into the last two weeks, starting with a mass casualty incident of assholes who deserved every bit of what had happened to them.

But Lazarus couldn't bring himself to do more than just lean in close behind her and kiss Grace lightly on the ear, letting her smell overpower him.

She purred in his arms and they laid like that for a while.

It was good.

At some point, he drifted off, because her moving brought him to wakefulness like a slap to the face.

She slid off the couch and stood, reaching a hand down that he took.

"You need to go to bed and sleep," she announced firmly, pulling him to his feet.

Lazarus considered it for about a heartbeat, but she was right. Anything they might do now would keep them both up far later than they needed to be.

And he would need to be sharp in the morning. *Pancho Oliveira* wasn't twenty-two anymore.

"Thank you," he said.

She smiled.

He headed for his cabin.

Tomorrow would be here too soon.

SIXTEEN

ADDISON

ADDISON STUDIED his bridge crew as he prepared for something that had most likely never even been anticipated, let alone undertaken.

It even sounded like the beginning of a bad joke: *A Churquen, a Vaadwig, an Ilount, and a NavCrawler come into a bar…*

But on the planet below, those pirates were looking forward to randomly shooting people. They were even bragging about it on the radio as Addison and the others listened. Mayhem, rape, and murder.

There wasn't anyone around that could do anything about it, except him.

Addison swallowed heavily.

"Helm, what is your status?" he asked in a hard voice.

Like Kuei, he had been watching training videos in his spare time to look and sound more like a Rio Alliance Navy commanding officer. At least the Humans had a lot of educational materials for that sort of thing. He had already been a Director of his own civilian ship for two decades.

"Jump is plotted and locked in, Commander," Kuei

replied, just like she was supposed to. Same video library and all that.

"Sensors, what is the vicinity like?" Addison turned to Cormac next.

"*One hostile vessel identified, Commander,*" the NavCrawler said. "*No other vessels have been detected.*"

"Fusilier, arm the Star Lances and prepare to engage enemy forces," Addison said. "Raise all shielding and reinforce the forward array."

Wybert's entire lower section shimmied once, with his spinnerets clacking loudly, but he nodded and tapped several keys on the console.

"*Ajax* is ready for combat operations, Commander," Wybert replied in that high voice of his.

It always reminded Addison of a songbird, and made him smile, but today it seemed more like a vulture getting ready to tear chunks out of a still-warm body.

A Churquen, a Vaadwig, an Ilount, and a NavCrawler sail up to a pirate…

He opened a radio channel on the same frequency that the Westphalian pirates had been using to talk to their ground forces, then immediately muted the line. They were two light-hours out right now, but he needed secrecy.

"Helm, make your jump," Addison ordered, echoing everyone else's screens on his.

Ajax redshifted.

Over there, a sensors tech would note a new supernova that had just erupted politely on their tail feathers. Kuei really was that good at her job.

Ajax emerged from jump. A pirate warship of Westphalian manufacture hung right in front of them like a galumph sleeping in the grass as a hungry Churquen slithered up to it.

"Attention, enemy vessel," Addison growled at them as

their world just came unhinged. "This is the Rio Alliance Navy. Surrender or be destroyed."

Addison watched Wybert for sudden twitches, but didn't override the weapon controls. The Ilount doofus had nearly killed Lazarus that first time. However, being in control of this much firepower had brought a new level of reserve to the man.

Being able to destroy planets would probably do that to anyone. Even an Ilount.

The pirates opened fire with a rear facing, double-barreled turret. Twin Powerbolt configuration, from what Cormac's sensors showed. About normal for a vessel that size, but Addison knew that they would likely mount something like a Star Spear forward.

Which was why *Ajax* was behind them right now. Best not even tempt them, correct?

Wybert rotated his head one hundred and fifty degrees to look at his commander.

"Permission to wound him, sir?" Wybert asked seriously.

It was like a stranger had taken over that goofball's flesh.

Addison closed his shocked mouth and nodded.

"Wound only, Fusilier," he acknowledged, somewhat hollowly.

At this range, a Star Lance would probably break the pirate into pieces. Shatter them completely on a lucky shot, to rain fragments into the atmosphere below.

"Firing one Star Spear now," Wybert announced in a formal voice.

One hand tapped the console and a sound echoed through the cathedral of the bridge.

On his screens, Addison watched a ball of plasma erupt from the stern of the pirate, even as the vessel had started to turn.

Whether they were coming about to fight or to run

became immaterial as the vessel suddenly began to rotate upward and starboard on both pitch and roll axes, like a biped that had slipped on ice and was going over backwards.

Thadrakho's people moved so slowly at all times because they were from a world that was mostly ice covered. Small steps, mincing, so you didn't fall backwards and crack your skull on the deck.

The pirate ship didn't have any deck to slam its head against as they tumbled.

The Powerbolts in the turret were suddenly signaling other planets, rather than being effective weapons.

"Pirate vessel, this is the Rio Alliance Navy," Addison continued in a slow, terrible thunder. "That was your only warning shot."

Warning shot. Fired into his tail at short range.

Humans were insane. Even Rio standards usually called for a warning shot across their bow, but the enemy vessel had immediately opened fire on something several times its size, so technically Addison was within his rights to just annihilate them.

Especially as they were in the process of attacking a Human colony on the ground.

What was Rio Alliance Command going to do, turn him back into a civilian?

A court martial over this might even be interesting, at least from an academic standpoint.

The pirate vessel managed to right itself on gyros pretty quickly. Finally.

It was upside down relative right now, with their deck pointed at deep space and looking up that the planet hanging over their head, but their bow was pointed this way.

"Reinforce shields," Addison ordered, but Wybert's hands were already in motion.

The pirate fired something from the bow. Addison didn't

have anything to compare it against, but it was more powerful than the turret weapon.

His screen identified it as a Star Spear. About what he had been expecting that size of a hull to carry.

That was your last opportunity, Human.

"Fusilier, destroy the pirate vessel," Addison called across the space.

Wybert rotated his head again. All four mandibles opened and then slammed shut with a clack. A Churquen's mouth and eyes would have fallen wide.

Wybert hissed a frightened breath and then turned back to face forward.

"Firing Star Lance One now," Wybert said in a shaky, uneven voice.

Lazarus's first shuttle had been the only thing Wybert had ever actually damaged with his guns before today.

A hand tapped the console. The result was a deeper sound echoing through the hull as the beam on the bottom fin lit.

The pirate exploded. Simple as that. A ball of plasma appeared a second later, already well away from the hull before it cooled.

"Cormac, locate fragments large enough to impact the plant intact and feed them to Wybert," Addison ordered. "Fusilier, destroy anything large enough to pose a falling risk."

No use letting a chunk of steel and radiation land on someone below.

"One of the vessels has already landed on the surface, Addison," Cormac noted. *"The other has aborted their approach and are currently accelerating vertically."*

"Kuei, track the one fleeing and get over its head," Addison ordered. "Wybert, prepare to destroy the pincke if it does not surrender."

Seriously? Addison Wolcott, police officer? Knight slithering to the rescue, like some Innruld legend?

"Remaining vessels, this is Commander Addison Wolcott," he called over the open channel. "You will surrender to planetary authorities or I will destroy you, on the ground or in the air. Reply on this channel."

Kuei already had the bow coming down and sliding to one side. From up here, there was no chance that the smaller vessel could escape him. Their choice was death today or imprisonment. Which probably meant death tomorrow, considering that they were pirates, but that would not be his problem.

He was just here to see justice done.

And maybe teach Westphalian-associated pirates some manners. After all, that wasn't a Rio Alliance ship that had been retired from service.

Hells, come to think of it, that might not even be retired, but a Westphalian crew just pretending to be pirates. They had certainly reacted to a Rio Alliance warship hostilely.

"Commander, the first vessel has also lifted off from the surface," Cormac announced in that flat voice of his. *"Course plotted well away from that of the second fleeing ship."*

Made sense. If each went in a different direction, Addison might not be able to get both of them before one got out of beam range and could jump to safety.

"Fusilier, charge Kirov's Lance," Addison ordered. "Lock on to target number one."

In for a scale, in for a tail.

The bridge had fallen into an eerie silence only broken by the vents pushing fresh air around.

"Kirov's Lance is charged," Wybert said in a firm, tiny voice. "Target locked and gyroscopic deflection programmed in."

Addison took a deep breath and considered his place in Human history when today was done. Probably not pleasant.

But necessary.

"Fire Kirov's Lance."

The pincke had enough altitude that the beam didn't strike the ground, passing through the craft like a knife through cheese and then exiting the far edge of the atmosphere.

The ship didn't explode. Merely flashed to hot gas and fragments of metal and flesh raining back down on the surface of the planet below.

"Helm, bring us around and line up to pursue the final raider," Addison ordered quietly.

Everything was quiet. Attacking a Human world had been a theoretical possibility before Yisan.

Now they were actively engaged in the anti-piracy business.

"*Remaining vessel has grounded,*" Cormac announced a few minutes later. "*Scanners are picking up large numbers of Humans on foot moving away from the vehicle at this time.*"

"Transmit the coordinates to the outpost on the ground," Addison said.

"*We are being hailed,*" Cormac replied.

Yes, I suppose we would be.

Addison located the communications controls he wanted and routed the return signal to be audio only. The Humans on the ground didn't need to know who had just rescued them.

"9087 Geminorum IV, this is Commander Addison Wolcott of the Rio Alliance Navy," he announced gravely. "The pirate warship in orbit has been destroyed, as has one of the two vehicles attempting a landing. The other vessel has grounded and the crew fled. Are you able to take charge of ground operations?"

Just like you were supposed to say it, from a manual that had too many pages in it. But they were attempting to cover situations like this.

If you could.

"Affirmative, Commander," a Human female appeared on the screen. Older, from what his studies had shown. Heavier than Grace Savidge. "Will you be transporting them?"

Not on your life.

"Negative," Addison said. "We are technically on a secret mission and you don't even know we were here. My ship will be returning to our orders as soon as we can."

She nodded. Grim-faced.

"How many of them are we dealing with?" she asked. "I'm Mayor Mila Henders, by the way."

Addison muted the line again.

"Cormac?" he asked.

"Forty-seven Humans, including the two pilots, Addison."

"Forty-seven," Addison repeated to the woman, leaving out the part where they were Humans. That would create more questions right now. "They have departed the vehicle and fled into the bush at present."

He watched her face brighten suddenly. She did something and muted her line. Addison watched the Mayor talk to someone offscreen for a moment and then turn her attention back to him.

"Thank you," she said. "We might be able to simply capture their shuttle and then they have the option of surrendering or turning feral. I doubt they'd be able to maintain military cohesion on a hundred mile hike through hostile terrain."

She paused and stared at what was hopefully a blank screen at her end. Certainly a Human would have had more reaction to the first Churquen she had ever heard of.

"What were you going to tell the authorities about us?"

she asked a moment later.

Addison considered his words carefully.

"My current mission is top secret, Mayor Henders," he offered. "At some point, I will update the sailing directions to note that this planet is inhabited. Presumably other authorities will wish to consider their response at that time."

He watched her deflate just a little, which told Addison that this was probably an illegal colony. Squatters.

But what had he been looking for, if not the exact same thing? A place where he could hide a colony of Churquen, Vaadwig, Yithadreph, and others, away from Innruld influence.

He couldn't exactly fault the Humans for getting here first.

"Understood," she said. "Thank you, Commander."

"Thank you, Mayor," Addison replied. "My crew appreciates the chance to do something good and strike a blow against piracy, even if my superiors will perhaps be perturbed."

He cut the line and turned to the two heads, and a pair of cameras, twisted to face him.

"Any debris needing to be cleaned up?" he asked Wybert.

"No, sir."

"Any other issues in orbit?" he glanced at Kuei and Cormac.

Neither replied.

Addison nodded.

"Stand down from combat operations, Fusilier," he ordered the goofball. "Helm, turn us outward and plot a track to our next waypoint. We'll mark this as a maybe on the charts."

Maybe.

After all, how would the Humans already here illegally react to more refugees arriving on their doorstep?

SEVENTEEN
RODRIGO

RODRIGO HAD DONE ALL he could. Sent the various reports in to Headquarters with some of the details ambiguous, hoping that the news of new alien species might deflect people from paying too close of attention to the possibility that *Pancho* was right.

That there was a spy somewhere in the organization that had told Westphalia about *Ajax*.

Hell, he didn't even know much about the missing warship, other than that the Admiralty Staff had a number of super-secret projects underway, any one of which might hopefully break the war in their favor.

And Rodrigo had left out the bits where an alien crew had possession of *Ajax* right now, without any of the Humans remaining behind with it. That was likely to cause an explosion of outrage when it got out.

But *Recife* was sailing down-system now. Next stop: *Fleet Base One*, orbiting the planet itself.

They would arrive tomorrow, and it would all be out of his hands.

Off his conscience.

Except something wouldn't let him sleep. Some detail kept niggling at the back of his head.

He didn't want to put another meeting with *Pancho* on the record right now. Those all had to be recorded and the evasions necessary to have a personal conversation would require too much work and make everyone look guilty.

Plus, the way the Yithadreph and Churquen had reacted to his Atomarsk engineer told him that they were from an extremely long ways away from Brasilia.

He had an idea.

Rodrigo keyed the intercom and an aide stuck her head into his office a moment later.

"Sir?" she asked innocently.

"See if Commander Enjehn is available and ask her to join me," he ordered the Lieutenant.

It took the woman a moment to process the words. She knew every senior officer on *Recife*, but people tended to forget that *Pancho* had made the Yithadreph woman a Commander as well. And she continued to act like a successful *90-day wonder*, which said a lot about the woman's competence.

"Immediately, Admiral."

And then he was alone in his office again. Sixteen hours or so from not being involved anymore. No skin off his back, either way, except something just didn't feel right.

Ten minutes of paperwork later, a knock preceded the door opening.

Rodrigo considered standing, but he was an Admiral and she was just a Commander, so he smiled and gestured to the chair.

"Please, sit, Commander," he invited her in a friendly manner.

After the last few days of meetings, he understood that Human chairs didn't fit a Yithadreph's physiology worth a damn. Short legs and a stubby tail. However, she would be gone tomorrow, presumably off his deck forever.

Or at least until they started recruiting actively among all the other species and had to reconfigure all the interiors of their vessels.

"Sir?" Enjehn asked once the door was closed.

"Presuming that *Ajax* needs to lay in supplies at some point, I thought that I should take it upon myself to interview the Quartermaster of the ship directly," Rodrigo replied in a vague, somewhat ambiguous tone.

He hadn't spent enough time around the alien to truly learn her body language, but she seemed to radiate a knowing smile. Her whiskers (**WHISKERS!!!**) came forward and her ears seemed to be tracking him on a sub-sonic level or something.

"The original mission, before I joined the crew, was a three week sail with a dead-minimum operations crew and a number of mechanics and such from the shipyard to fix anything that went wrong," she replied in a formal tone that almost sounded like a training video.

Had that been how she had learned the language of the Navy? Interesting.

Rodrigo nodded to her to continue.

"That meant roughly nine to ten weeks of supplies, with a number of check-in points," she did continue. "The star drive engines had already been tested and approved, so Lazarus didn't need any other ships along."

Lazarus. *Pancho* as he had apparently been reborn. Lazarus of Bethany.

"And where are you at now?" he asked.

"Nobody likes coffee," Enjehn said flatly. "That left Lazarus about a century and a half worth to drink on his own. Roughly two thirds of the remaining food stocks are adequate to the crew's needs, according to Khyaa'sha

Ramarkhay, our chef who originally was responsible for keeping us from poisoning Lazarus when he came aboard Addison's ship, *Shiva Zephyr Glaive*. Addison has enough food and fuel to not need a port call for roughly two years, if they are careful."

Rodrigo considered his next question. That was the one nobody had been willing to approach in an open meeting being recorded for posterity. In fact…

"Commander, unlike previous meetings, this one is not being recorded," he said. "I would like an assessment between Rio Alliance officers, off the record. Are you willing to do that?"

The ears went to midmast. The whiskers slid back. Straight out sideways, rather than back against her cheeks. Thoughtful, perhaps.

"Possibly, Admiral," she said.

"Will Addison Wolcott seek to recruit more crew members to expand his current staff?" Rodrigo asked carefully. "If Lazarus returned to *Ajax* with your group, would he be set to return to Rio service, or head back to Innruld Space and do things over there?"

Her eyes got shrewd. In that, her body language was much closer to Human than the Churquen woman's. But a Yithadreph was a mammalian biped, unlike some of the truly bizarre aliens apparently left behind on *Ajax*.

"Overthrowing the so-called Masters of the Galaxy is very near the top of Addison's list, Admiral," Commander Enjehn replied. "But he'll have concerns about people he doesn't know. Lazarus will be able to vouch for some, but even the civilians we brought with us from Yisan have not been keyed into *Ajax* as officers."

Oh? That hadn't come up earlier. Or maybe nobody had asked the right question, and *Pancho* and his friends were playing it even closer to the chest than he had anticipated.

"But *Pancho* Oliveira, Lazarus, would prefer not to return to duty directly, if given the choice?" Rodrigo asked. That was the million cruzeiro question.

She leaned back now, then shifted to one arm of the chair as her tail got pinched painfully from the sudden flash of irritation on the woman's face.

"Lazarus is family," she said obliquely. "We took him in when he had nothing but the suit he was in and a beer logo for a jacket, Admiral. Protected him from folks that did not have the best intentions. Now, he wants to help us be free. However, he has trust issues, as you might imagine."

Rodrigo considered her words. And the implications. The greatest thing since an Atomarsk miner accidentally encountered a Human exploration vessel, but trust was going to be an issue.

Because there was a whole other war being fought across the galaxy.

"Thank you, Commander," he replied after a long thought. "You've given me much to think about. Did you have questions for me?"

"Will the Admiralty deal with their spy?" she asked bluntly. "Or will there be another Westphalian GunWall jumping down on us one of these days? Lazarus said that with enough crew members, he could take one apart, but we're not there yet. Plus, as Quartermaster, I'm still responsible for twenty-eight Humans who did not make it home. Their bodies are in my freezers right now, until you can come get them."

Yes. Human dead, being cared for by an alien woman. How much stranger would it all get before it was sorted out?

"Understood," he replied. "I cannot vouch for the Admiralty, but I have noted various things in my report that should guide them towards a spy. But it is now out of my hands. Until tomorrow, then?"

She left him alone with his paperwork and Rodrigo considered how he might be able to help.

If *Pancho* was right, really right, the rot was at a very high level, and neither *Pancho* nor his friends were going to be safe until it was dealt with.

How long would Addison Wolcott wait before he did something irrevocable?

EIGHTEEN
OLUCHI

THEY WERE a couple of hours from departure and Oluchi had no idea why a cute, female lieutenant had asked him to accompany her. Didn't feel like an assassination, or even an assignation. Most of the sailors had looked down their noses at a civilian like him.

Fair, he wasn't after any of them. Had there been a woman as Captain or Admiral, maybe a different story, but nobody here needed a fixer and he was retired from being a gigolo.

He hoped.

She led him to a side door, opened it, and gestured him in without following.

The Admiral was alone in a small office with a single chair. Nobody had found out about any of those warrants that quickly, had they?

But he sat when the man silently gestured. The woman closed the door and Oluchi stared at the man.

Lazarus had said nice things about the Admiral as a former officer he had served with. Everything had been generally pleasant up until now, and Oluchi would *presumably* be departing with everyone else shortly for a political reception likely to be much different from the military one on their arrival aboard *Recife*.

"Oluchi Pryce," the Admiral said in a slow, heavy voice after he sat.

He smiled at the man, still being dressed as a civilian in as good a style and fashion as a tailor like Thadrakho the Necherle had been able to handle.

The opera cape worked wonders disarming sailors trying to be formal and superior.

"What happens when all this comes out, Pryce?" Admiral da Silva asked.

"Trade through Yisan expands significantly," Oluchi answered. "My principals make even more money than they already have. Without knowing too much, I presume that Rio Alliance trade with Innruld Space perhaps uses Yisan as a nexus. I get rich in the process."

"Is that all you care about?" da Silva pressed.

"No," Oluchi countered. "I helped rescue Eha from kidnappers intent on killing her, Admiral. Killed people in the process. These are my friends, however strange that sounds even to me. But I was sent here to do a job."

"You describe yourself as a Fixer, Pryce," da Silva's voice took on an edge Oluchi recognized now.

Cop who can't prove anything criminal yet. Won't stop him from trying.

"That's right," Oluchi smiled more serenely. "What would you like to buy? I have a cousin."

In this business, you always have a cousin. A favor. A number to call.

da Silva took a deep breath. Gritted his teeth some.

"I want to establish and maintain a secondary channel of communication, Pryce," he finally admitted. "Our politicians may lose track of themselves in the process. They might make this Addison Wolcott over into an enemy because they get too pig-headed for their own good."

"And you think I can help?" Oluchi marveled.

Most Navy folks took civilians like him for granted.

"Commander Aileen Enjehn is responsible for twenty-eight sailors who died aboard *Ajax*, Pryce," da Silva said. "Eventually, someone will get around to remembering those men and women, but I want to make sure that there is an easy way to get them home. Even if Wolcott ends up heading into deep space because Oliveira's spy turns out to be real and not just bad luck or timing. I want a way in case something else happens."

"And what do you think I can do in that case?" Oluchi asked.

"Find a way to get them home." The Admiral surprised him with the emotion in the man's voice. "I don't care if we have to become enemies after that, but those men and women deserve a proper burial and ceremony, Pryce."

Oluchi would have normally said something there. Trite. Perhaps sarcastic. Biting, at least.

But that was a different Oluchi Pryce. The one who had been charitably described as a gigolo of no import. A playboy card sharp making his way on looks and brains, without ever working an honest day in his life.

This Oluchi still had the faintest bruising on his legs from where Eha had wrapped her tail tight around him and leapt into a storming ocean, something he later discovered was the single greatest fear a Churquen might ever face.

She had trusted him to save her. A stranger named Lazarus of Bethany had relied on him.

This was not a moment for levity. For anything but deadly seriousness.

"I'll see to it, Admiral," he nodded.

Addison might object, but Oluchi doubted it. And he would have Lazarus and Eha and Aileen on his side.

NINETEEN

LAZARUS

LAZARUS STARED at the two shuttles that had drawn up in the bay. Never a good sign. The number of people assigned as escort was double what it had been for the last week as well.

Troubling.

He stood at semi-attention and watched. Aileen had drawn herself up beside him. Eha and the three Human civilians were separated slightly.

Admiral da Silva walked away from the group where he had been talking quietly and gesturing extravagantly, a barely-controlled rage on his face. He came to rest in front of Lazarus and took a deep breath before speaking.

"They *insist*," he growled in a rage so potent it seemed to come off him in waves. "Stupid *varkash!*"

"Sir?" Lazarus asked quietly, noting the gap that separated all the security marines from the people they were guarding. And the way those men and women were keyed up for violence again, like that first meeting.

"You and Commander Enjehn will be taken to your former headquarters for debriefing, *Pancho*," da Silva ground out the words as though pounding a chicken breast flat for dinner. "Ambassador Dunham and the others will be taken before the High Council's representatives to be interviewed."

Admiral da Silva flexed his entire body downward angrily for a moment. His skin wasn't as dark as Grace's but he'd seen her do the same thing, mostly right before practicing her dance.

Admiral da Silva looked more like a man about to start a bar fight.

"I told them that they would be best served keeping the entire group together," he continued. "And got politely patted on the head for my troubles. Morons."

"Two years' supplies aboard, Admiral," Aileen spoke up in a bright voice that didn't seem to say anything Lazarus understood.

Rodrigo da Silva did, however. That much was obvious from the look in his eyes as he turned to Aileen and nodded curtly.

"That, Commander, is my greatest fear," he said simply. "If Wolcott has to act alone, he will not assume friends here. That is an unnecessary mistake."

Lazarus nodded. Addison would eventually just assume something bad had happened if nobody came and told him the story.

Hopefully, he would just go annihilate the Innruld rather than starting a war with the Rio Alliance first. Even *Ajax* couldn't do that much damage.

Hopefully.

"I'm sending Lt. Commander Slani with you, *Pancho*," the admiral continued. "And Lt. Lam with the others, so I at least have some contact. Not sure what I can do, but we'll burn that bridge when we get there."

"Understood, Admiral," Lazarus said, turning to pick out his new minder.

Atomarsk. Best described as a bipedal peacock with a small beak, large eyes, opposable thumbs, and dewclaws, except that she generally had maroon fur. The seven-feathered fan tail on the woman was at rest right now, pulled in so that it looked like a single upright blade, a closed Chinese fan, perhaps.

Engineer. Nerd like him. One of the few people aboard that probably had enough tech grounding to actually talk about some of the crazy, top secret things he and Kirov had done, but Lazarus doubted that she had anywhere near enough to the right clearance to even know him.

At least up until now.

Lazarus found it interesting that da Silva hadn't flipped the assignments, sending the Atomarsk woman with Eha and keeping the security marine officer with the Rio Alliance people, but he had to presume that the man knew what he was doing.

It was his superiors who had overruled his decisions.

He saluted the Admiral. Felt Aileen do the same beside him. Rodrigo da Silva grimaced and returned it sharply, before nodding and stepping past them, his face inscrutable.

In the other group, Eha had turned questioningly towards him. Lazarus shrugged. Not much he could do at this point without adding charges of mutiny to the dereliction of duty he was already facing.

To say nothing of losing his command at sea. Even if it was still out there.

Addison wouldn't bring it into dock without confidence in the situation.

Lazarus didn't even have that at this point.

At least Lam was acting politely. Lazarus watched him bow to Eha and gesture for her to board the other shuttle as if she was an Ambassador and he was her chief bodyguard, rather than her jailer.

Self-perception is everything, after all.

Oluchi glanced his way and nodded, so Lazarus felt better. That one still looked like a dandy. Probably would be mistaken for one, right up to the moment he slid a knife between someone's ribs.

Eha had three killers with her. Four with a trained security marine, although Lazarus wasn't about to tell Lucas Lam that he was the fourth or fifth most dangerous person in that group, depending on how angry Eha got. Hopefully, it would never come to that.

"Sir?" Lt. Commander Slani stepped up now and gestured for him to precede her to the other shuttle.

He'd worked with Atomarsk before. After Humans, they were the most common species in the Rio Alliance, even if Humans were still ninety percent of the population on most worlds. Technically, the Alliance represented nine species, but five were tiny fractions of populations spread thin. Possibly refugees from places like Innruld Space, although Lazarus had never given it any thought before.

Nerdy engineer building a better warship to go beat up Westphalia. Not a species liberator set to save the galaxy.

That had come much, much later.

Lazarus nodded to her and glanced at Aileen. The two women fell in beside each other as the remaining marines escorted them onto the second transport.

Lazarus looked over at Eha's shuttle and silently promised her that he would see that she got home safely.

Whatever the cost was going to be.

TWENTY

H'BRIGE

H'BRIGE SLANI HAD NEVER MET a Yithadreph before. Nor a Churquen. Nor had they an Atomarsk, apparently. If she was understanding the subtext correctly, where those two women came from, Atomarsk like her were merely legends.

She considered fairy tales her mother had told her, ages ago, and wondered if they contained a kernel of truth that her kind had once lived much closer to this Innruld Space. Or at least traded with them for a time.

The Innruld had risen to dominance two thousand years ago. Like the Human stories of Exodus, the Atomarsk had something similar, but it was entirely oral, even in a space traveling species.

Had her ancestors fled their own pharaohs in the distant past?

She took her seat next to Captain Oliveira and buckled herself in. Interestingly, Commander Enjehn chose to sit on H'Brige's far side, putting her in the middle instead of a periphery.

H'Brige took the opportunity to turn and study Commander Enjehn at close quarters.

Short legs and arms. Long, sinuous torso. Brown fur everywhere. Lively whiskers and ears. Bright eyes staring back at her now.

A Human otter, in a Rio Alliance uniform.

But she was Atomarsk, and her kind were almost as rare.

"Commander," H'Brige nodded to the woman.

The rank was semi-honorary, enlisted in the field and then promoted into a slot on need. Not unheard of, but H'Brige was interested to know what the 4-star admirals in charge of the fleet would do with her.

But for now, they were all under military order.

H'Brige supposed that was why the civilians were being separated off. Diplomats would take charge of the Churquen Ambassador. She had admirals in her future.

With any luck, good things would happen, rather than bad. Admiral da Silva had selected her because of her species, so she should have gone on the other shuttle.

But…

"So how many Atomarsk are there, really?" Enjehn asked in a whisper.

H'Brige blinked at the randomness of the question.

"We are the second largest population in Rio Alliance Space," she replied after a moment of thought. "Perhaps twenty-four billion sentients, although that is just an estimate on my part. How many Yithadreph are there?"

"Maybe a billion," Enjehn replied grumpily.

"Why so few?" H'Brige asked, intrigued now.

"The Overlords keep a tight rein on us," the woman replied. "The Churquen are the largest, and that's maybe ten or twelve billion across all sub-species and cousins."

"Oh."

H'Brige hadn't given much thought to the sociological aspects of such a place, other than to be deeply offended that Westphalia was replicated over there. But it made sense that one species trying to control so many others would have to exercise all manner of subversions. And probably perversions.

She really was facing Westphalia in another form, wasn't she? H'Brige had not connected that circuit, even in her own head.

Captain Oliveira's underlying anger at everything made a great deal more sense in that instance. She had not been privy to the design and construction of this new thing called *Ajax*, but apparently he believed that it would be sufficient to alter the balance of power with Westphalia.

"What would *Ajax* do in Innruld Space?" H'Brige asked carefully.

Admiral da Silva had been rebuffed in seeking that answer. Commander Enjehn leaned back now to look over her head at Captain Oliveira, who nodded to some unvoiced question.

"Break them," the Yithadreph woman said simply. "Free us."

H'Brige recoiled and turned to Captain Oliveira.

"Then why are we not doing so, sir?"

"That is the question I have been asking myself, Slani," the man replied in a dark tone.

H'Brige didn't have a good answer to any of this, so she fell into silence. The two officers apparently recognized that and let her be.

TWENTY-ONE

OLUCHI

OUT OF THE FRYING PAN?

Oluchi wasn't sure where he'd ended up this time, but he'd been in tighter spots. It was doubtful that a husband would accidentally come home early and nearly catch him upstairs with a wife.

Today, anyway. Tomorrow would sort itself out. They did that.

Eha was tense, but that was nothing exceptional. She had three Humans along as allies, but not the two friends she had brought to Yisan originally. He would just have to try to get as close as he could to what Lazarus represented to her.

If that was possible.

Oluchi turned to Lam. The man had an odd smile on his face. Subversive, lacking a better term to use. Oluchi understood subversive.

"Where are we going?" he asked the man.

"Greenbriar Starport," Lam replied. "From there, I don't know. Admiral da Silva instructed me to be your escort, but the locals will provide guides."

Interesting. Didn't make a damned bit of sense, either.

One would expect that the government would welcome additional alien species, since that was the literal core of the Rio Alliance in the first place. Why were they treating all this with such secrecy?

Unless Lazarus had been determined to be a problem? Oluchi had already spent a lot of time working through all the puzzle pieces and most of them just didn't align.

And he was good at puzzles.

Did someone in fleet command think that Lazarus was the spy? Or that he'd been captured and turned by Westphalia? Then why go through the effort to send Eha and Aileen?

None of it made any sense.

"What happens after we land, Lam?" Oluchi asked, but he was rewarded with a shrug.

"Not a ticker-tape parade, which surprises me," the marine replied grumpily.

Oluchi nodded thanks and turned to Eha on his other side.

Somehow, he always ended up at her right hand when Lazarus wasn't around. Left hand when the big man was. Grace and Xiuying watched with bright eyes.

"Why are you not being celebrated?" he asked in a low voice that Lam and the other marines in here would miss.

"I don't know," Eha replied. "I had somehow expected the Rio Alliance to throw a massive party at the thought of forty other species out there that they might welcome with open arms."

Food for thought.

Oluchi fell into meditation as the shuttle cut through the thickening atmosphere. He had never been to the core world of the Rio Alliance. Just the first tier out, in terms of wealth and society. He'd done much better out beyond the border, in places like Yisan where money and power spoke its own language.

Here, there were other currents at play. Deeper, colder ones. Even without *Ajax* in hand, Lazarus should be welcomed as a hero, doubly so with friends who could blast open the galaxy.

What the hell was going on?

Eventually, they landed, where most of the marines were separated off by what appeared to be Council Guards, if he heard the term correctly. Lam refused to be moved, even when all his men were hustled back onto the shuttle and instructed to depart.

"Lam, maybe you should go?" Oluchi leaned close as the Council Guards huddled up across a short distance and contacted someone remote via comm.

The air was lovely today. Clear, blue skies and just enough breeze to make everything feel peaceful, except for the ring of armed troopers around them and the shuttle. It felt rather like when arriving at *Recife*, come to think of it. More guns, but he'd brought more marines.

"Admiral da Silva specifically instructed me to remain with the Ambassador under any circumstances, Pryce," the man murmured back.

Oh, did he now? So the Admiral didn't have any better feeling about this than Lazarus or Oluchi Pryce?

The goon squad got an answer. Didn't like it, but weren't going to argue.

"You alone may remain with the Ambassador," the head Council Guard said. "But you will be disarmed."

"Fine," Lam said.

He slowly removed his gun belt and handed it to one of the other goons.

"Mark that as in possession of the Council Guards if I

don't get it back," Lam called to his own troopers loud enough to be a bureaucratic threat across departments.

Oluchi was a bit surprised that a marine would know that trick, but all the Council Guards flinched as if affronted. Insulted, perhaps, that they might lose the weapon and have to account for it later to someone important.

And they couldn't easily come back with a sob story about a misplaced Ares pistol now, could they?

From there, everyone was hustled into an aircar almost as good as the one Fernanda Flores had back on Yisan, and that woman was a gearhead for such things.

It was crowded, with the Ambassadorial party increased by one, plus the head goon in this vehicle. As they lifted off, Oluchi caught sight of two other vehicles escorting them.

Quickly, it became obvious that they were not headed into the city, but south, towards a hilly area covered over with trees supposedly seeded from original Amazonian stock, back on Earth.

Remote and quiet, again at a time one might expect noise and celebrations. What was the Council all about?

Or, more interestingly, how many spies were there, perhaps working in concert?

Oluchi kept his thoughts to himself as they flew, since the head goon himself was seated across from him, watching the group with hostile eyes.

Enjoy your moment, my friend. Strav Ardna had thought he was untouchable, too.

Look how that turned out for him.

TWENTY-TWO
LAZARUS

LAZARUS WATCHED on a remote screen as the shuttle came in to dock at *Fleet Base One*. The anchor of the Navy itself. The most heavily-defended and armed platform known, depending on maybe new mods to *Earth Prime Station*, but Westphalia wouldn't have much of an edge regardless.

The back of the shuttle was comfortable, but the others were at a cold reserve. A social gap that separated he, Aileen, and Lt. Cmdr. Slani from the rest. Just a bunch of marines who apparently had orders to keep their distance.

They docked and the inner hatch opened as everyone unbuckled and rose.

Lazarus followed a pair of *Recife's* troopers out into a larger concourse area where more marines waited, as well as a small assembly of senior officers. The only one Lazarus recognized was Admiral Santos. Not exactly a friend, but not someone who had been an enemy.

As far as Lazarus knew.

Lazarus wondered what the man thought as he saw the two alien women following behind him. The three of them came to rest and saluted sharply. Santos returned it somewhere between professionally and negligently.

Santos stared at them for a long moment, some internal dialogue playing out that Lazarus could not read in his eyes.

"This way," he gestured abruptly with a thumb and started walking.

Lazarus and the two women fell in with him, surrounded by all the armed troopers, rather like landing on *Recife* had been. Maybe colder. Hard to tell yet.

After all, a captain went down with his ship, right? And Lazarus had failed three times with that now.

Maybe next time he would be able to just send Oluchi and Grace and trust them.

Maybe.

Conference room.

Lazarus wondered what percentage of his life had been spent in rooms exactly like this. Throw in years spent on a bridge or in some ship's main engineering deck and you were probably getting close to half, even with time to sleep.

He came to rest behind a chair, still more or less at attention, with Aileen on his right and Slani on his left.

Santos sat, studied them again, and gestured for them to join him.

"I've read the reports from da Silva," he began in a hard, voice. "Normally, I would be disinclined to believe them, but Rodrigo does, and the presence of two new species, and suggestions of dozens more, weighs in your favor, Oliveira."

Lazarus nodded and remained silent, unsure where the man's temperament might take him. Technically, a court martial was the next step, according to all the rules and statutes.

"Where is *Ajax*?" Santos asked flatly.

"Right now they are hiding out in the darkness until the Ambassador and I could be sure what kind of reception we would receive," Lazarus replied. "Yisan had a significantly negative impact on Addison Wolcott's trust reserves, sir."

"So you left an alien crew in command of an experimental Human warship, in Rio Alliance Space, Oliveira?" Santos's voice got harder.

"That's only a problem if we make it one, Admiral," Lazarus replied, letting his own voice get a little harder. "I consider all of them my friends. My greater concern here was that there might be a spy relaying all this information directly to Westphalia."

"The ambush," Santos said negligently, one hand brushing an invisible dust bunny out of the air. "I think it was just bad luck on our part. Or a leak at a low level and Westphalia was able to deduce your rough path. If I had heard something about your ship, I might have set several GunWalls out and left them in your possible paths."

Lazarus had considered that. It made a sort of sense, other than those ships had been firing almost as fast as they detected his blueshift. They had been literally lying in wait.

"What happens if you do not return to them by some appointed time, Oliveira?" Santos asked abruptly.

"Addison Wolcott takes *Ajax* back into Innruld Space and uses his contacts there to recruit enough of a crew to use the ship offensively, Admiral," Lazarus replied.

Around the walls, the marines stirred unconsciously. Just little twitches, but it was like wind passing through a wheat field.

"What can *Ajax* do by itself?" Santos leaned forward a little, both palms flat on the table top.

Lazarus considered asking the Admiral to clear the room before he spoke, but then he decided that rumors and gossip would work in his favor, since the lords of the fleet seemed intent on keeping him quiet.

He smiled at Admiral Santos.

"*Ajax* is more powerful than any vessel in their entire fleet, sir," Lazarus said. "Addison could probably overthrow the Innruld if he played his cards right, just by blowing up enough Security Barcs and frightening the rest."

"And then what?" Santos demanded. "They come this way and roll over us?"

Lazarus shook his head emphatically.

"No, sir," he said. "All of Innruld Space, every single person alive over there, sums up to about one hundred billion sentients. Total. Across more than forty species. Addison's original fear was that we would overwhelm them, because there are so many more Humans. The Churquen are the largest species group at twelve billion, sir. We also breed faster than they do. And have a higher technology level than the Innruld. In short, Admiral, they are more afraid of us than we should be of them."

Again, wheat stirring as breezes rocked them. That information would get out. Marines couldn't help but jabber to each other. He'd spent enough time around them in his crazy days to know the mindset. They would be thinking about how to fight Yithadreph or Churquen. That would leak out as well.

The information would not be contained for long.

"And all the secrecy, Oliveira?" Santos demanded.

"The Species Underground, of which Eha Dunham is our Ambassador and Addison Wolcott the Field Commander, fear that Humans would sail in and displace the Innruld instead of overthrowing them, Admiral," Lazarus let a hint of cruelty into his voice now. "Not free them, but turn into another set of overlords. Another Westphalia. I've tried to explain to them that the Rio Alliance is different, but we're working with a culture of fear and rebellion over there, and their first exposure to Humans, at Yisan, was a decidedly *mixed* affair."

"Mixed?" Santos leaned back now, perhaps taken aback by Lazarus's tone and words.

"Eha and Aileen got kidnapped at gunpoint, Admiral," Lazarus stuck the knife in and twisted it a little, nodding to Aileen. "Commander Enjehn was severely beaten. The Ambassador was going to be murdered. I had made some contacts when I arrived and they were able to help me recruit some help."

"And then what happened, Captain?" Santos bored in now. Those details hadn't been in a report.

"With the assistance of retired Senior Chief Marine Bălan and the two Humans that accompanied the Ambassador today, I penetrated the security on the kidnapper's boat while it was at sea in a storm." Lazarus fell back into the old patterns of speech. A young and crazy *Pancho* and the things he had done back then. The marines stirred again, understanding the rhythm of the words. "Ascertaining that the entire crew was hostile and implicated in the crime, we rescued Commander Enjehn first, then went to the main chamber and rescued Ambassador Dunham at significant loss of life on the part of the kidnappers."

"How?" Santos asked sharply, but his voice had fallen off from anger and was more curious now.

"The Senior Chief had a Battlerifle," Lazarus said. The marines around him would appreciate using something like that in a confined space. And the kind of trooper willing to use it. "I kicked the door in and he killed most of the people in the room. The main kidnapper had a pistol to the Ambassador's head, so we shot him, too. Afterwards, we blew the entire boat up by sabotaging the engines and let it sink in a hurricane off-shore. Those details were not made public at Yisan before we left, so I doubt anyone there knows the truth. I rated the alternative to direct action as too great a threat, Admiral."

"What was the alternative?" the man asked, less hostile now than he had been perhaps. Possibly even a little nervous now.

"*Ajax* annihilating the colony at Yisan from orbit, sir," Lazarus said. "Addison Wolcott is Eha's mate and he would have reacted badly had something happened to her. I would have as well."

He didn't bother explaining Kirov's Lance to this man. Or the marines. The fact that Lazarus thought he could do it would be enough for most of them.

"That would be a serious crime, Captain." Admiral Santos's voice got deadly now.

"Indeed it would have, Admiral," Lazarus replied. "I'm just glad that it did not become *necessary*."

The room fell into silence. An awkward, pregnant kind of stillness as folks digested things. The marines might recognize him now as one of them in a previous life, nearly twenty years ago. The Admiral was seeing a different officer than he had expected, apparently.

Santos turned to his right now.

"Lt. Commander Slani, do you know why Admiral da Silva sent you with Captain Oliveira?" he asked.

"Negative, sir," she replied. "I would have expected to accompany the Ambassador as some sort of species representative, perhaps. At present, I could also serve as an engineering officer aboard *Ajax* if you ordered us to return to that vessel."

Lazarus kept his smile to himself. Sending him politely on his way hadn't seemed like the outcome on tap up until now. Maybe da Silva was herding things in his own, quiet way?

"And you, Commander Enjehn?" Santos turned that way. "Were you expecting to remain in uniform?"

Ah, that might be it. The man might have been insulted

that Lazarus had commissioned an alien in the field. The statutes did allow it, however far Lazarus had stretched them in interpretations.

But the Devil had most assuredly been on his heels all the way.

"Actually, sir, I'd rather return to civilian life, given the choice," Aileen smiled up at the man now. "However, Lazarus needs me in place handling supplies for his crew. At least as long as he remains in command."

Again, Lazarus kept his face serious. It wasn't a threat, per se, but the Rio Alliance would make its reputation with the Species Underground by how they treated Aileen and Eha. As well as the others, but it started here. Today.

Now.

Admiral Santos suddenly realized that he was negotiating with two other alien ambassadors, and not just officers he could issue orders to.

He shook his whole body and took a deep breath.

"My orders were to determine where things stood, Captain," he said flatly. "To see if you should be held accountable for losing your command and crew. That still remains, but I am also instructed to keep things quiet for now, rather than dragging you before a court. The three of you will be confined here for now, while the Admiralty Staff determines its next steps. Do you have questions?"

"Will they reach a conclusion in less than forty-three days, sir?" Lazarus asked.

It was a polite way to indicate that a clock was running. And how long Addison might wait.

Maybe.

TWENTY-THREE
ADDISON

6357 WEI XIU.

Also marked in Addison's records as *Vilga's Stand.* He'd had to dig to find the reference, but Addison also had access to a Rio Alliance military database here, and was interested in the notes about one of the first battles that had erupted between the Rio Alliance and Westphalia, back when independence had been declared.

They weren't on the theoretical frontier itself, but back some, still inside Rio Alliance-claimed space. The battle itself had been an engagement between small fleets on both sides. Oversized squadrons, perhaps, depending. A full GunWall, plus other Westphalian vessels, against a roughly equal tonnage of Rio warships.

The Alliance had won, of course, and that had helped establish some level of border and separateness. There were still shattered remains of metal and debris out near the seventh planet, where the battle had been fought, but *Ajax* was down listening in quietly around the fifth planet.

"Still nothing?" Addison asked.

He and Cormac were alone on the bridge, with Kuei and Wybert both off doing things. Or maybe sleeping.

"*That is correct, Addison. Ongoing passive scans have shown no indication that Humans have visited this system in a considerable period of time. There are a series of satellites in orbit, tracking the surface of both the fourth and fifth worlds, but they are non-intelligent systems.*"

Yes. Lazarus had said that Humans did not, as a rule, fully trust sentient computer systems, after errors in their distant past.

"Can we tap those systems secretly?" Addison asked.

"*I have already begun, Addison.*"

"And the planets themselves?" Addison asked.

"*The fourth might be a better fit for Churquen and Yithadreph,*" Cormac replied. "*It is much hotter as a rule over most of the surface, with significant water resources. Large portions of the fifth are cold enough for Necherle to enjoy. Human terraforming efforts in the past have seeded both with a variety of plants and lower animal forms. The current prognosis is positive.*"

He'd wondered why nobody lived here, but if they were waiting for the worlds to settle down into some balance of alien forms and Human, then he could understand that. This system would be a good place to establish a colony of peoples from Innruld Space. Two planets instead of one meant a wider variety of ecosystems into which folks could settle.

Of course, he would be trespassing, if they did establish a colony here. But it might be a risk worth taking, especially if things went well with Eha.

TWENTY-FOUR

EHA

EHA STUDIED the group waiting in the middle distance as the flying vehicle finally landed on a wide grass area near a magnificent stone manor house. The kind secluded in the middle of an enormous nature preserve, from the lack of other settlements nearby.

Isolated and remote, that was her impression.

Her four Human associates, including Lucas Lam, were a bit on edge, but that was partially a reaction to cultural touchstones she did not share, so Eha decided to take things at face value for now.

It was hard to insult someone who didn't give you any authority over them. To her, these folks were just politicians, not rebels or revolutionaries.

Bureaucrats, but she would never call them that to their faces. As Lazarus had said, the true power lay with the fleets of warships that defended the Alliance from Westphalia. And the men and women who wore that tan uniform he prized so much.

She emerged last from the vehicle and let her keelscales

be seduced by the feel of grass. She'd been on stations too much over the last few years, rather than planetary surfaces. It would be good to get out more when she got home.

When. Not if. She was not here as a beggar with galumph in hand. Nor was she a prisoner of their system.

If they thought otherwise, Eha would tell her friends that she needed to depart and let them sort things.

Eha still had nightmares about the amazing prospect for lethal violence contained in her Human friends, from Xiuying killing almost everyone in the room to Grace firing a shot so close that Eha could still feel the heat on her scales.

The Council Guard formed themselves up into something loosely interpretable as an honor guard, two lines for her. Unlike the tan of the fleet, these men and women wore a dark maroon, the kind of color that suggested fresh blood tainted with black ink.

The faces were an interesting mix of curious and hostile, but she took that as professional paranoia. Her own team had something similar going.

As Eha crossed the meadow and approached the group of politicians, she noted six Humans, plus one each Moah, Gnashiiley, and Atomarsk. The first two, like similar specimens on Yisan, were taller, larger, and in better shape than the kind she knew from Innruld Space. The Rio Alliance was a better place to live.

One Human male stepped away from the group and approached. Like the others, he wore robes instead of a uniform. Or perhaps as a uniform. His were a dark blue and billowed in a way that disguised most of his body.

From his face and head, she presumed him to be tall and thin. White hair as a thick mane. Skin much darker than Lazarus, but more red/brown than Grace.

But Eha already knew that Humans came in an amazingly diverse mixture.

The man did not smile, but his face was merely calm, rather than anything hostile or negative.

"Ambassador Dunham," he bowed as he spoke. "I am Roald Cavalcanti, Chairman of the High Council of the Rio Alliance."

She gave him the sort of bow reserved for equals. Again, not a beggar. This planet didn't even have galumphs yet, although someone would eventually import them for food.

"Chairman," she smiled. "Thank you for taking the time to meet with me. I look forward to negotiating trade agreements and alliances. Captain Oliveira has been a great help to me."

Eha caught a flash of something across the man's face, gone so quickly she might have imagined it. He turned to the others and quickly introduced them.

Human flesh was cool and damp compared to Churquen. The three non-Humans were all impressive, seen up close.

Cavalcanti led them onto a rear patio of the estate and into a door that deposited them in a dining hall that could have comfortably fed fifty, even as large as Humans were.

Eha found herself at the center of one long table, facing Cavalcanti with his eight split evenly to his sides. She considered her four an even match, even though she knew that Oluchi was likely to be the only one that spoke today, except in direct response to a question from someone.

This was her show. The Humans on her side of the table had turned into friends, but they could remain in Rio Alliance Space, while she would have to face the Innruld at some point.

An armed fleet of some sort at her back would be most helpful.

"I have read reports from the naval officers who met you aboard *Recife*," Cavalcanti began after everyone was settled and stewards had brought coffee and tea. "It is my understanding that you are requesting our assistance to overthrow your current government?"

Eha didn't like the way he phrased it. The tone suggested that perhaps the Human government facing her was more interested in using the Innruld to fight Westphalia, without thought to the other species being oppressed.

"According to Lazarus, Captain Oliveira as you know him, the Innruld and Westphalia bear striking similarities to one another, with a single species elevated to authority and all others subordinate by law and custom," Eha replied, making eye contact with the three non-Human Councilors. "We are seeking your assistance freeing the forty other species so that they can have their own liberty."

Quando no curso de eventos Humanos…

When in the course of Human events…

Right out of the founding documents of the Rio Alliance itself, but apparently drawn from their distant history as well. A Human thing, obviously, but supposedly universal.

Eha was willing to challenge them on that ground.

The effect on the group was electric. Literally as if a shock had been applied to their chairs by the way they all twitched and flinched.

She could see the nine split into groups by personality. Interestingly, the other two male Humans and the Gnashiiley Councilor, Pascia Nkali, seemed not quite hostile but perhaps sour. The Moah and the Atomarsk, Whrlaxu C'Vorloo and Ch'ani Zen respectively, plus two of the Human females seemed friendly. That left Cavalcanti and a Human female named Ruby Martins as what Eha might call deciding votes.

"And how did you come to rescue Captain Oliveira, Ambassador?" Cavalcanti asked. "The documents are vague on that topic."

"I'm afraid you'll have to ask Aileen," Eha smiled at the group. "I only came into the picture much later, when Director Wolcott reached out to me for help with an unknown and potentially dangerous new species."

"Dangerous?" Cavalcanti pressed.

"You have height and mass, Councilor," Eha noted, gesturing to all the Humans. "Shoulders designed to throw weapons as well as wield exceptionally heavy tools. Greater strength and endurance compared to most species, as I am given to understand."

"I see," the Human said, leaning back some in contemplation.

"Why come to the Rio Alliance then?" Erlyn Teixeira, one of the friendlier-seeming Humans, asked.

Eha turned to the woman.

"Westphalia would not liberate us from slavery, madam," Eha replied, studying her. She had a similar air to Fernanda Flores, back on Yisan. Hopefully a good sign. "There was some concern that the Rio Alliance might not be able to send forces to assist us, although I am given to understand from Captain Oliveira that a full crew on *Ajax*, trained up, would be sufficient to tip the scales in our favor."

"Where is *Ajax*?" the Gnashiiley Councilor, Pascia Nkali, asked abruptly.

Lazarus had called them Kitsune, from some ancient Human legend. A head taller than Aileen, but still shorter than Lazarus. Whiskers and ears like a Yithadreph, but a more pointed nose and snout.

In Innruld Space, the species tended towards red fur, while here apparently they were generally gray-brown. And larger.

"Patrolling Rio Alliance Space, if I understand the term correctly," Eha replied with a smile. "Surveying, on the hopes that one of your uninhabited worlds might be a good place for refugees from Innruld Space to come and start a new life. A new colony."

Again, an electric effect, but shifting. The group smiled or frowned in different patterns.

"It is a warship," Nkali noted sternly.

"It is heavily armed, yes," Eha agreed. "But Lazarus also told us that it was a ship that could do scientific research as well. While he and I sorted things out at this end, Addison and the others decided to do science."

And not just return you your silly warship, thereby depriving us of all leverage. That includes the coordinates of Innruld Space, although you might be able to eventually guess. Good luck finding Zhoonarrim from here.

But she didn't say that. Just smiled enigmatically.

"How many refugees?" Cavalcanti spoke up now.

Eha shrugged her narrow shoulders in the Human manner.

"We have many more worlds than you do, but are much more thinly spread upon them," Eha said, giving them the first taste of a true interspecies alliance. "There are more Humans, if you combined the Rio Alliance and Westphalia populations, than there are everyone else I am aware of."

The effect of those words was explosive, as Eha knew it would be. But it was necessary to slither along a thin ledge now. She needed the Humans, but they needed to be equals and allies.

Not threatened by the Species Underground, nor suddenly besotted with the possibility of grand conquests.

She had not come all this way to replace Innruld overlords with Human ones.

"So you foresee that we will need to become allies?" Cavalcanti said, speaking to the entire group, both sides of the table. "You are offering us assistance against Westphalia, while we help you free your kind from the Innruld?"

"That, Councilor Cavalcanti, is why I am here," Eha said. "Let us negotiate."

TWENTY-FIVE

GORE

"YOU'RE SURE?" Gore Wescott asked the man across the gap separating them in the tiny room.

This meeting had to be outside the office. Outside even the building. Too much risk for Benedict ever coming to his official space. They were allowed to be occasional drinking buddies after work, but should never be seen together on-hours. Thus Gore could invite him to a private club for drinks, but only infrequently.

After all, it required significant wealth and connections to belong to an organization such as this. Gore had faked both sufficiently.

Gore watched as Benedict glowered for a moment, his aquiline face growing dark.

"They believe it," the tall, thin agent murmured. "Is that not sufficient?"

Gore looked around the private room in the private wing in the private club, and hoped that the native paranoia of the Rio Alliance elite would keep the place secured.

He was too young to be executed for treason. Too poor,

without regular payments from Earth's Westphalian government.

And he still had people he owed for their treatment of him when he was younger.

Gore studied Benedict again, looking for something, but he could not place it, and it was not there. He supposed that this was not an elaborate trap, wherein his own double agent had been turned against him. That armed troops were not about to storm the room and arrest him.

That he might yet be safe.

"*Pancho* Oliveira has returned from the dead?" he asked, still doubtful. "Worse, he has allies with him?"

"So the reports I have seen confirm," Benedict replied. "The ship was not lost, as we had been led to believe, but is hidden now, with an alien crew. Two previously-unknown species accompanied the man here to Brasilia, along with several Humans apparently recruited at a place called Yisan, outside Rio Alliance borders."

"I know Yisan," Gore noted simply. "A trade outpost that refuses to allow politics to interfere with getting rich, so that both Westphalian and Rio hulls may call, as long as they behave. Do you have copies of the reports?"

"Images," Benedict said, somewhat evasively, reaching into a pocket and withdrawing a small datacard that he passed to Gore's hand. "And only partial at this point, as I was alone with paper copies for a few moments and unsure how significant this information would be."

"Critical at the highest levels," Gore decided. "Perhaps worth blowing your cover over and fleeing to Westphalian Space. Am I clear?"

He appreciated the way Benedict gulped once, eyes huge at the implications. But the man had been a minor functionary in the organization for several years. A clerk with access to parts of the library, but not the whole. Never the whole. Rio security reserved that greedily to only certain players, none of whom ever looked like the types of people Gore might approach.

Not if he wished to keep his head attached.

Gore reached into an inner pocket of his uncomfortable jacket, noting that as a member, he was still required to hew to sartorial standards more than a century old, while his guest was allowed more leeway. He pulled out a wallet and extracted a stack of bills, then added a few more.

"Add this to your operational budget for bribes," he said, passing the bills to the younger man. "Keep what you don't use, but don't stint. This might be the most important case of either of our careers, so we will be richly rewarded for our efforts later."

"Assuming we're not dead," Benedict murmured.

"Just so," Gore agreed. "But we will all hang at this point if any of us are suspected, so exercise care."

Benedict nodded and rose, his half-finished drink forgotten on a side table.

"What does it mean if *Ajax* has returned?" he asked, taking a single step towards the closed door but not touching it yet.

"It means the Rio Alliance might somehow win the war if we don't do something," Gore replied. "Especially if they have found alien allies somewhere that might tip the current balance further in their favor."

Benedict nodded and compressed himself around a heavy breath.

He bowed and opened the door as he smiled, becoming almost a different man.

"And thank you again for the invitation, sir," he called out in a louder, brighter voice that would most certainly be overheard down the hallway. "I only regret that duty calls."

"We shall do this again," Gore called back, again too loud.

Setting the stage for future visits. Perhaps someday Gore could retire and nominate his old friend Benedict for a place at this club, when an opening appeared. Another spy—long since retired to Earth—had gotten Gore in this door, decades ago.

Benedict left the door open as he departed and a waitress appeared with a pretty face and a low-buttoned shirt. Her bright eyes asked if he needed anything without a word being spoken.

Gore considered his glass. He held it out for her to take with a smile and let her pull the door closed again while he meditated.

The art and decorations in here were soothing. Wood paneled walls, with seascape oils done in a professional hand. Gore had enough seniority and apparent family wealth to have his own private room, for those times he didn't wish to sit in one of the common areas with other Greenbriar elites. The stress of the job always seemed to melt away when he was alone here.

The woman returned quickly enough that perhaps she had already prepared a second glass and just needed to retrieve it. But Gore's needs and standards were known and exacting. He took the glass and was alone.

Only then did he open his hand to study the datacard Benedict had passed him. He slipped it into a reader from an inner pocket and studied crisp images of paper reports. Seventeen pages of thirty according to the page numbers at the bottom, plus several missing appendices, but sufficient to read the executive summary prepared by an admiral's communications staff aboard *Recife*.

Yes, Captain Oliveira had returned from the dead. And brought two alien species with him as ambassadors, with a promise of either a dozen more, or three dozen, depending on how it was interpreted.

Three dozen new species out there, just waiting to be encountered?

It made logical sense. For all the volume Humanity covered at present, it was a small oval tucked into one corner of a single galactic arm. A rounding error on the number of stars known.

And those apparently inhabited.

This Admiral, da Silva by name, had not understood what *Ajax* represented. That was good. Few people did, outside the original *Project Ajax* team that had designed and built the ship. Oliveira and Kirov, most importantly.

Gore would pass this information along the pipeline immediately, but he already knew what his superiors would demand. The aliens assassinated. Oliveira captured, since most of his original crew had been unable to provide any useful information about the vessel after they had been taken, other than it was a revolution in naval warfare they believed would eventually rout Westphalia.

That would never do.

And yes, it was possible that Benedict would need to drastically overplay his hand and then be extracted to retirement someplace safe afterwards.

Gore closed the image files and composed a vague message to another one of his spies, arranging a meeting.

TWENTY-SIX
LAZARUS

AGAIN, a locked suite representing a gilded cage, but Lazarus was not surprised. He had a pair of trump cards with him, in the form of Aileen and H'Brige.

The Rio Alliance was just that, Humans *and friends*, resisting Human supremacists intent on conquering the galaxy. Admiral Santos might have four stars on his shoulder and represent the fine, high lords of the fleet, but this was bigger than just the Navy. Forty more species who might— and might not—be willing to join, depending on how the Humans treated the non-Humans.

He was just sorry that Grace wasn't here. They had never slept together, not counting that half hour on a couch, fully clothed. But there was a spark there. Both of them had recognized it at the end and Lazarus was pretty sure it went above and beyond whatever Eduardo had ordered.

Tonight, he sat in a living space with a view of a river and forest in the distance and contemplated the future. A door opened and he looked over as H'Brige emerged.

"Am I intruding?" she asked.

Lazarus smiled. The suite was for an ambassador or senior

admiral who had brought a sizable staff and wanted them all close. The three of them rattled around the twenty rooms like peas in a bucket.

He gestured to the couch, remaining in the overstuffed chair. Aileen was either asleep in the bathtub in her room, or just hiding from people, having had other people breathing her air all day.

The Atomarsk woman sat, her tail rigidly upright. She still wore her day uniform, but hadn't been acting like a senior officer on detached duty the last few days. Then again, Lazarus had never been a particularly strict disciplinarian. Get the job done, keep yourself and your space clean, look professional when someone important was touring.

"Was this what you anticipated, sir?" she asked after a moment.

"Call me Lazarus," he said, almost automatically. "The rest of the crew does, because they never met *Pancho* Oliveira before we came here."

"Lazarus," she nodded, carefully. He could tell she would only do it a few times.

"Yes and no," he continued. "There is a huge mystery that they need to solve, but I'm only part of it. I've cast a wide net of accusations that are causing any number of people to take notice. Some to start looking. Others, I'm sure, to start burrowing deeper. But I am convinced. The odds of all of that being random chance are so laughable that I should take up gambling professionally if they're true."

"So what will Fleet do?" she asked.

"In my perfect world, send me and a full crew on a long survey mission," he smiled at her.

"With guns?"

"The Innruld will not be displaced voluntarily, Commander," Lazarus replied. "I don't think much violence would be necessary, but some, yes."

"Can *Ajax* do it alone?" she leaned forward now. "I thought she was a Light Starcruiser, sir. Lazarus."

"She is," he nodded. "Built around a new weapon system unlike anything in the galaxy right now. Call it a super beam, at least until you're cleared for the details. Bigger than a Star Lance."

"Oh," she leaned back now, the engineer in her coming to the fore.

He watched her eyes flicker back and forth, possibly remembering rumors she had discounted before now. Or wondering what you might do to a Star Lance to make it a more deadly thing.

Kirov would explain it, but not until someone upgraded this woman's security clearance significantly.

"Wouldn't we want to overthrow the Innruld?" she finally asked after a time.

"If we weren't afraid of hordes of new aliens overrunning us," Lazarus said. "They can't because there are so few of them, which in turn is why they're afraid of us, both politically and personally. We are individually bigger, faster, tougher, and breed prodigiously, compared to anything they know."

Lazarus had never known that an Atomarsk beak could pull sideways, like a Human's mouth, when they were deep in thought. But he hadn't spent that much time around any in his previous jobs.

"Still, won't that alter the balance of the Rio Alliance, Lazarus?" she asked after a few moments.

"The Churquen are the largest individual species in Innruld Space, I believe, H'Brige," he replied. "If all of them came over here, they would still be fewer in number than the Moah or the Gnashiiley, to say nothing of Humans."

"Then why should the bosses be concerned?" she asked, confused now.

"Change always makes people nervous," Lazarus grimaced. "Some will be all in favor of doing the thing. Others will want to remain detached and possibly keep them at a distance while they sort out Westphalia."

"I see. Should we be looking at how to break out of here and get back to *Ajax* then?" she asked, concern and confusion warring in her voice.

"Not yet, H'Brige," he laughed. "I think they'll do the right thing. It will just take time."

"Do we have the time?" she perked up. "How long will Commander Wolcott wait if we're not on time?"

"I don't know, H'Brige," Lazarus said. "Or what he'll do."

TWENTY-SEVEN

ADDISON

ADDISON HAD TAKEN to spending his awake hours on the bridge, rather than back in the office he technically shared with Lazarus. Cormac had everything under control, and Addison and Kuei ended up mostly supervising anyway.

Aft, Ereshkiki Nisab and Thadrakho were mostly doing the same, as the ship was automated to a degree that had surprised him, considering the way Lazarus had reacted to the possibility of fully sentient systems like Cormac or Lenox.

Ajax was a close-enough cousin, at the end of the day. But incapable of making decisions. Just making them easy.

Hells, only Khyaa'sha really had anything to do, keeping the crew fed and motivated as they rattled loosely around this enormous hull.

"Addison, I have begun receiving strange signals," Cormac suddenly spoke up. *"Radio traffic indicating at least two vessels have begun moving into approach of Four. They are attempting to remain quiet."*

Addison checked his screen as Cormac relayed sensor reports.

Ajax was running as silent and quiet as possible, in a trailing, gravitationally-stable orbit using the complicated LaGrange points generated by Five's one large moon and two small ones. Close, but not all that close, as astronomical distances went.

More importantly, they had been listening, rather than sending out sensor signals. The optical and electrical telescopes on *Ajax* were sufficient to study the planet, especially once they had tapped into the signals given off by the survey satellites.

"Have you identified them?" Addison asked.

"*Not yet,*" Cormac replied. "*Neither vessel is transmitting signals or scanning the area. Both are using tight-beam communications to talk, but their laser wash has been almost akin to shining a spotlight on one of the hulls. Presumably the more distant one.*"

Why keep quiet? Unless, of course, you were up to no good. Addison wasn't up to evil, but he certainly didn't want to announce his presence to whomever might come along. Too many questions best left unanswered.

"Shift all the telescopes and passive sensors to watch and track them," Addison decided.

"*Should I bring Kuei to alert status?*"

"No, let's let her sleep for now," Addison said. "We need to know who it is before we do anything. Multiple vessels suggests something more complicated."

"*Smugglers, perhaps?*" Cormac asked with what could only be a smug tone.

But then, they'd made a career of being smugglers, before they turned into pirates and revolutionaries.

"As good a working hypothesis as any," Addison replied, studying the signals as they slowly built up.

It would take time, but Cormac would not grow tired or

distracted. Yet another benefit of sentient Crawlers attached to bridge systems.

"Make sure to keep our emissions minimized," Addison continued. "And be ready to jump out as soon as anyone notices us or approaches. We're not supposed to exist."

"Understood, Addison."

Hopefully nothing but smugglers. He'd already had to deal with pirates, if that Westphalian hull had been civilian and not a military probe disguised. No way to have been sure, short of landing and having a conversation with the illegal colonists.

Let them handle themselves.

Still, right now they were close to what might look like front lines on a star map showing Westphalia and the Rio Alliance. Addison had never contemplated what a war might look like. However the group of them had rather significant experience on the wrong side of the law.

TWENTY-EIGHT
GORE

GORE WOULD HAVE PREFERRED to handle this meeting at his club, but even that facility was not secure enough for this, so he had to rely on his personal security, in his home.

He could still count on one hand all the people who had ever been inside here, including the older woman who played the part of a long-time family retainer and was in truth probably just another Westphalian agent. Possibly also an assassin sent to keep tabs on him and eliminate him if he ever started to deviate from the party line or grow lax.

This high-wire act allowed him no off moments, if he didn't wish to plummet to his death. Maybe she was here to push him, if he did get tired.

Berka answered the doorbell with a nod and admitted Ferdinand Knef silently, showing the man into the library and closing the door.

They would be safe while they met. She would see to it. Probably was standing just outside the door with a blaster pistol even now.

Gore had a glass of whiskey with ice and gestured Ferdinand to fix himself something.

Small talk was just wasted in these circumstances, so Gore watched the man work. Steady hands indicating steady nerves. No twitchy glances over a shoulder expecting an attack, either verbal or physical.

The life of spies in unfamiliar terrain.

Finally the man finished and joined him, taking the other chair and sipping something vaguely blue from the bar.

Ferdinand watched him over the rim of the glass.

"Two new aliens," Gore said simply. "The lost Rio warship *Ajax* not lost and now a threat to everything. Briefing materials will be supplied, but they are currently being assembled from partial data. What you carry to our superiors will not be sufficient. I am aware of that, but believe that they need the partial data now, rather than after I have a more full picture. By then it will be too late."

"Why?" Ferdinand asked bluntly, no doubt memorizing every aspect of this conversation to repeat later. Eidetic memories were useful in couriers.

"The Captain of the returned vessel did not sail into port with it," Gore said. "He left it in the possession of other aliens, and suggested that we have just over thirty days from now before he will have missed some important meeting with them."

"Then what happens?" the courier asked.

"Presumably they take that ship into the depths of the galaxy and use it to fight a war with other aliens," Gore stated.

He noted the slightest twitch in the man's eyes, but they were all Westphalian. The concept of other aliens out there that might be a threat to Humanity was enough to unnerve the strongest men and women.

"Is it in our benefit to encourage a war between aliens, fought elsewhere?" Ferdinand probed.

"It is," Gore agreed. "I am working to insert assassins, but the target party has been divided into two groups, one with the High Council and one secured at Naval Headquarters. It is quite likely that the attempt, success or failure, will blow so many covers and agents that a mass extraction might be necessary. By the time you reach Earth with your news, things will be close to culminating here, so I need to inform your superiors, our superiors, so that they are prepared if a mob is following close on behind you. I will try to shield as much of the organization as I can, but this might be worth destroying all that work, if we can keep Rio from gaining new and potentially powerful allies."

The man licked his lips once and nodded. A slow blink seemed to confirm everything in deep memory, where it could be drawn out later.

"When should I depart?" Ferdinand asked.

"Immediately," Gore said. "All teams have been activated and tasked. It is out of my hands, except where the failure might reach the stage where I am endangered."

"Does anybody know where *Ajax* is located?" Ferdinand asked.

"The Captain of the vessel," Gore said. "Probably the two aliens. It is doubtful that any of the others will be privy."

"And capturing them for interrogation?"

"Too risky," Gore replied, nodding. "I had considered it, but the evidence suggests that eliminating them now pushes *Ajax* out of the current sphere of concern. It hopefully reduces the chance of a Rio/Alien alliance for the time being, while we work to reduce Rio."

"Should surveys be sent out to locate the aliens?" Ferdinand asked, speaking the first question they would put to him on Earth, most likely.

"Only if you wish to open a multi-front war," Gore fought not to sneer at the man. He was just the messenger. "We cannot afford it. If there are as many aliens as the report you will take home suggests, we are probably surrounded on all sides. Better we work on technology research, so that we can overwhelm any aliens we do encounter."

"Understood," Ferdinand said. "Do you have anything else to transmit?"

"No," Gore said. He pulled a reader from a pocket and handed it to the man. "Read and memorize this material and you will be ready to depart."

He leaned back and watched the man's eyes flicker over each page. There was significant intelligence in there, but the man only took fifteen minutes to read it all, barely pausing to sip at his drink as he did.

Finally he handed the reader back.

"Thoughts?" Gore asked. "Questions?"

"Negative, sir," Ferdinand replied in a quiet voice. "Compelling and dangerous."

"We should assume that the Rio Alliance must be broken in the next five years, if not utterly defeated," Gore said. "After that, the chances are good that another Atomarsk mining vessel will stumble into a Human explorer, with yet another set of aliens that will resist our efforts to expand our colonies. Go."

Gore finished his drink as the man exited the library.

He would make it to Earth and let those people know that trouble beyond their worst nightmares had erupted. And there was nothing they would be able to do about it, but Gore had been given sufficient authority to make those decisions, by the nature of his position in the government.

On the surface, just another senior bureaucrat from a good family with an inheritance and sufficient cover. How could those fools know what went on inside the sanctum of his mind?

He would see the Rio Alliance fall.

With any luck, his hand might even hold the blade.

TWENTY-NINE
OLUCHI

OLUCHI SMILED at the woman who was a representative of the High Council, as they attempted, yet again, to question his motives, his position, and his authority.

"Because I am attached to the Churquen Embassy," he answered her, again, in a bright innocent voice that would brook no silliness. "Ambassador Dunham has accredited me to speak partly in her voice, at least as far as negotiating pacts of trade and such."

"Yisan is not part of the Rio Alliance," the leader of the small group across the table from him retorted.

Oluchi paused to study the three of them. One man on his right. The woman across from him with the authority. One more woman on his left. The outer two were just bureaucrats. Faceless and interchangeable, although the junior woman was rather cute, once he thought about it.

"Innruld Space is not part of the Rio Alliance, either, madam," Oluchi noted. "I also speak with trade authority for the merchants of Yisan, through whose space I suspect a significant tonnage of cargo bound for Churquen worlds will pass. I might remind your masters that they will wish to be on good terms with those merchants at Yisan, if they wish to consider future expansion or colonies in that direction and not any sort of organized polity one of these days."

He could almost see steam coming off the woman's head. The two on her flanks were even less skilled at maintaining their façades.

Oluchi figured he was only slightly bluffing. Eduardo Martìnez had specifically ensured that Oluchi was part of the team to rescue Eha originally, hanging up on Lazarus, seated all of three feet away, to call Oluchi two seconds later with key pieces of information.

Eduardo had understood immediately that this was going to be big. And trusted Oluchi to keep his interests, and all of Yisan by association, in mind.

"I am not authorized to negotiate with representatives of Yisan," the woman said the words slowly. Painfully. Angrily.

"Then I will continue to speak with you as a representative of Ambassador Dunham," Oluchi smiled warmly, just to frost them an extra layer.

This was even more fun than seducing rich, older women with needs and nobody willing to treat them as people rather than meal tickets. But that was why Oluchi had been so successful for so long.

A willingness to simply listen when a woman wanted to bitch, hold her when she wanted to be held, and take her off line at the appropriate times, too.

This main bureaucrat didn't look like one who needed his services. Still, the one on the left, a dark brunette with the sort of dark brown skin that was common in this sector of space, was giving off subtle signs as he watched them all.

None of them would last twenty minutes across from him at a poker table.

"I will need to consult my superiors." The woman in the

center grimaced and rose, awkward and off-balance physically as well as mentally.

The other two were a moment slower.

Oluchi watched the brunette with a smile. She briefly smiled back. Could he seduce her for information? Or let her seduce him, depending on whose orders meant what?

Eha was a spymaster of great skill. Oluchi had figured that out pretty quickly, back on *Ajax*, but then, he'd listened to her talk. Understood her words and context.

And was more than willing to let her set him on these bumbling bureaucrats, as long as he was able to get a thin slice of things going by. Even a few basis points would be fun, when there were going to be that many zeroes involved.

Oluchi rose after the others and saw them to the door of this conference room, where he could see his minders waiting patiently in the hall. None of them were likely to break responsibility long enough to fool around, which was something of a shame, but he could appreciate them not wanting to risk their jobs.

The main woman stomped off, followed closely by the man. The brunette hesitated for a long moment, glancing at him. Oluchi smiled an invitation, to which she nodded and departed quickly after the others.

He took a long breath and let them have a head start to the lifts. It was close enough to lunch time and he could head there now.

None of the guards were apparently allowed names around him, but again, Oluchi wasn't offended. The High Council was trying to keep control of things by maintaining something of a dignified distance, even as everyone was more or less confined to a large, rural estate.

He nodded to the man assigned as a minder today and turned left, headed for the stairs instead of the lift. The guard fell in a step behind and followed. Presumably the man would eat after going off duty, regardless of previous suggestions that he could just sit and have a cup of tea or something.

They didn't do that.

The lunchroom was sparsely inhabited. Oluchi stayed away from the formal restaurant where important personages were served, preferring to eat with the staff. The decor wasn't anywhere near as good, but the ambiance and cheerfulness more than made up for it. And it all came from the same kitchen, as near as he could tell.

Down the communal line, with food deposited on plates and his tray. Stop for a tea pot while his guard glowered at people to keep them at a polite distance. Out into the main area and taking a table currently unoccupied, so as to not put anyone off their lunch.

He ate, wondering. Waiting. Something.

It had been a week of dickering and bickering, with little to show for it. The Rio Alliance wanted names, dates, and places. Eha wanted assurances before she offered up Innruld Space to potential new overlords.

Deadlock was the result. Or gridlock.

He ate. The food was pretty good today, pasta with meat and a pink sauce, but that was him getting here twenty minutes before most people.

Oluchi had a view of the main doorway from where he sat.

He saw the brunette woman from earlier enter, look around, and spot him. No blush marred her elegant face as she turned and went for a cup of coffee and a bowl of soup.

Interestingly, the minder chose this moment to supposedly absently wander to a corner of the room, far enough away not to eavesdrop but close enough to watch.

Oluchi wondered if they thought he was that dense or not paying any attention, but wasn't going to point out bad tradecraft, just because it was aimed at him. They might decide to send professionals instead next time.

And seducing a spy and seducing a woman required the same skills, most of the time.

Anya, that was her name. She hesitated cutely as she approached and sat down across from him.

"Sorry about this morning," she offered carefully.

He smiled and tried to look innocent. Oluchi Pryce had a *LOT* of experience at that sort of thing.

"Eventually, the wheels of bureaucracy will grind far enough," Anya continued. "But everyone has to have their hand in things first, adding a signature or getting a bullet point to their approval."

Oluchi nodded.

"My concern, however, is still with the timing," he offered, just as blandly, to see where she would go with it. "At some point, we need to go check in with Addison."

"Surely not all of you?" Anya asked.

"Actually, I would presume just the opposite," he countered. "Eha has only spoken briefly with Lazarus since he and the others were diverted, but Eha has some nervousness about that sort of thing, especially after the events at Yisan."

"Did you really storm a yacht?" she asked, eyes glowing just a little.

"Lazarus did," he corrected her. "And we snuck aboard, stunning several people at first, until we realized how complicit the entire crew was. At that point, everyone took their gloves off. I doubt any of the crew survived after we blew the boat up, considering the size of that storm."

"Would they do anything like that here?" she asked, faking a pretty good breathlessness.

"The whole reason they did it in the first place was to keep *Ajax* from setting the colony on fire in retribution for some moron hurting Eha," he leaned forward, just so he could whisper the words and see the impact.

She was a pretty good actress, for a cute bureaucrat. Amateur, but well-meaning.

"So if all of you don't go out to meet the others…?"

"I would presume that the Rio Alliance would have blown its chance to achieve a meaningful working relationship with Addison Wolcott and the Species Underground," Oluchi repeated the key piece that probably nobody in authority had really believed. "He'll still have a warm spot for the Humans at Yisan, who helped him in his time of need, but that's because we had already killed everyone for him."

Someone really engaged emotionally would have flinched, or something. Reacted, however viscerally. He'd made enough of a living at poker tables to read layers deep on people.

Anya did react, but it was a calculated thing. Just a shade off, but fish that's gone bad is *just a shade off*, as well. Her eyes gave her away. Too shrewd for this sort of conversation.

He nearly chuckled when one of her hands crept across the table and rested next to his. Just touching, rather than holding, but more than his minder would have allowed, if someone hadn't ordered the man to move far enough away to make this look and feel like a casual assignation.

Her hands were cold.

"So you'll go away with them?" Anya asked in a soft, throaty tone.

"Briefly," he smiled.

Hell, if they wanted to throw this woman at him, he wasn't about to say no. Would trust her about as far as he could throw her, but he'd let her set the pace on verisimilitude. And take advantage of it.

There hadn't been any women around since Fernanda,

after all. Not counting several alien females who had not expressed any sort of interest. And Grace only had eyes for Lazarus.

"But that's just to sort out the bad guys," Oluchi continued, letting himself even sound sincere.

Faking that had been the hardest lesson to learn. And the most fruitful over his career.

He smiled into her eyes and put all his experience to work.

"Once the Innruld are handled, I'm sure the next stop will be to return here for an extended period," he said in an open-ended, inviting sort of tone, just to see what her orders were.

Oluchi felt like a shit, but he hadn't set these rules. Just understood on Day One that the fools in Greenbriar and the vicinity didn't really understand how the rest of the universe worked, once you got away from all the silly, meaningless, bureaucratic squabbles.

Most of these people had never been shot at, and those that had had been serving in the military, probably.

"How would you feel about a private meeting for a while?" she asked awkwardly, going so far as to bat her eyelashes at him. "I've reserved a conference room and you don't currently have anything on your calendar for two hours."

Oluchi smiled. He'd done dumber, riskier, crazier things. And it wasn't like they could blackmail him with video. He might insist on a copy for himself, just to seed various video services with as an advertisement for his services, if he ever had to go back to that kind of life. Lazarus was too serious to appreciate performance art as a practical joke, but he didn't need to.

Eha would get a good laugh out of it.

Oluchi finished his tea and nodded.

If she had any sense or experience with this sort of thing, she would have immediately walked out the door and waited down a hallway for him. Instead, she rose and nodded at him, almost making the whole scene *kabuki* in case any of the secretaries had missed the subtext of what was going on over here.

They walked side by side, with his minder casually—and more importantly silently—following along. Oluchi wondered just what they might think they could demand of him later, since they were going all this way to set him up, presumably for blackmail later.

Or maybe they thought they could set him up with a girlfriend to whom he would spill all his secrets?

Inwardly, he shrugged. Pillow talk required pillows, rather than conference tables with full audio/video functionality.

He'd let them figure that out on their own.

Or not.

THIRTY

ADDISON

ADDISON STUDIED the readout on the screen, ever so happy that he had decided to park the ship out here in a LaGrange point to watch as a way of killing time when *Ajax* was ahead of the original schedule. A far better alternative to having been in orbit of the planet at the wrong moment.

That was a Westphalian Task Force over there, intent on something more than mere mischief.

He'd listened to Lazarus talk about the GunWall, but never really understood the concept. Innruld Space was a police state, to use the Human conception. One authority exercising control with no overt challenges. No war fleets. Just occasional Security Barcs or Innruld Pyramids.

Westphalia had brought a fleet. A GunWall. Each of the little ships looked like a flying mushroom, with a shield around the bow gun and a Star Spear on the central mount, plus eight Powerbolts around the rim. About midway back on the hull they had an articulation point that let the engines and rear half of the ship rotate forward past ninety degrees. A Phalanx-class destroyer like those could keep the bow centered on an enemy force while maneuvering sideways.

Each set of four Phalanx ships protected a leader, known as an Archer, where the Star Spear had been upgraded to a more powerful Star Lance and the number of Powerbolts cut in half.

A team of five would be a terrible thing against anything in Innruld Space lighter than one of the bigger Security Barcs. When you had four such teams, you added a CommandWall, where they kept the eight Powerbolts but replaced the cannon with added space for a senior Director to control all twenty-one vessels.

Lazarus had said that *Ajax* could take on an entire GunWall like that, if it had a full crew of trained sailors. Truly a frightening thought.

Addison had Kuei, Wybert, and Cormac. It would not be enough to even consider, since the Westphalian force had two GunWalls and something the encyclopedia called a Heavy Starcruiser, plus any number of cargo vessels coming and going.

"Cormac, what are they building?" Addison asked.

"*Speculation, Commander.*"

That was how Addison knew just how spooked his NavCrawler had gotten. Cormac had turned himself into a Rio Alliance officer in his speech patterns.

"Speculate," he ordered the junior Lieutenant who was seventy years older than he was.

"*If I extrapolate outward from the current structure in orbit, it would appear to be growing into an armed station, Commander,*" Cormac announced. "*At current rate of construction they will finish sufficient to defend themselves in under four Human weeks.*"

Addison swore under his breath. That was just about the time that he was supposed to meet Eha and Lazarus at Checkpoint Six. Assuming all went well with their mission to Brasilia.

At that point, Lazarus would be able to determine the correct course of action. This was obviously a Westphalian invasion, landing in secret and functionally capturing a future colony, then dropping enough force in place to hold it, unless the Rio Alliance had another Admiral named Vilga that could have another last stand here.

Addison took a breath and activated the shipwide comm.

"Kuei and Wybert, come to the bridge," he announced. "Ereshkiki Nisab, make sure all power systems are on line and ready to deliver. We will be maneuvering shortly and then going to jump."

He closed the line before anyone could ask him any stupid questions. They were aware of the enemy force sitting over there. At some point, scouts might come this way and realize that *Ajax* was more than just a rock floating in space.

They needed to leave.

Worse, they needed to go get help.

THIRTY-ONE
LAZARUS

IT HAD BEEN another day of waiting. Lazarus knew that the bureaucracy was going to drive him crazy, but he had made his case. The infrequent messages from Eha and Oluchi suggested that they were just as frustrated as he was, but the Rio Alliance was simply not prepared to deal the current situation in a timely manner.

Or they thought he was a spy and this was all some elaborate game to set up a trap.

Except that the only trap here was the one Lazarus was currently stuck in, waiting for the spider to come out onto her web and eat him.

Lazarus was seated in the common area, reading. Aileen was in her cabin, probably also reading, but doing it alone. H'Brige was clear across the space, seated and quietly studying for some exam that she needed to take for certifications. He didn't miss those days. If he turned into a full-on pirate instead after all this was done, he would never have exams again, except where he was administering them.

The outer door opened with a squeak indicating that the

tracks needed to be cleaned, and Admiral Santos walked in. Stomped in, perhaps. His face was hard and focused.

Training took over and Lazarus was on his feet at attention immediately with a call of "Admiral on the deck."

H'Brige was up a moment later.

Santos came to rest a dozen steps inside the entryway, trailing a handful of junior officers in his wake. They slowly coalesced about the time Aileen exploded out of her room and came to attention. She wasn't wearing shoes, but she almost never did except when they left for meetings.

The Admiral looked at the three of them, all rigid and focused on an invisible horizon, and seemed mollified, a shade. Lazarus had enough peripheral vision to see the man come to rest as well, rather than start yelling, which had been what his face had promised when Lazarus looked up.

Santos took a deep breath and looked around.

"At ease," he said in a quieter voice than maybe he had originally intended.

Lazarus fell to parade rest. H'Brige did the same. Aileen was even passably close, for never having marched around parking lots to learn the rhythms of the Navy.

Santos turned to his staff and gestured most of them out, except one woman holding a briefcase.

"Commander Almeida, you remain," he said. "Everyone else wait outside."

Lazarus watched the two strangers move to the oversized dining table and sit.

"Join me, Captain, Commanders," Santos ordered.

Lazarus moved to the table and sat. The two women flanked him and watched.

Santos seemed to be rethinking anger as an opening gambit.

"When was the final scheduled check-in with Commander Wolcott?" Santos asked as an opener.

"Twenty-seven days, sir," Lazarus replied. "There are three others before that, but if Addison had heard nothing at that point, he will presumably assume the worst."

"And his orders in the meantime, Captain?" Santos asked, as if they hadn't already discussed this to death previously.

"To keep as low a profile as possible, sir," Lazarus replied. "There were a number of worlds they were going to survey, all currently uninhabited, with an eye towards possibly resettling refugees and immigrants from Innruld Space at a future date. Training and familiarization with the equipment, for the most part. May I ask why, sir?"

"Two things have occurred in the last five hours, Captain," Admiral Santos declared in a voice that seemed to hold Lazarus responsible for all the sins in the universe. He turned to Commander Almeida.

She put the case on the table and opened it, pulling out a file and handing it to the Admiral. Santos passed it immediately to Lazarus and studied him like a hawk watching a mouse emerge from his den.

"Five hours ago, a civilian vessel came into the inbound lanes with an emergency call for naval assistance," Santos began before Lazarus could do more than flip the file open and note the date at the top right. "The vessel was an unregistered pincke of **Westphalian** manufacture. *Recife* happened to be closest on station, and responded."

Santos paused and studied the three of them now. He did not smile.

"The story they shared was one of a pirate raid on their colony, broken up by a Rio Alliance warship on an otherwise secret mission, Captain," Santos said as Lazarus felt his stomach drop. "The attacking destroyer was shattered. One pincke annihilated by a beam so powerful that it was able to fire a lateral kill shot through a significant depth of atmosphere. The other vessel grounded and all the pirates aboard abandoned to flee into the bush."

Again the pause. Maybe a gritting of teeth, even.

"At that point, the commander of the warship instructed the colonists to capture the pincke," Santos said. "They did, and as a result most of the surviving pirates immediately surrendered. However, the colony was an illegal one, located at 9087 Geminorum. The warship in question did not offer marine assistance. It also did not stay put afterwards. The commander warned the colonists that he would eventually update this world as inhabited, so the Mayor of this *unregistered and illegal* colony flew herself here in said captured pincke, to turn herself in, and request military assistance for the forty-seven captured pirates they are now holding at 9087 Geminorum IV, all of whom seem to be recently employed as members of the Westphalian Navy. This woman, Mayor Mila Henders, had an obviously interesting story. Because da Silva was on station, he routed it immediately to me, once he got everything sorted out. Would you care to guess the name of the Rio Alliance warship that broke up a pirate raid, killed a number of pirates who might have been Westphalian sailors, and then disappeared into the darkness, Captain?"

"*Ajax,* sir?" Lazarus asked.

"*Ajax*, Captain," Santos replied bluntly. "Commander Addison Wolcott was on the bridge, and he even spoke with the people on the ground, but without visuals."

"As would be appropriate, given the situation," Lazarus replied.

"Indeed," Santos nodded. "That would be bad enough, Captain."

"Sir?"

"Two hours ago, *Ajax* herself arrived in system with

details of a major Westphalian fleet incursion at 6357 Wei Xiu," Santos continued.

"Vilga's Stand?" H'Brige gasped before anyone spoke and then covered her beak with both hands, the tips of her tail flickering outwards from that normal central blade in embarrassment.

"Correct, Lt. Commander Slani," Santos nodded. He turned back to Lazarus now like gun turrets tracking. "Commander Wolcott delivered complete scan logs showing two GunWalls, a Heavy Starcruiser, and what he estimates is a full base under construction over the fourth planet of that system, Captain Oliveira. He requested fleet assistance to help him remove the threat."

Lazarus could not help but smile.

"Something amuses you, Captain?" Santos growled, obviously not pleased.

"Chapter and verse out of the manual, Admiral," Lazarus replied. "Addison is acting like a Commander temporarily in command of a Light Starcruiser of the Rio Alliance Navy. Anti-piracy patrol and forward surveys, sir."

"Do you trust the man, Oliveira?" Santos asked bluntly.

"With my life, on more than one occasion, Admiral," Lazarus said. "If he says that you have an incursion, then you do and we need to figure out how to deal with it."

"He seems to be of the opinion that they will be fully operational in four weeks," Santos said. "I do not have the resources available to do anything about it in that time, Oliveira. Further, Wolcott refused to remain on station. He has jumped randomly several times. Never far, but he is not acting like a proper line officer."

"He is not one, sir," Lazarus pointed out. "He is an alien posing as the ship's captain. A *director* to use their terminology, who has volunteered to be pressed into service as my First Officer, as has his old crew, including his Loadmaster who is now my Quartermaster."

Lazarus looked over to see Aileen smiling. He knew she had a pretty low opinion of the Admiral, but that was personal, rather than anything else. She rather like Lucas Lam and H'Brige Slani as companions.

"However," Lazarus said, overriding whatever the man was going to inject, "he has acted correctly. Twice now, if I understand the situation. Both times he could have simply kept sailing, so as to not jeopardize his own mission. Now, he is at the greatest risk, because he has come directly to Brasilia for help."

"There is no help, Captain," Santos snapped. "That is a Heavy Starcruiser and two GunWalls, plus whatever they have done to assemble that station by the time I get a fleet there to do something about them. We're looking at six months, minimum, as I would have to shuffle significant forces around so that I did not open up some other hole in the defense wall that they could exploit."

Lazarus paused before he spoke. Considered how crazy it sounded, even in his head.

"Send me, Admiral Santos," he said in a calm, quiet, *rational* voice. "Get me about two hundred sailors, heavy on Gun Teams and engineers, and *Ajax* will surprise you. All I need is a trio of light escorts to keep a GunWall from swarming me while I go about destroying their forces."

"*Ajax?*" Santos asked in disbelief. "Against a full Westphalian fleet?"

"Aye, sir," Lazarus replied.

He paused and flipped open the file, finally finding the description he wanted and turning the folder around to show it to the other officers.

"A pincke, running for their lives low in an atmosphere, with significant atmospheric degradation and deflection on the shot, Admiral Santos," Lazarus pointed out. "The weapon they used is called a Kirov Lance, after the man who designed it. I built *Ajax* around that weapon. You could add a zero to a Star Lance and not be that far off in your power estimation."

Slani gasped just as loud as Almeida. Admiral Santos stopped and read the half page in detail before he looked up.

"The prior shot broke a pirate destroyer into multiple pieces at short range with a single shot, Captain," Santos noted. "Your Kirov Lance again?"

"Aye, sir," Lazarus nodded and smiled.

"Why were you so ineffective in your first battle, then?"

"We came out of blueshift and were immediately in the kill zone of a full GunWall, Admiral," Lazarus felt his voice get growly at the man. "Everything I had went into ray shielding and evasive maneuvers as we were getting the shit pounded out of us before we even knew what had happened. I was not cleared for action, and by the time we could have managed that, I already had twenty-eight dead, an unknown number of wounded, and the ship needed to be destroyed before it could be captured. I ordered my crew to abandon, and set a course that should have destroyed me. That was the only failure I will admit to on that day, Admiral Santos. Surviving when the ship should have slammed into a star and been destroyed."

Lazarus watched the man lean back and study him. H'Brige reached out a hand and pulled the file close, turning it to read.

"And I've served with Addison for a decade, Admiral," Aileen spoke up to break the silence. "We were rebels against the Innruld, smuggling the sorts of narcotics eventually guaranteed to destroy them, or get us executed for it. Because we want to be free. If he's here, he's serious. But as Lazarus has told you, and as I've told you, there is a clock ticking. Two, actually, if they'll be unmovable in a month."

Santos studied them for a long moment. Lazarus could not tell what the man was thinking, but he was the senior admiral in the system, so his decision would be the one that stuck, whatever it was.

He gestured to the file, for them to keep it, as he rose. Commander Almeida was a beat behind him, grabbing the briefcase as she stood.

"You have given me much to think about, Captain Oliveira," he said in a far more pleasant tone than his face had promised when he had arrived. "I will keep you apprised."

Lazarus and his two officer had risen, as well. He saluted, because it felt like the right thing to do. Aileen and H'Brige did the same.

Santos let go a breath and returned it after a moment.

He turned and departed without another word, Almeida in his wake.

"And?" Aileen asked as the hatch slid shut.

Lazarus stepped back from the table and massaged the spot on his neck that had gotten tense.

"And Addison has managed to put them in an unwinnable position, without even realizing it, I'd guess," he said. "He's come here for help directly. Offered to help. They have to either take him up on it, or measure that mistake in generations."

"Generations?" H'Brige asked.

"Addison will take *Ajax* and go home," Aileen said across his body. "Then he won't need Human help. Might not accept it later, when they finally do find Innruld Space."

"What about us?" H'Brige asked.

Lazarus grinned at her use of *us*.

"Either they let us go be heroes, or maybe they throw us in jail for the rest of our lives," he replied. "Easy, right?"

THIRTY-TWO
OLUCHI

OLUCHI CHECKED the clock as someone knocked quietly on the door to the suite he was still sharing with Eha and the others. He had been reading to kill time, unsure why he was up so late, other than everyone but Lucas was as well.

He rose because he was closest to the door and caught glances from Grace and Xiuying. Eha shifted out of her nest of pillows and moved closer to the dining table. Lucas had already gone to sleep. Or at least into his room to read privately.

Oluchi opened the door just a crack and peeked out.

Anya, the bureaucrat who had been assigned as his girlfriend by some wannabe spymaster in the Rio Alliance government.

He pulled the door open just enough and gestured her to slip in, closing it behind her as she did.

She looked around, a bit surprised to suddenly be on stage in front of his friends, but after her performance in that first conference room, and a few closets and such later, Oluchi did have an understanding that the woman was something of an exhibitionist.

But this situation didn't feel like a late night assignation where she might rap on his window to sneak out after curfew. Anya did, however, take a breath and slip close enough to kiss him. It was without emotion, or maybe the emotion was already loss.

He couldn't tell.

"The room is being monitored on audio channels," she murmured in his ear. As if that was a surprise. "But something has happened and I thought you and the Ambassador should know."

"Video monitoring?" Oluchi asked, stiffening just a shade, even as his arms closed around her in something approaching a hug between two lovers.

Or whatever term appropriately classified the sorts of sweaty interludes the two of them had stolen in quiet spaces over the last few days. Not that he was complaining.

"No, just sound," Anya whispered tersely. "I brought something for them to read. You and I should slip into a bedroom as a distraction for the guards listening in."

Not the most callous way to put it, but Oluchi was still surprised that she had such a mercenary approach. Of course, the entire thing was utterly a sham, at the end of the day. He just didn't know who she was working for.

He let her slip from his arms while watching the woman. She smiled and pulled a data chip from a pocket and handed it to him.

Oluchi turned to everyone and put one finger to a most serious face. He held up the chip with his other hand, and then gestured to one ear and finally the ceiling.

People are listening to everything you say, but not watching.

Nods greeted him, so he tossed the chip to Grace, trusting her to catch it.

"Don't wait up for us," he called in a sardonic tone at odds with the situation.

Taking Anya's hand, he headed towards his bedroom for some verisimilitude.

Or whatever you wanted to call it.

THIRTY-THREE

EHA

EHA WATCHED the two Human lovers retire to the bedroom as Grace approached and handed her whatever prize the bureaucrat had brought.

Standard data chip. Huh.

Eha slipped it into the tablet she had been reading from and called up a menu. Grace and Xiuying silently rose and moved behind her to read over narrow shoulders, no doubt.

The file was a copy of a military report, marked top secret and most urgent and several other things. Eha wasn't sure how the woman had gotten her hands on it, or who had sent her as a courier with it.

Obviously, Anya and Oluchi would be making enough of a scene in the bedroom, if she understood the body language correctly, so Eha was to read this now and then presumably prepare questions.

The profanity that almost slipped out of her mouth wasn't one Humans were familiar with. And not something to yell in a quiet room. Eha barely managed to bite it back.

Ajax *was here? Now?*

She read deeper, amazed at the insanity that had

apparently overtaken her mate when she had left the man without adult supervision. Eha could see that she would need to remain extremely close to him for the rest of his life, if he was going to keep being a hero like this.

Pirates destroyed. Westphalian incursions detected.

And he was here in the system, right now. Somewhere overhead.

How did she get to him?

Eha turned to Xiuying.

"Wake Lucas," she said almost silently. "Quietly."

The man nodded and moved on ghost's feet to the fourth bedroom.

Hopefully, Oluchi and Anya would be making just enough noise and entertainment to distract whoever was supposed to be listening to the rest of the suite, although she had no doubt that everything was being recorded.

Eha returned to the report and kept reading.

Good, they were consulting with Lazarus as to how to handle this new development.

He would have the best understanding that Addison Wolcott was not just another game piece they could move around. It had taken Eha years to appreciate that about the man.

What would the Rio Alliance Navy choose to do at this point? Eha was uncertain, but obviously wheels within wheels were turning.

Xiuying emerged a moment later with Lucas, still in uniform as something of their guardian, but unarmed and without shoes.

Eha read through the cover details and then handed it to Grace, trusting that woman's esoteric background to extract details that might have gotten missed.

While Grace read, Eha slithered silently close to the front door of the suite into which she was being held. The curtains were drawn on the windows for the evening, and she could not unlock them. And probably not shatter one with anything less than four people heaving a table through it. Faint noises emerged from behind Oluchi's door. From the tenor, Human sexual encounters were more vocally robust than Churquen, but they couldn't wrap tails around each other, so Eha wasn't entirely sure what form it might take.

At least Oluchi and Anya seemed to be impressively involved with the process, even if she was as much a spy and imposter as Oluchi. But Oluchi was Eha's spy. Cunning and diabolical.

Eha shot the bolt on the door. It might stop the guards for all of two seconds, if they were committed to gaining entry. Those two seconds might be the difference between a complex misunderstanding and treason, depending on how you wanted to cut it.

Decades as a spymaster had taught Eha much about the craft.

She returned to the table as Grace finished reading and began slowly typing notes. Eha slid close to watch the woman as Xiuying apparently was bringing Lucas up to speed on what he had missed by whispering directly into his ear.

Lucas was another one she had accumulated in this misadventure, but like the three from Yisan, he had apparently gone in with her mission.

Or he was waiting to betray her at the worst moment, which might be now.

Grace raised a hand to get her attention, so Eha slid close.

"Would Ambassador Dunham agree to return to Brasilia, after rejoining Ajax for a short combat mission?" someone had scrawled on the last page, which turned out to be a picture rather than text.

Eha considered it. If Addison was here, someone in a position of authority had finally determined that he would leave if not welcomed at present. Possibly return to Innruld Space shortly, assuming that the Humans had captured her, Lazarus, and Aileen, and be unwilling to give them up.

The Innruld would face all of Addison's rage, even for those few things they had never actually done.

They would fall. And the Species Underground would have access to the technology that would begin to make them an equal of the Humans. And perhaps not a friendly one, if the Rio Alliance made a mistake here.

But why were they not approaching her openly? Or were Lazarus's suggestions of a conspiracy being taken seriously, and a spy even now being sought?

Eha had been forced to hunt down intruders in her own networks over the years. Willing accomplices of the Innruld or lackeys being blackmailed, it made no difference. Death was still the outcome of such a game.

She really needed Oluchi at this point. He was her expert on those sorts of things. Xiuying and Lucas were killers. Grace was an assassin of unexpected depths.

Oluchi was the con artist whose skills would be the most useful, if this was a true offer of alliance. Or at least good faith on their part with an expectation of the same on hers.

The chance to break the Innruld, and not replace them with Humans.

All she had to do was find a way to convince Anya's true boss.

Whoever that was.

THIRTY-FOUR
ADDISON

ADDISON STILL WASN'T USED to the star drive. To be able to simply open a hole in the universe and emerge over there in an instant. Trans-space drives were slow and steady. You opened a tunnel that allowed you to navigate around obstacles, instead of landing and hopping, however much faster it would be.

Worse, he had been bouncing like a rabid Galumph around the edges of the Brasilia system, waiting until he got a response. It had been twelve hours on the Human clock since he had sent his message packet. Long enough for them to have come to some consensus.

Addison lacked the physiology to truly understand Humans, and all the games they might play, but he had spent enough time around Lazarus, he hoped. And he had seen the man at his worst, and his best, ranging from that first moment when they had brought a homeless refugee aboard with nothing but a beer logo, all the way up to returning to find *Ajax* waiting for him.

Addison looked around and contemplated this bridge.

Cormac was at his duty station. Kuei was flying. Wybert

was seated as Fusilier, but had all four of his hands off the console and had locked everything to boot.

There were no targets in this system Addison wanted to shoot at, under any circumstances.

"Kuei, you do have an escape route plotted, right?" Addison asked.

The Vaadwig woman rotated her furry head back over a thin shoulder to grin at him. Despite her modifications to Rio Alliance uniforms, she didn't look anything like an officer right now.

"You bet," she laughed, perhaps confirming his suspicions. "Any problems, and we'll go straight down."

"Down?" Addison asked, perplexed.

"Humans are surface dwellers who learned to fly later," Kuei said. "They tend to go sideways when surprised. Up if they think about it and can jump. Nobody ever would consider going down. Their mind reads that as face planting into a deck. Lazarus told me that one before he left."

"Oh," Addison shook his head in surprise. "What's down? Who do we run into?"

"Nothing and nobody," Kuei said. "But I can jump a thousand light-years without hitting anyone. That gets me clear beyond the galactic disk if I'm feeling frisky. From there, I can go any which way easily enough, and the chances of someone landing close enough to follow me from there are almost impossible."

Addison wondered how long she had been planning something this crazy. It smelled like exactly the sort of thing Kuei would have in her pouch for a surprise. She liked that sort of thing. Just look at Zhoonarrim Station and their escape.

Hopefully, she would never need to use it.

He could hope that the Rio Alliance Navy would come to their senses and treat him like just another sailor, right?

Even if he was well past insubordination at this point and it was only going to get worse.

You can issue me all the orders you want. I will follow only the ones I choose. And yes, I can always go home and overthrow the masters of the galaxy before coming back for Eha.

And I will be back for Eha. Whether I take your souls in the bargain remains to be seen.

But he didn't let that thought make it as far as his scales. Didn't want to spook Kuei or Wybert with the contained rage.

"Helm, bring us to a spot close enough to talk to *Recife*," Addison formally ordered her. "Preferably in a blind spot."

"Way ahead of you, Commander," she said, losing some of the snarky goofiness as she settled. "Course plotted and executing NOW."

Addison blinked, but he didn't see the blueshift that others would see looking this way. Other vessels had arrived in a blink of azure light, so he knew what it looked like now, but *Ajax* had simply stepped over to where *Recife* was parked. Close to the inbound lane for traffic wishing to approach Brasilia itself.

Not too close.

Now, to see which way the Humans would coil.

THIRTY-FIVE

LAZARUS

LAZARUS HAD LEARNED the knack to fall asleep anywhere at the drop of a hat. You picked that one up early, when a fifteen minute break might be all you got on a twelve hour surprise alert that woke you from your normal down time. Aileen and H'Brige had both retreated to their cabins, but he was in the main room, stretched out in a chair with his feet up and the lights down, meditating more than sleeping.

That hatch squeaked again, breaking through his rest and bringing him to full wakefulness. His body clock said middle of the night, a few hours before dawn.

Zero-dark-thirty.

He rose, somehow not surprised that someone had come in the dark of night. But if they were here to assassinate him, they should have fixed the door.

The room lights were just enough for Lazarus to make out a shadow stepping into the room, where hallway lighting would illuminate enough to see Lazarus rise from the chair.

"Good, you're awake," Admiral Santos said. "You wake Enjehn and I'll get Slani."

That sounded almost personable, but Lazarus didn't read too much into the words or the tone. But the fact that the Admiral was alone spoke volumes.

Lazarus had been unconsciously expecting a wall of marines.

He moved to Aileen's hatch and rapped hard three times. There was an override to open it, but she was likely in the bathroom, asleep in the tub in a foot of water.

Nude, with fur.

These hatches didn't give him the option to open just enough to yell.

It wasn't that he hadn't seen Aileen nude. The second day aboard *Shiva Zephyr Glaive* had involved him scrubbing her back in the shower. And then having her scrub his.

Admiral Santos didn't need to know that.

Lazarus counted to ten and rapped again. Three times.

She was a light sleeper. Loadmaster on a cargo ship taught you to come to full wakefulness quickly in any emergency.

The hatch opened a moment later.

Aileen, wearing pants and pulling a modified T-shirt down, still damp enough that it was going to stick. And she was close enough to Human female in form to distract.

At least she had a towel, drying the fur on her arms and head.

"Dry and fully dressed," he said simply. "The Admiral is here with news."

Lazarus turned away and walked back to the middle of the room so he didn't stare at the Yithadreph woman.

Santos had gone ahead and opened H'Brige's hatch enough to turn on a light, and then returned to the dining table. Atomarsk weren't mammals, so seeing her nude or in whatever she slept in wasn't going to be that much different than clothed.

Still, Lazarus appreciated the Admiral treating this professionally. The man had enough rank to do damned near anything he wanted.

Lazarus came to attention.

"No, sit," Santos said immediately. "We're past that."

Past that?

Sounded ominous, but Lazarus wasn't sure which way.

Aileen joined them first, still damp around the edges, followed a moment later by H'Brige. Santos looked a little askance, but he had also showed up in the middle of the night and awakened a sleeping Yithadreph.

Those were the risks you took.

"The Rio Alliance High Council has been in continuous session since I alerted them to *Ajax*," Santos began simply. "Oliveira, your offer to go do something about the incursion at Vilga has generated the most interesting and ugly arguments, both with and between the Admiralty Staff and the High Council, that I have ever seen in my long years as a sailor."

Lazarus kept his face serious. Admiral Santos didn't look like he had enjoyed the experience, but Lazarus also couldn't tell which side the man had been on.

And whether his side had won or lost.

Both of the woman commanders remained silent and poised, but they were probably just witnesses at this point. Innocent bystanders caught up in the currents of history, as it were.

Santos nodded to himself, satisfied apparently at the lack of response. Or arguments.

"We are detaching a pair of Protector Escorts, along with a Leader, to accompany you to Vilga, Captain Oliveira," Santos said. "da Silva is thinning out his own crew to provide you sailors from *Recife*. If there were any other officers in the navy capable of commanding *Ajax* in battle, you would be remaining here and I would send them instead, but you and Wolcott have either blundered into the most luck any sailor should ever have, or this is a trap and the most I end up losing is three escorts, because I can crew *Recife* back up in a week."

Again, he watched.

"You will shake down your new crew, Oliveira," Santos said, his voice taking on a harder, more formal note now. "Not later than two weeks from today, you will assault the fortifications and moorage at Vilga IV and destroy it. Am I clear?"

"You are, sir," Lazarus said.

He could smell the flavor of *with your shield or on it* in the air, but he had asked for the chance to prove what *Ajax* was capable of doing. And any damage he could do now would make it easier for whatever fleet Admiral Santos and the Admiralty Staff sent later, assuming he failed.

Lazarus didn't think he would fail, but that was a determination you made after the battle was complete, not before. Any fool can get lucky once.

"Commander Slani, you will join the crew of *Ajax* as an engineer, supporting the…person currently handling that task," Santos said, stumbling over a good description of a Qooph. Doubly so as he had never met one. Certainly not one with a sense of humor. "Your transfer is already in motion, according to Rodrigo da Silva. How quickly you will return to duty on *Recife* is yet to be determined."

"Thank you, Admiral," H'Brige nodded.

Lazarus saw the tips of all seven tail feathers separate like seaweed in a current, but that was excitement on her part. Going from being a junior engineering officer aboard a Heavy Starcruiser to Assistant Engineer on an experimental warship would look good on her resume when it came time for her next assignment.

"Commander Enjehn, you will be accompanying Captain Oliveira as Quartermaster for this mission," Santos continued, turning to stare at Aileen now. "I will need your supply situation as soon as you can provide it once you get aboard."

"I can provide you solid estimates now, sir," Aileen spoke up. "I've served with that crew for a decade, so I know how quickly they consume various perishables. Plus I have a list in my head of everything we used from the time we boarded *Ajax* until we departed in the pincke."

Santos did a double take. Lazarus did allow himself a brief grin, but wiped it away immediately.

There was a reason she was the best Quartermaster he had ever served with. Aileen smiled, whiskers and ears both forward to show how serious she was.

"How quickly can you join me?" Santos asked her.

"Would you like me dry and semi-formal, or damp and available immediately?" Aileen replied, turning serious now.

"Take twenty minutes," Santos decided. "I will have an escort return for all of you then and bring you to where the next stage will play out."

He rose, causing the three of them to bounce out of their chairs with him.

He paused at the hatch and turned back as it squeaked open.

"Captain, Commanders, good luck," he said simply, and then he was gone.

Lazarus blew out a breath and turned to the two women.

"Do or die?" Aileen asked in a careful voice. "Did I understand his implications correctly?"

"You did," Lazarus nodded soberly. "We get them all, or die trying."

"Then what?" she asked.

"We'll cross that bridge when we get there."

THIRTY-SIX
OLUCHI

OLUCHI UNTANGLED HIMSELF and studied the woman more or less draped across his chest and side. Certainly Anya was a fantastic actress, if she hadn't actually enjoyed that, but he suspected that she had gone well beyond her original assignment by now.

His heart rate was almost back to normal. Hers, echoing through his chest as she pressed against him, was recovering as well. The smell was ripe, pure sex that someone might not manage to wash out of the sheets on their first try.

He rolled onto his left side so that they were facing each other. Oluchi leaned close enough to breathe in her ear.

"Should we join the others?" he asked almost silently.

Her hands clenched around his back for a moment and then she nodded, albeit reluctantly from the look on her face.

Forty minutes of an audio performance should have been enough to convince the guards listening. He would need a nap first if she wanted another round, but Oluchi suspected she would need a nap as well.

They slid from the bed and located clothes that had been

more or less piled on the chair. Interestingly, she was as silent as he was when she moved.

Oluchi doubted that it was a skill taught to bureaucrats like the one she was possibly impersonating, but she might also have had to sneak out as a teenager. The woman didn't move like Grace did, thank all the gods that might take pity on him.

Anya paused as he finished and pulled him into a hug and a deep kiss. Warm and passionate, when many of their encounters had been more like a three aircar collision in rush hour traffic.

He returned the kiss, wondering if that was her saying goodbye at a moment when she could not speak without giving the entire game away to whoever might be listening.

Oluchi took her hand and silently opened the bedroom door, moving out into the light that was far too bright, considering what he had just been up to.

Xiuying and Lucas both grinned at him, as expected. Grace had a scowl, but it might mean anything.

Eha almost seemed excited. That hit a frightening chord in his soul, but he already knew Anya had been sent in as a spy for someone.

They just didn't know who.

Eha gestured both of them close. Grace rose and moved to the end of the table, leaving two chairs. Oluchi took the nearer one, with Anya immediately beside him, still holding his hand under the table.

Eha placed a reader on the table and gestured for him to begin.

Oluchi twitched as he did. Anya did not, but she probably had already been briefed on the contents and had just been waiting for now to complete her assignment.

Oluchi was absolutely certain the woman did not have

any weapons concealed on her body. He had carefully checked. Twice.

Ajax? Addison? Westphalia?

Crap.

He turned to Anya and studied her face. She nodded, somehow both serene and serious at the same time.

She reached out with her free hand and clicked the next page, so Oluchi went back to reading, feeling her pulse in his fingers. The shape of a conspiracy took form in his mind, but he'd spent more than two decades conspiring with pretty women, or rich ones, to accomplish things, so he was an expert.

Someone had drawn an obscure conclusion, after all the arguing about precedent and propriety. Addison was here right now. He needed help, but was also offering help.

The Rio Alliance had just run out of time to drag their heels. At least someone had been smart enough to understand that not sending Eha and her embassy to the ship would look an awful lot like they were being held as hostages.

Strav Ardna had made that mistake. It had proven to be terminal, once Oluchi Pryce, Xiuying Bălan, and Grace Savidge had gotten involved with the Lazarus who was occasionally known as *Pancho* Oliveira.

He turned to Eha and mouthed the obvious question with his face and eyes.

Are we going?

She nodded.

Oluchi turned to Anya, studying her far closer than even those unguarded moments when her brain had been turned to mush by a particularly strong series of orgasms.

This had just stepped over from being a casual infiltration to a full-bore conspiracy. If they weren't saying anything out loud, then someone of a high enough rank had put a foot down to stop them.

On the High Council, three of the people were generally referred to as the Humanist Block, while four made up the Alliance Block. Chairman Cavalcanti and Ruby Martins frequently cast deciding votes. That much Oluchi had been able to research in his spare time.

How had this vote broken out? So many new species available might roil the old coalitions and force some new configuration, but apparently freeing a potential hostage in Eha Dunham had been too much?

Oluchi had no illusions that he and the other Humans in the room were just collateral damage. The Churquen Ambassador to the Humans was the prize.

Collateral damage.

Oluchi saw another conspiracy perhaps. Shadowed by the first half dozen he was aware of.

Maybe it was his paranoia speaking, but he'd had to go out too many windows or through too many air vents when husbands or wives suddenly came home early. He had a nose for the change in scent or air pressure warning him to run like hell without even doing more than grabbing a pile of clothes.

What if someone was setting things up to get Eha and her embassy off-planet as a way of embarrassing a rival? Ruining their good name by associating them with the behavior of a thief in the night? Or a cuckolder?

Something must have shown in his face. Anya was suddenly on edge again, although her hand did not pull away from his.

Eha was the prize. The only prize, but maybe the situation needed a consolation as a wild card. One-eyed Jacks, as it were.

He leaned to Anya, as if kissing her ear.

"Eha and the others, yes," he said quietly. "I will remain behind to continue negotiations in the meantime."

Her flinch of surprise was honest. Not necessarily damning, but certainly telling.

Nobody had discussed that option, at least with her, so she was unprepared for it.

That should throw off other calculations.

He turned to the rest and included them with a wave of a hand, indicating that they would be leaving.

Oluchi pointed to himself and then the ground.

He would be staying.

Who was this going to surprise the most?

THIRTY-SEVEN

AILEEN

AILEEN WANTED TO PINCH HERSELF, just to be sure she was awake and not dreaming. It made no sense, but she'd always thought of the Atomarsk as legends, not real people. H'Brige Slani was indubitably real, but Aileen still had moments.

Her slow legs set the pace as they moved through the hallways, going someplace interesting maybe. Damned Humans were just storks. The legs on Lazarus always seemed as long as she was tall. Even H'Brige had a half a head on her. And legs.

Aileen wondered if she should challenge them all to a swimming race sometime, just to remind them.

But she kept her mutters to herself. She was in the Navy now, however temporarily *that* weirdness had gotten. Her example would be necessary for the next dozen fool Yithadrephs that decided to actually try this as a career.

She'd go back to smuggling or maybe honest cargo at that point. Whatever Addison ended up doing. Certainly not going home and making pups.

They entered a space certainly heavy in militariness. Reminded her of the bridge of *Ajax*, multiplied by several times but crammed down instead of open and elegant.

Obviously, Lazarus had wanted a comfortable place to spend his time. After looking around this room and the noise, she could understand why.

Aileen gritted her teeth and entered the fray.

"Slani, you accompany Commander Enjehn," the Admiral guy announced, pointing them to an excited-looking Human off in a corner. Aileen knew it was her destination because somebody had actually found her a chair that she might find comfortable.

Humans just did not understand that a solid back on a chair kinked a tail all wrong.

She considered suggesting a few of them surgically graft one on for a year, just to understand, but that was probably petty. And rude.

Lieutenant Commander Hernandez, from the rank tabs and name written on his chest. Human. Dark-skinned like most of the people around here, at a time when she had gotten used to Lazarus and Oluchi, only to find out that they were pale compared to most.

Apparently some sort of latitudinal biological category from the original homeworld that always left her confused.

Aileen climbed into the chair and levered it up to the point that she was comfortable. Still shorter than the Human, but that was almost a given. H'Brige had a similar chair, so maybe they were made for Atomarsk. Or at least a species with tails.

Hernandez had several tablet computers in front of him, showing all manner of charts, grids, and data. Aileen recognized them from having to keep records on *Ajax* using similar tools.

"I've set the baseline up as *Ajax* originally sailed,

Commander," the Human said excitedly. "And I am given to understand that you also removed consumables and cargo from your other ship at some point?"

"That's right," Aileen replied, trying to keep her grouchy under control. Too many people, too much noise. "When we turned fully pirate, all the cargo we had been carrying got broken down, cataloged, and much of it transported onto *Ajax.*"

"How much was that?" he asked, eyes wide and bright with what she would have called exhilaration in another Yithadreph. Maybe the same in a Human.

"Thirty-seven Human tons," Aileen said. "Not counting all the water and air we pumped over when we shut down *Shiva Zephyr Glaive* for long-term storage."

Rather than answer more questions, Aileen grabbed a tablet out of his hands and started typing. She had all the numbers in her head, and if she missed the consumption rate by more than a tenth of a point she'd be amazed. Feeding a crew was a daily exercise in logistics and she'd been doing it with those folks for years and years.

"How many crew members are we adding?" H'Brige asked into the gap.

Aileen supposed she should be asking, but that sounded a lot like peopling. It could wait. Or she could sort of hide behind a nerdy engineer's tail feathers and let H'Brige do the work.

"Two hundred and seventeen," Hernandez replied. "Mostly Human, with four other Atomarsk, six Gnashiiley, and nine Moah, in addition to the three of you and whatever crew is currently aboard. I am not familiar with any of those species."

Aileen grunted noncommittally and started adjusting the load order. Ereshkiki Nisab and Khyaa'sha were allergic to some of the food stuffs being delivered, but she already knew what to swap out. Wybert and Remahle had both fallen madly in love with Human oatmeal spiced with a healthy mix of local and Innruld stuff. And honey.

"Khyaa'sha will need at least two assistants to cook," she looked up and speared Hernandez with her gaze. "Others can mop and paint, but with two hundred crew members, the kitchen will be running hard and pretty constantly. Tarni don't need as much sleep as Humans, but she'll still need to be off-line, so I want a Chief who can handle the kitchen when she's off-duty."

The Human gulped and began furiously typing onto another pad.

"Tarni?" he asked absently.

"You might call them pinwheel spiders," Aileen noted. "Lazarus has also called her a centaur spider more than once."

She was rewarded with a shiver. Apparently arachnophobia was far more common in Human Space. But that made a rude bit of sense, in a place where Humans were seventy-five percent or more of the population.

"I have a cook we can pull from *Recife*," Hernandez said. "Petty Officer First Class instead of a chief, but he had good recommendations for promotion in a wardroom, when a slot opens somewhere."

"Good enough," Aileen agreed, looking over the notes when he turned the tablet her way.

In addition to Quartermaster, was she turning into *Ajax*'s Administrative Officer as well? Normally, that would be Addison's job, or one of the senior officers, but she supposed that she fell into that category now, since Lazarus had made her a Commander, along with Addison, and everyone coming over were going to be junior to her. Mostly, they were enlisted personnel, with a few Lieutenants and exactly one Lieutenant Commander, currently seated next to her and about to become Assistant Engineer on a Light Starcruiser.

Crap, had Lazarus set her up to become Second Officer? She'd have to tickle him in the shower, next time, just to get even with the man for that.

Worse, as she considered all the paperwork laid out in front of her, she might actually enjoy this job.

THIRTY-EIGHT

EHA

EHA COULD TELL, just by the delay, how much Oluchi had disrupted someone's plans by deciding to stay put. She wondered if they had been planning to send the Human woman, Anya, up as a spy to travel with them, exactly in this circumstance, and now couldn't coil back, not without causing enough of a scene that word got out elsewhere.

Why would the Human Pryce stay and send his girlfriend on?

Whispers would compound rapidly.

In the end, the woman had taken the data chip with her and left, then returned less than an hour later. Eha had been expecting them to move immediately on news from Anya.

Too bad.

She studied the returned Human for clues as Anya stood there quietly. Humans were still weirdly shaped and exotic, but she had spent enough time around Lazarus and the others to have a better handle on body language now.

The woman was nervous, but not in a bad way. Conspiracy-moving-to-fruition-way, perhaps.

"The audio system has been overridden," she said in a

conversational voice after Oluchi closed the door. "Right now, it is playing back a copy of last Tuesday morning, which was a completely mundane day that should not get the attention of anyone. At least not until it is too late to stop us. You."

Eha appreciate the pause to correct her language. Yes, the woman had originally expected to travel to *Ajax*, whether as a spy, a saboteur, or a messenger was unknown.

The Humans would have to come right out and ask now, if they wanted someone else aboard. But Lazarus was apparently getting a crew from somewhere, so perhaps that would be the way they infiltrated if something inimical was planned.

Eha wondered if Wybert had kept up the training Xiuying had started. And if the Ilount would need it later.

"How will this happen?" Oluchi asked. "I presume we can't just board an aircar or a shuttle and fly somewhere."

"Correct," Anya said. "I am to get the group of you down to the loading dock immediately. Guards have been moved around to open a path without observation. From there, a bakery truck will get you off of the government grounds to the civilian port, where you will transfer over to a military shuttle. That will take you to the ship, according to what I have been told."

"How much trouble will you be in, staying put?" Eha asked, insinuating that she could not join the party fleeing into the night.

Or early morning. The sun would be up in about an hour.

Anya grimaced and shrugged.

"With Oluchi remaining as the Ambassador's representative, I will probably come in for some negative approbation," she replied. "But that will not affect me in the short term, and my other masters will see that I am covered, if someone starts asking awkward questions."

"Were you a spy in the department before we arrived?" Eha asked, just to watch the woman blanch and press her lips together.

"I was," Anya finally admitted after a moment. "My engagement with Oluchi does not necessarily break my cover or expose me, since I was already something of a double agent for certain elements on the High Council who wished to keep track of the bureaucracy around them. With him staying, I will probably maintain that connection as a method of communication."

Anya turned to Oluchi and fixed him with a warm smile.

"The sacrifices we make in the name of good government," she said licking her lips in a manner that could only be described as lascivious.

Eha didn't think anything could make Oluchi Pryce blush, but she was wrong. The pale Human turned red for a moment.

"We are ready to move," Grace spoke up now, taking charge as instructed by Eha.

They were past the time of subtle words and innuendo. Past where Oluchi excelled.

She would need Grace, as well as the two warrior men.

They were moving now to direct action.

THIRTY-NINE

GRACE

GRACE WATCHED the Rio spy as she stepped close to kiss Pryce, adding a significant amount of passion to the effort. Grace let the twinge of jealously spike through her whole system and then recede, like an ebbing tide.

Lazarus had left her with implied promises, as yet unspoken. She just needed to protect Eha and get the woman back to Addison. Then she and Lazarus would have that opportunity to finally talk.

And perhaps more.

Everyone had their gear. Quick bags packed with a few things, while leaving most of their clothing behind for now. Grace had no reason not to be returning for them at the present time, but she also understood that *Ajax* and Lazarus would apparently be heading into a major battle.

Bad things could happen at the best of times. A lucky enemy is worse than a good one.

Lucas and Xiuying wore Rio Alliance tan uniforms, which would actually make them stand out around here, but she and Anya were dressed as civilians.

Nobody encountering them in a hallway would be able to mistake a Churquen for anything else, but that was the risk they would have to take.

Anya opened the door, sticking her head out enough to look both ways before glancing back and nodding. Grace followed immediately behind. Eha after that. The two men trailing and looking like military aides minding their own business.

Grace approved of their tradecraft. She had already figured out all the hallways and stairwells in the building, but had also formulated a plan to shatter a windowsill if she needed out. The glass would be unbreakable, but the frame was still wood and could be dismantled from the inside. Quietly, even, if you have patience and need.

She had not gotten desperate.

Down the hall, they took two turns and ended up clear at the rear of this floor, in an area Grace had never seen before. If she was correct, they were above and a little behind the kitchen right now. Call it the service end of the palace. Or whatever this place was classified as on a map.

Palace, for now.

The hallway was deserted. Only a wide, shallow staircase greeted them.

The stairs weren't as tall as she had seen other places, and that confused her for a moment. Then she decided that perhaps that would make it easier for older legs to climb. More steps, but each less work than normal. No other explanation made sense, and it felt awkward to descend.

Anya moved with poise, but Grace assumed that the woman used these stairs frequently. On Yisan, you just had private lifts, when someone was too frail for stairs.

A circular clock on the wall proclaimed the time. Grace noted it and adjusted herself. False dawn was perhaps twenty-five minutes off on this planet. The quietest part of the night and Human cycle.

Down a flight of stairs, Anya paused at an open doorway and gestured Grace close. Grace motioned the others to stay put and slid over to the pale Anglo.

"I heard voices down the hallway," Anya whispered. "There should be none. If I have to distract them you take everyone down to the basement, exit right and look for a door close by that will lead to the loading dock. Stay just outside it for two minutes. If I don't arrive by then, you go through and look for a panel-sided airtruck with a bakery logo."

Grace nodded. That sounded like the set up for an excellent trap, if someone wanted to get them separated from Anya for bad things to happen.

Still, the woman had been upfront so far.

And it was doubtful that she understood just how dangerous Xiuying was. Or Grace for that matter.

Anya stepped into the hallway and vanished from sight. Voices rang out in quiet conversation.

Grace stepped back and motioned Eha and the others to follow her down.

Second floor. Ground floor. Basement.

She grabbed Xiuying and pulled him close.

"Turn right from here in two minutes," she said simply. "Out through a door onto the loading dock. Panel van from a bakery."

"Is it a trap?" he asked professionally.

"Not on the surface," Grace nodded grimly. "I am going to look for Anya. If I am not back in three minutes, leave without me."

He started to say something, caught himself, and nodded.

Grace went back up the stairs as quickly as she could without making noise, pausing at each landing to listen.

Silence, broken only by the sounds of the building itself settling and adjusting. She counted seconds in her head.

Anya was just entering the third floor stairwell as Grace came into view. The brunette woman stopped cold, surprise etched on her face.

"What's wrong?" she whispered hoarsely, hurrying closer.

"Nothing," Grace lied. "Came to make sure you weren't in trouble."

"Accidentally caught one of the High Councilors emerging from a bedroom belonging to someone else," Anya grinned. "Had to route him the other direction, lest he follow me this way and ask where I was going."

"Whoops," Grace grinned back.

"Indeed," Anya said quietly. "My next report will be filled with all manner of gossip and innuendo. Are the others safe?"

"Yes," Grace whispered. "Left them below."

"Then let's get all of you to safety," Anya started moving, barely making any noise.

They found Lucas first, poised to race this direction to confront trouble. His face conveyed concern, but Grace shook her head and the man fell in.

Xiuying was listening at the door when she and Anya approached.

"So far, so quiet," he murmured, stepping out of the way.

Anya opened the door out onto a concrete dock. Grace followed on her heels. The others trailed when she glanced back.

Wide and deep, but only twenty feet tall. Grace had the impression of a vast underground cathedral, polished gray concrete in all directions marred by age, water, and stains.

And a bakery truck, backed up to the dock itself. The back was open and a man dressed like a civilian stood there.

Thirty-five. That reddish-brown that natives of this planet had, itself originally colonized from *America del Sur* on Earth. Black hair under a flat cap. Thin build.

Unarmed.

"No names," Anya said firmly as the group got up to the man.

As if anyone would mistake Eha Dunham for anyone else. Or Grace, since blacks had been pretty rare on this planet. In a pinch, she maybe could pass for darker than most, but they tended to straight, heavy hair, and her ringlets would mark her.

The man nodded to Anya, then studied the group.

"In," he said simply, a quiet tenor that didn't sound as rough as his appearance might have suggested.

Grace entered.

The rear was empty, but they had walked by a number of rolling racks that had delivered bread and pastries no doubt. The entire box was empty, so she went all the way forward and stood right behind the driver's seat, just in case this was a trap of some sort and she needed to lay hands on the man.

Or kill him and fly the vehicle instead, although she had no idea where she might go.

But that was just her paranoia speaking up. She had gotten infected by Lazarus and his vision of a spy. Another double agent like Anya, feeding information to Westphalia that had nearly gotten him killed.

One of the reasons Eduardo had sent her.

The others crowded into the rear, the two men pressing hands against the ceiling to brace themselves while Eha coiled as low as she could get.

The driver entered the front as Anya closed the rear with a call of "Good luck," and then the darkness descended, with only the dim lighting on the dock itself coming in the windshield.

"Ready?" the driver looked back at everyone.

He didn't wait for an answer as he powered up the lifters and edged away from the loading dock itself.

Next stop, space?

FORTY

LAZARUS

LAZARUS STUDIED the vessel through a porthole as it came in to dock. Standard personnel transport, designed to rapidly convey a large crew from point to point instead of tying up a warship. Compact, with one hundred rows of seats and two aisles, running two/four/two.

He had fallen into parade rest. Around him, others moved quietly, but he ignored them. This would be his second crew, after he lost the first one, killed or captured and being held by Westphalia against a future trade.

If they would be willing to trade home some of the engineers who might yet be compelled to give up their secrets.

Still, while Westphalian vessels might recognized *Ajax*, they would not be expecting her, assuming Addison had been successful in sneaking away from Vilga's Stand.

A presence manifested close by. Lazarus looked over and realized that Santos had come to rest next to him, hands crossed behind his back in that manner pounded into new recruits from day one.

The space around them was almost empty.

"There are any number of things I might say, Oliveira," Santos said quietly. "You've certainly kicked over an ant's nest. Several of them. The Admiralty Staff and the High Council will both be years sorting all of this out."

Lazarus nodded. He'd figured from the beginning that the best way to do this involved making the biggest splash possible. He would have landed that pincke illegally in Freedom Square, down in Greenbriar, had that penciled out as a better result, but he had gotten his message across.

Now, he needed to go act like a sailor.

"Your new crew are arriving, and you will depart shortly," Santos said. "I am informed that a smaller vessel has departed from the surface, with a crew and equipment for you to offload all the fallen currently in your freezers. They will rendezvous with *Ajax* about two hours after you board, giving your current crew time to prepare for ceremonies."

"Thank you, sir," Lazarus said.

That had been a fear at the back of his mind. Those twenty-eight men and women would not be returned before he went into a new battle where he would expect more to join them.

Or fail and truly be destroyed this time. Those orders still stood. *Ajax* could not be captured by Westphalia under any circumstances, up to and including setting the scuttling charges and destroying the ship.

Or flying it into the middle of a massive nebula and somehow managing to not hit anything.

Lazarus had in his head the rough course and bearing that would get him halfway through the Phraettis Nebula without passing too close to any of the gravity wells that might have torn him apart. If he had to run, that might be an option, but most likely he would be in such bad shape that he would need to overload everything instead.

The first battle had been one GunWall. This would be two and a Heavy Starcruiser.

At least this time, he would be surprising them, instead of the other way around.

"I will expect you back here when the battle is done, Captain," Santos said in a way that managed to convey more warmth than the words suggested. "I look forward to meeting Commander Wolcott. He's already been put in for a medal for the events at 9087 Geminorum IV."

Lazarus flinched and turned to actually look at the man, after he had been focusing on the ship in the porthole.

Santos had a wry grin on his face.

"As you yourself reminded me, Captain," Santos said, "upholding the best of the Rio Alliance Navy, even when he didn't have to. Stopping pirates. Detecting a Westphalian invasion and getting us the information, Paul Revere style, to maybe do something about it. Taking great personal and professional risk, because it was the right thing to do."

"Thank you, Admiral Santos," Lazarus managed. "I'll let him know."

Further words were interrupted by the clanging of the arriving ship attaching to the dock.

When Lazarus looked again, Santos had moved off to a corner of the room with a firm smile on his face. Lazarus looked at Aileen and H'Brige and nodded. A handful of other enlisted sailors had been quietly waiting and rose now, somewhat cowed by the Chief of Staff himself being in the room.

"Good luck, *Pancho*," the Admiral called.

Lazarus saluted and stepped into the lock as it started to beep. The others followed.

Inside, the vessel was a wide, flattened cylinder, oval shaped with space for cargo below and a narrow crew compartment above. The pilot, a Lieutenant named Lopez, was standing just inside the door, obvious who he was from the flight wings over his heart.

"Welcome aboard, Captain," Lopez said with a sharp salute.

Lazarus returned it, feeling almost like he was back in the Navy again after nearly a year off-duty. He stepped out of the airlock vestibule and looked to his right.

Most of the men and women were standing for a better view of their new commander. Admiral da Silva would have asked for volunteers, and hopefully only sent good ones, but none of them had any idea what was happening.

He could tell when Aileen followed him by the gasps and shocked looks on faces. Lazarus stepped all the way across the gap at the front of the seats and gestured everyone following him to grab seats.

"I'll explain as soon as we button up," he yelled over the murmuring, causing it to pause for a moment, and then redouble.

Lopez saw to the hatch and then stood in front of it.

"Attention to orders," H'Brige suddenly yelled in a voice that didn't seem like it fit in such a slim, tiny body.

The room fell to silence quickly and she grinned at him, her tail feathers parting just a flicker.

Most of the crew members were seated forward, and he had to trust that he was only carrying two hundred and change, and that they were sailors and not a disguised marine assault force intent on retaking *Ajax* from the pirates who held it right now.

Even if they all wore tan uniforms.

"This mission is simple," Lazarus lifted his voice enough to carry. "We are going to rendezvous with the Rio Alliance Light Starcruiser *Ajax*. She is an experimental warship far heavier than you would imagine, and we'll need that. A Westphalian fleet has snuck over the border and is currently building a secret base. We have to get there before they are operational."

"We taking a fleet, sir?" a woman yelled from the back. Probably a Chief from the gruffness of her voice.

"Us and three Protectors," Lazarus yelled back. "Plus surprise, a big gun, and the sort of attitude problems I asked Admirals Santos and da Silva to provide for me as a crew."

He let the laughter build and recede before he spoke again.

"A few of you saw Commander Enjehn when she boarded," Lazarus continued, watching the heads turn to the seat where she was out of sight right now. "Aileen is a Yithadreph, and will be Second Officer and Quartermaster on *Ajax*. My First Officer is a Churquen named Addison Wolcott. All you need to know is that he is a Commander and outranks you. Similarly, I have Atomarsk Lieutenant Commander H'Brige Slani here as Assistant Engineer and Commander Ereshkiki Nisab as Engineer. He's a Qooph, and is smarter than the rest of the crew. He also outranks you."

Lazarus paused to let all that sink in. He studied the hungry faces. Volunteers would be looking for action and promotion opportunities. Serving on an experimental warship with new alien allies would look good in a personnel file later. As would a few words from their new commanding officer.

"There are other aliens aboard *Ajax*," Lazarus continued. "Species you have never met. All of them will outrank you, regardless of the number of stripes on your arm, so be prepared to take their orders. I needed engineers to handle all the power that *Ajax* can put out and gunners to help fight the ship. That's you people. Then we're going to go kill some Westphalian invaders and return as heroes."

He turned to Lopez and smiled as the crew cheered.

"Lieutenant, take us out."

FORTY-ONE
EHA

EHA LOOKED out the windshield as the truck backed into another loading dock with an annoying beeping. It came to rest and someone rapped twice on the rear door. A moment later, whoever it was grabbed the handle and rolled it upright.

Human. Female. Rio Alliance Navy tan uniform without rank or nametag. Young Brasilian native woman with dark skin and straight hair.

She counted tails, or noses, maybe, since Humans didn't have a tail, and nodded.

The driver had not moved from his seat.

"We need to move quickly," the woman announced, gesturing them to exit the vehicle.

Lucas went out first, Xiuying hard on his heels like they expected combat to break out at any moment, even though the woman was unarmed.

Lucas nodded to her a moment later and Eha uncoiled to join them, Grace remaining inside until last.

Another loading dock.

The uniformed woman rolled the door shut again and

slammed a palm on the door. A moment later the truck lifted and left without a word.

"Ambassador Dunham, we have transportation for you and your party if you will follow me," she said simply, turning and walking through a set of double doors into whatever this building was.

The two men led, bodyguards now. Eha followed, trusting Grace to cover the rear.

Whatever was about to happen next.

She was not expecting a small commuter train.

The woman stepped in and grabbed a vertical rail, chromed steel scuffed with age. There were no seats, just a number of such rails.

Eha smiled and coiled her tail around of the posts. At last Humanity had found something she could do comfortably. The others spread out, still guarding her.

"We're aboard," the woman said simply.

Someone was listening, as the doors closed immediately and the capsule began to move a moment later.

Eha assumed that Human soldiers handled acceleration better, because most of the people she knew would have at least stumbled, but everyone here had hold of a rail.

The car rocketed down a tunnel in the sort of silence a good maglev system exemplified.

Since the female was not communicative, Eha studied her body language instead. She reminded Eha of Grace in the way both women moved and stood, so perhaps some higher level of close combat training, since all Humans apparently studied several in their spare time.

Humans were just a frighteningly violent culture.

They flew through several stations without stopping. Eha saw Humans on most of them, all wearing tan, so she presumed that she was on a military base now. This almost reminded her of the usual mass transit systems at stations like Dormell or Aceanx.

Finally, the car itself spoke, a Human female voice that was just enough off to probably be generated electronically.

"Now arriving at Bay Seven serving docks sixty-four through eighty-one. Bay Seven shortly. Exit on your left."

Sure enough, they came to rest and the doors opened. Lucas and Xiuying were moving with greater confidence now, like perhaps they knew where they were, with the nameless female leading everyone. Eha slithered in their wake.

Out onto a platform and then up a moving slidewalk but one built with steps instead of flat.

Humans and steps.

They didn't know any better.

Up top, they crossed another platform and emerged at Dock Seventy-One, according to the enormous Human numbers painted on either side of the doorway.

The sun was up now. Clouds threatened, but there were enough breaks to see sky and sunlight through them.

A Human starship awaited them. She knew it was Human because it was perfectly symmetrical down the centerline and generally streamlined unnecessarily. Innruld ships could do anything, including the ammonite-style design of *Shiva Zephyr Glaive* that Lazarus had compared to a musical treble clef.

Eha didn't perform music, but he had shown her the notation and she had to agree that the looks were similar.

Human ships were supposedly fast and efficient.

And dull, but she didn't offer her opinion out loud. They were assisting her covert return to Addison, at least for a while. It wouldn't do to insult them in the process.

Their fashion sense already left so much to be desired.

The woman led them to the vessel's rear hatch, a ramp up

into the vehicle, since the engines were on outriggers to each side.

A man in brown descended the ramp as they approached. This one wore rank tabs and a name tag.

Lieutenant Commander Mohammed. A pilot, if those were supposed to be wings on his chest.

"Yours now," the woman said with a nod.

She turned and studied them for a long moment.

"Good luck," she said and left without looking back.

Eha turned back to Mohammed.

"We're ready to depart as soon as you board, Ambassador," he said in a pleasant baritone.

He turned and walked up the ramp and everyone followed.

The inside of the ship was a long, low cargo bay, already filled with individual boxes on what appeared to be pedestals. It made no sense to Eha, but Xiuying stepped up and laid a hand on one of them.

"Hey, mate," he called, causing the pilot to pause and look back. "These full?"

"Not yet, sailor," the man snapped. "That's where we're headed now."

"You got too many, then," Xiuying called back, unwilling to grant the other man an inch. "Only twenty-eight where we're going."

"This is a standard configuration, Chief," Mohammed replied. "You die, I fly."

He turned and kept walking, gesturing for them to accompany him forward.

"What was all that?" Eha asked.

"These are refrigerated coffins, Eha," Xiuying replied.

"Coffins?"

"Yeah, for all the dead currently being stored aboard *Ajax*."

FORTY-TWO

ADDISON

ADDISON WATCHED the first vessel slowly approaching, with the second one just now clearing the atmosphere of Brasilia.

"Cormac, confirm with a hard scan of the closer vessel," Addison said simply.

Cormac was a NavCrawler, so he relayed his pique by just updating the information on Addison's personal screen and changed the presentation font and color to something less pleasant to read.

Two hundred and twenty-one life forms scanned. Thankfully, one of them was a Yithadreph, so he knew Aileen was aboard. Plus Atomarsk, Moah, Gnashiiley, and a bunch of Humans.

What he had been told to expect.

"We're being hailed."

"Conference mode," Addison replied, still not quite sure which set of buttons or sliders would do that.

"*Ajax*, this is Lazarus," the man's voice came in. "On final approach with crew. Password is Aceanx."

"Understood, Lazarus," Addison replied. "Stand by."

He did know where the mute button was. He clicked it and watched the comm screen get a flashing red border.

"Wybert, stand down the guns and head aft to meet them in the docking bay," Addison ordered.

"Do I have to leave my spear here?" the Ilount goof, Lieutenant Wybert of Capantzina the Goof, asked.

"Not at all," Addison reassured him. "They will be expecting a fierce, Ilount warrior to greet them, after all."

"Yippie!" he cheered as he carefully locked everything, popped up off his gunnery nest, and skittered to the main hatch like a small avalanche of limbs and blue silliness.

Addison waited until the sound died down before he opened the line again.

"Lazarus, you are cleared for approach and landing," he called into the line.

"ETA four minutes."

Cormac cut the line. Addison watched the vessel begin to maneuver carefully. It was too big to actually land, so they had to mate airlocks and come aboard individually, where they would be greeted by someone who really looked awe-inspiringly dangerous, if you didn't know any better.

"*Addison, the second vessel has an interesting scan signature,*" Cormac announced in that droll way he did.

The screen changed and the life form reading stood out. Four Humans, one of them forward in a piloting bay, and a Churquen.

There was only one other Churquen in the system besides himself, but he restrained himself from cheering right now.

Nobody had mentioned that she would be on the second vessel, when Addison would have thought that was the first thing they would say. Had they stolen the vessel? Convinced the pilot to sneak them off?

Except that the same orders telling him that Lazarus was

returning on the first vessel included details on the second, making a later rendezvous.

"Cormac, once Wybert gets aft, lock down most of the frame bulkheads along the neck," Addison said a shade louder than perhaps necessary. "Just in case."

Kuei and Cormac both looked back over their shoulders at him.

"Why did nobody mention Eha?" he asked them.

"Oh," both said in harmony.

There was something deeper going on, and Churquen did not swim. Did not like water in any instance. This felt like a pool of still water hiding a predator.

FORTY-THREE

LAZARUS

LAZARUS HOPED he would never get over that spike of wonder as he watched *Ajax* on an overhead screen, filling up the entire frame like a wall as they flew right up next to her. Docking was quieter than normal, but that just spoke well of the pilot they had selected for this mission.

Maybe he was used to hauling senior officers around.

Lazarus unbuckled and rose, turning to face aft as about half the men and women rose to stretch and watch.

"Your first orders will be to identify your new section leaders when we board," Lazarus called. "Wybert of Capantzina and Ereshkiki Nisab, respectively. However, before you do anything else, this entire crew will form up as a Color Guard and march aft with me."

Faces grew serious at those words. An Honor Guard was escort duty. Color Guard meant that the people in question were fallen sailors being sent home.

The room grew sober.

"Captain Oliveira, I show positive pressure on the airlock," Lopez called over the intercom. "You are cleared to debark."

"Thank you, Lieutenant," Lazarus replied. "That was about as smooth a flight as I've taken."

Lazarus moved to the hatch, Aileen and H'Brige in his wake. The space was a hallway, but the door would only allow one at a time, so he was going first.

Something caught in his throat as he touched the cold steel panel.

Aileen tapped him on the hip and caught his attention.

"It's okay," she said quietly. "We're home."

Home.

Yes. Not his final home. Or maybe it would be, since he had so many things yet to do and *Ajax* would be central to them.

He smiled down at her and hit the switch, stepping back as the hatch opened towards him.

The air pressure was just slightly off, or maybe that was the smell of all the sailors with him, rather than the life support systems.

Still, the air in his face smelled cleaner. Better.

He stepped across the threshold and he was indeed *home*.

Right down to the Ilount warrior in breastplate and powerspear, standing more or less at attention at the far end of the loading dock. Getting everyone in here would be a little crowded, but they'd make do.

"Permission to come aboard?" he asked Wybert.

All five eyes lit up and his four mandibles flexed outward as far as they could in a smile before returning to his normal fierceness.

"Permission granted, Captain," Wybert chirped happily, thumping the butt of his spear on the deck once for emphasis.

Lazarus walked out of the shuttle and gestured Aileen to join him.

"Oh, wow!" Wybert called as H'Brige exited, the first

Atomarsk the Ilount had ever seen outside of a book of fairy tales.

Lazarus gestured H'Brige to one corner.

"Form up on Lt. Commander Slani," he yelled as more and more folks debarked. Most stepped normally, right up until they saw Wybert, and then balked, flinched, or stumbled, making the going slow.

The big goofball practically preened with the excitement of looking like a badass warrior.

He certainly had the image down. And had painted his old blue breastplate to look like the same uniform everyone else was wearing.

After all, a Captain has a good deal of leeway on uniforms in the field.

"Form up," Lazarus yelled again and again until it was taken up by the men and women still on the transport.

After that, the movement became more orderly.

Wybert wasn't tall enough to be seen by folks in the back, but the ranks ended up a little off-set by the way folks came to rest, craning around to see their first Ilount male ever.

"Transport is clear, Captain," someone yelled from the back of the room. Maybe that same female chief that had yelled earlier from the tone.

"Lock us up," Lazarus called back.

Beeps signaled, followed by the clang of the doors closing and the thump of bolts setting.

Lazarus took a deep breath to say something when the hatch behind him opened. He glanced back to see Ereshkiki Nisab making the grandest possible entrance.

And then he spoke, and topped it.

"Humans, fear not," Ereshkiki Nisab sang with all six voices.

Lazarus could tell that *someone* had been into the Bible database and read the appropriate bits of Ezekiel 1. Then all the other parts where bizarrely alien creatures came down and the first thing they had to do was convince the poor herdsman that they were indeed Messengers of God.

The noise peaked after the initial surprise.

"Silence in the ranks!" was heard as that female chief's voice overrode everyone else and quiet fell.

"On my left is Ereshkiki Nisab," Lazarus said to the assembly. "He is a Qooph and your Engineer. On my right is Wybert of Capantzina, Ilount Fusilier."

Another gasp and earthquake in the ranks caused Lazarus to glance over and grin at Khyaa'sha as she skittered in and then rested back on her abdomen and rear six legs.

"Khyaa'sha Ramarkhay, Mistress of the Wardroom," Lazarus called. "She will be responsible for feeding all of you, so make sure your personnel records indicate any allergies or other problems. I'd hate to have her poison you *unnecessarily.*"

That got a laugh out of the group.

H'Brige broke ranks enough to step out of line a bit and turn so she had all of the room in front of her.

"Sir, what other species will we encounter aboard?" she asked rhetorically.

"Commander Wolcott is a Churquen," Lazarus began listing. "Lt. Commander Akeley on the Helm is Vaadwig. Remahle Mebarsu is Kr'Mari, acting as one of my Loadmasters. Thadrakho is Necherle, back in Engineering. Cormac and Lenox are Crawlers, Nav and Medical respectively. As a reminder, they will generally outrank all of you, so behave accordingly. I don't have time to deal with personnel issues because as soon as we leave here we're going to train for two days and then take you directly into battle. Questions?"

The room was silent.

"Chief Garcia, is that you in the back?" Lazarus called over the assembled ranks.

"It is, sir," she answered.

"Take charge of the troops, Chief," Lazarus ordered her. "From here, we're heading aft and I'd like us to look like a military unit, and not a pub crawl."

That got a laugh, as intended. Lazarus had always had a way with sailors, a calm confidence that had mixed well with his nerdiness to move him to where he could design a ship like *Ajax*.

Chief Garcia began pouring a layer of profane invective down on the ranks as she walked forward, getting them shifted about and organized into four columns.

Lazarus was finally able to step back and take one of Khyaa'sha's paws in his and just hold it.

It was good to be home.

Now, the hard part began.

FORTY-FOUR

EHA

EHA HAD FOUND a quiet place off to one side to wait as they reached orbit and then headed outward. The rear of the ship was kept dim and cool, which just reinforced the psychological effects on her.

Grace sat nearby, while Xiuying and Lucas had their heads together a little ways off, engaged in a low conversation that never got clear enough to be anything but sounds.

Docking made the ship ring and bounce just a little. Eha surged up, but held on to the chair she had coiled around.

"Sorry about that," Mohammed's voice came over the intercom. "Not used to having living passengers. Should have remembered to warn you. Docking complete. Airlock extending."

Eha nodded. She would have appreciated a notice.

On the aft wall an airlock light came on and beeped as a tunnel began to deploy itself outward, thumping again as it locked itself. More noise as it started to open, but Eha had already joined the others moving that direction.

It was still dim in here, but much brighter on the other side of the corridor, so she saw the first figure enter as a shadow, before lights began to come up in the airlock corridor and the bay.

Lazarus.

Anya's people had hopefully come through.

He walked right up to her and Eha wrapped her arms and part of her tail around the man, just happy. He returned it gingerly, Humans being so much stronger, and then stepped back.

Grace was there and their hug was even more intense, if silent. Topped with a kiss.

Aileen slipped around the two and smiled.

"Brought friends," she announced. "Xiuying and Lucas, you two move off to one side while my folks get everything going."

"Where's Oluchi?" Lazarus asked, stepping to one side but still holding hands with Grace.

Through the airlock, Eha watched a silent parade of men and women enter, intently focused on some task, but still reacting when they happened to look at her.

"He stayed behind on Brasilia," Eha answered. "So that it didn't look like a jailbreak in the morning."

"I see," Lazarus replied, the comment more like a placeholder than anything.

She ended up to one side as the new crew members began collecting the caskets. Apparently, they floated on lifters, because they had a person at each end, just guiding them as everyone began hauling them onto the ship.

Once the group left, Lazarus turned to her.

"Addison hasn't come aft yet," he said, his face slowly turning into a smile. "Been too busy on the bridge, but I suspect he might like to see you."

"Soon," she replied, gesturing. "As Ambassador, I need to be part of the ceremonies. Xiuying and Lucas have explained some of what's happening. We need to honor the fallen properly."

"That we do," Lazarus said. "If you all will join me, that's next, and will take a little while."

The other side of the airlock turned out to be one of *Ajax*'s main loading docks. The carrier she had arrived on was too wide to enter, so they had mated locks instead. Many men and woman stood in lines down the two sides as she entered.

"Ambassador on the deck," a female voice rang out and everyone snapped to attention like she was a visiting dignitary. Bipedal heels together. Hands down by the sides. Head up and spine straight.

Eha supposed she was. Ambassador to the Humans. And she was surrounded by them, as well as a few more Atomarsk, plus some Moah and Gnashiiley.

Perhaps a better title would be Ambassador to the Rio Alliance, if she could finally get them to relax about demanding her planetary coordinates as a prelude to anything good.

Lazarus led her and the others to one side, near where Lt. Commander Slani was standing at attention. Eha took a place and settled on her coil.

"At ease," a man yelled from one side and everyone moved their feet back to shoulder width.

A coil was so much more comfortable.

The room was remarkably silent, considering that there must be nearly two hundred people in here, so Eha sat and watched, picking out Human ethnicities around her as well as ranks from what she had studied.

Aileen had vanished with the others, leaving Eha with Lazarus and Grace on her left and Xiuying and Lucas on her right. And most of the new crew of *Ajax*. At the main hatch,

Wybert and Ereshkiki Nisab stood to either side, forming the lines that the rest followed.

Music started from overhead speakers. Slow and mournful. A dirge on instruments she could not identify. Pipes, perhaps, wailing strangely.

"Attention to the Colors!" a voice rang out and all the men and women snapped back to attention in sharp unison.

A hatch opened, the same one Aileen had left with her group, and a single Human entered. Female and approaching middle age perhaps.

She carried a staff in both arms, with a green and gold cloth hanging from the top half.

It took Eha a moment to understand that it was a flag. She had seen the logo of the Rio Alliance any number of times, painted on walls or as a patch on uniforms. And even in the background in rooms she had been meeting in.

She had never seen it actually used in a ceremony.

The woman stepped slowly, deliberately. At a pace Aileen would feel comfortable. Behind her, the first of the floating caskets entered, escorted by a pair of sailors.

The rest followed one by one, somberly transported onto the other vessel as the crew watched and the music played.

For Eha, she had a chance to see another side of Human culture. Up until now, it had been in different settings. Lazarus in various moods. The oligarchs of Yisan. The politicians of Brasilia.

Now, she could watch them at what was probably their most serious.

It impressed her, the way the crowd stayed perfectly still and silent. Only the sounds of shoes on the deck, mostly covered over by the music, gave any indication at all. Faces were sober and still.

Humans almost had a second language in the way the muscles of their face pulled and deformed to communicate emotions. For a Churquen, the closest equivalent might be the scales around the jaw and the tip of the tail, which was why they tended to sit on a coil when things got serious, precisely so nobody could tell what you were thinking.

One by one the caskets transited the room, until finally they were done.

Eha wondered what came next, but nobody moved or spoke, so she supposed that the ceremony was not done. Eventually, the woman with the flag returned, two columns of sailors marching in formation behind her and coming to rest in front of Lazarus.

Eha glanced over and noted that the last man in line had stopped and was closing the airlock from this side. The music tailed off as the beeping intensified, and then the door slammed shut.

"All hands accounted for, sir," the woman said into the sudden silence.

"At ease," Lazarus called.

Everyone relaxed again and settled into a more comfortable stance.

"Several weeks ago, a Westphalian Task Force arrived in secrecy at 6357 Wei Xiu, a system many of you will know as Vilga's Stand," Lazarus continued. "They have surprise and believe they have overwhelming force capable of withstanding any ships that the Rio Alliance can send against them before they are able to complete a Battlestation that will be harder to dislodge than a hungry tick."

He paused to look around the room and Eha saw more of the man known as *Pancho* Oliveira. Lazarus was much more laid back and friendly. *Pancho* was hard. Steel ground to a killing edge. If she hadn't known Lazarus first, she might never have recognized the transformation happening before her eyes.

"They're wrong, by the way," Lazarus continued. "You

and I, we're going to go show them that. Now, organizational work, and then dinner in a few hours, once everyone has a chance to claim bunks and find the heads. Dismissed."

The men and women broke ranks, but most seemed interested in studying her and the others from Innruld Space, rather than a quick nap or a shower. Many stepped near enough to perhaps speak, but nobody did.

Lazarus was close, and her other bodyguards, so she felt protected.

He turned to her now.

"Tell me what's up with Oluchi," Lazarus said.

FORTY-FIVE

OLUCHI

OLUCHI CAME out of a doze and realized that he had fallen asleep wrapped around Anya, warm and snuggled up against her bare bottom.

As she had said. The sacrifices we make in the name of good government.

"You awake?" she asked quietly.

"Yeah," he breathed in her ear. "How long have you been up?"

"Maybe twenty minutes," she replied, rolling inside his arms to face him.

"You could have rolled me over," Oluchi said.

"I was enjoying myself," Anya grinned, kissing him quickly.

"How soon until all hell breaks loose?" he asked, glancing at the clock and noting that for all the excitement, the sun was only an hour above the horizon and most of the palace grounds rarely got going before brunch.

"We probably have time for a shower and breakfast," Anya shrugged in a distracting way. "Unless you wanted to fool around some more first."

That was the best part Oluchi had discovered about most women, once they were into their thirties and past all that silliness of youth. They had hopefully gotten over themselves and started living to enjoy their life, rather than constantly worrying about what others thought. They could tell you what they wanted you to do, and where, and how. And maybe, if you were lucky, fix you breakfast in the morning.

Of course, as a reformed gigolo he didn't have a lot of space to talk. But we all grow up eventually.

Or should.

He kissed her and considered it, but his bladder was making demands and Oluchi knew that coffee and carbs were going to be better for him today than more fooling around, as much fun as that might be.

And if he ended up in jail in a few hours, a last meal from the good kitchen would probably be almost as good as a fourth romp with this woman in the last twenty-four hours.

Maybe.

"Food," he decided, kissing her yet again before rolling away and staggering to his feet.

At least he had offset all the good food around here with plenty of strenuous exercise.

Or whatever you wanted to call it.

Anya eventually joined him in the shower, which caused him to consider how much hot water they had available, but he still needed food.

Oluchi also needed intelligence, so he could plan a campaign of distraction and misdirection while the Rio Alliance government sorted itself out.

Somebody was going to be monumentally pissed that someone else had snuck Eha and the others out of the palace and off-planet. Oluchi wasn't sure who the names were, but it was obvious that some generally-hidden political fault line had emerged over the last week and a half.

Anya continued to distract him with a smile as she soaped herself and then him, chuckling.

"I'm trying to keep us out of jail, woman," he mock-growled at her.

That just made it worse.

"You," she laughed. "I'm just a simple career bureaucrat you seduced with your evil ways."

"I see," he said, unable to not laugh with her. "So that's how it's going to be?"

"That's my story," Anya said, grinning as she shut the water off and turned on the blower.

Warm air swirled around them for a bit, blasting the skin mostly dry and reminding Oluchi that he needed a haircut soon, unless he was just going to let it get too long again and pretend to be an artisté. Maybe he needed a peasant shirt redone with lace cuffs, or something extravagant.

Today, he would dress in his better outfit. If they were going to arrest him, at least he wouldn't be a slob in tomorrow's newsreels. That would never do, since Yisan would hear about everything just as quickly as someone could load up on data and race over to tell them.

Anya had brought a bag with her after seeing Eha and the others off, and apparently been of the same mind, because she went to the nines as well. Skirt instead of pants. Silk shirt. Paisley vest. Everything in shades of lavender and purple.

Nothing like a good hanging to focus the mind and sartorial choices.

The kitchen technically ran all night, but most of the morning staff had just started to come on duty when the two of them arrived, plus their minder/bodyguard in his faceless helmet trailing along like a pooch who really didn't want to get off the couch and go for a walk.

Because he could, Oluchi took Anya to the side of the

facility that fed the diplomats and Councilors. Same kitchen. Generally the same menu. But he wanted the cut crystal water glasses for his juice this morning, and the plates with a rim of gold around the edge. The good linen napkins.

He pulled out Anya's chair like a proper gentleman and seated her, ignoring the quiet snickers from the woman as he did.

They were putting on a show and she knew it just as well as he did.

The morning waiter was obsequiousness itself, so nobody had an arrest warrant out for him yet. Oluchi ordered a heavy meal, assuming that he'd be in an interrogation room for much of the day when the news finally got out.

Boy, won't you folks be surprised? Some of you, anyway. It will be interesting to see which group is faking.

But he just smiled and flirted with the woman seated across from him, wondering how he might convince Anya Persaud to transcend her mission and maybe consider getting a little more serious. If they didn't execute him for this, he stood a pretty good chance of getting filthy, stinking rich and having to retire as a playboy card sharp.

Or worse, play at Eduardo's table with his own money.

The horrors.

"What's so funny?" Anya asked quietly, after carefully glancing to make sure that they had the dining room to themselves and the staff.

"Wondering about the day after tomorrow," Oluchi offered.

"Oh?" One perfect eyebrow went up just enough to make him smile.

"Reasonably confident you've blown your cover," Oluchi murmured with the perfect amount of sarcasm smeared on it. "What happens to old spies who are no longer useful?"

"We get put out to pasture," Anya replied, making

something of a sour face. "Pensioned off and largely forgotten, for the most part, except for annual physicals and interviews to make sure nobody from the other side has attempted to seduce us into giving up secrets."

"I see," Oluchi nodded carefully.

"Whyyyyyy?" she asked in that long, slow, sarcastic drawl that just pushed his buttons in the right way.

"Well, there's a reasonable chance I'll either be in jail or excommunicated to someplace like Yisan after this," he offered. "Didn't know where *out to pasture* might be, or how you might feel about being seduced, if I promised not to ask any important questions about your current employer."

She got perfectly still. Eyes speared him with a hard, cold look that hopefully was caused by some other moron in her past and nothing he had done.

Oluchi wondered if nobody had ever looked beyond the cute brunette and really gotten close enough to touch her. Anya was attractive, but not beautiful. Nice bottom, but not a body that caused traffic accidents on a street if she went with the tighter pair of pants. Hazel eyes that didn't seem to miss anything, though.

He wondered, not for the first time, if there was a genius-grade intellect up there and she'd had to hide it all these years because she was a deep-cover spy pretending to be a mid-level bureaucrat. Some women started doing that when they were teenagers, so as to not intimidate all the boys around them.

Occasionally, they forgot how to not be bubbly airheads, which was a shame, but Oluchi Pryce wasn't here to save the galaxy.

Well, not intentionally. That might turn into an occupational hazard, if he had just become the Ambassador-designate to the Species Underground and Innruld Space.

Weirder shit had happened in his life. At least he didn't

know anything useful about where to find a Churquen world.

Anya started to breathe again. He only noticed it because she had stopped.

"Wrong time to ask?" He tried to play it off sideways, giving her an out.

An hour ago, she'd seemed like she was playing this role to the hilt.

Had they moved beyond roles? She didn't know many of the embarrassing parts about him, and Oluchi supposed she probably should at some point. Except that they weren't that embarrassing, on the face of it.

Many pretty women have used their charms and their bodies to get ahead, especially when they come from the poor part of town. Oluchi just happened to be male, even as he had been doing the same things.

Before Lazarus. Captain Francisco Luiz *Pancho* Oliveira of the Rio Alliance Navy.

And friends.

Before it became time to grow up.

"What's your game, Pryce?" Anya asked in a harsher tone than probably either of them expected, from the flinch and little look of surprise she suppressed afterwards.

Oluchi glanced around, but they had enough coffee and he shook his head at the waiter to keep the man at bay. Perhaps a lovers spat and the waiter didn't need to get involved.

Oluchi studied her face, but she gave nothing away.

"Six months ago, I was a gigolo on Yisan," he said quietly. Slowly. Teeth-grittingly. "Dress it up any way you want to. I was also a gambler, a thief, and a dozen other things, but I made most of my money as a free agent kept man."

He paused, but she didn't have anything to interject. Just those sharp, hazel eyes studying him back.

"Then Lazarus landed, with Aileen and Eha," he continued. "I saw a chance to break out of my old life. Others must have trusted me, even liked me, because when all hell broke loose six hours later and I needed help, the biggest players on Yisan came through. In a powerful way. Now, I represent a significant proportion of the economy of Yisan and that sector of space in the names I could call on."

"Why are you telling me this?" she asked. It wasn't a snap, but it wasn't short by much.

"Because of the day after tomorrow, Anya," he replied, keeping his voice and his body language calm. If he had stepped into a minefield, it was his own damned fault. "Maybe it arrives today. Or a month from now. But it will arrive."

"And what happens?"

"I will have to reinvent myself as a power player," Oluchi said, letting serious become his byword. "Or go back to being a nobody. Today, I am standing in for the Ambassador to forty alien species. And all the money on Yisan. And whoever else comes along who needs my help."

"So?" She was almost cast in copper today, darker than him by a considerable amount, but still a few shades lighter than most inhabitants of Brasilia.

Oluchi wondered if she might yet turn him to alabaster.

"So when this is done, I would like to inquire if you might be interested in joining me on that adventure," he said in a precise, almost-formal tone rather at odds with where the conversation had started.

Mine field.

Her eyes got almost deadly. Hopefully she was still reacting to some other moron, and not him.

She leaned forward so they could whisper deadly nothings to each other. He joined her.

"I am a spy, Pryce," she hissed quietly.

Oluchi nodded.

"What will you be, that day after tomorrow?" he asked, watching her eyes for any sign.

There was none.

"What are you asking for?" she demanded in a harsh whisper.

Oluchi understood that question. Hoped he had not been the one to hurt her or make her angry.

"Your body," he said. "Your mind. Maybe your heart at some point. Not your soul."

Let us at least be honest with one another, then.

She gasped a tiny fraction. He hoped it was at his audacity and honesty. And that she wasn't about to slap him.

"Maybe you go back to being a deep cover agent with one hell of a story to tell around the department when tomorrow happens," he continued in a hard, calm voice. "Whatever happens when the news gets out. And maybe your cover is completely blown and you have to reinvent yourself. That's the sort of thing that happens when you get put out to pasture. I've been there more than once. And until Lazarus and the others came along, that was the precipice I had been edging along. Now, I have a chance to change everything. To get rich and maybe turn myself in a power player of significance, instead of just another pretty, forgettable face. I had asked how you felt about being seduced away from your current job, or maybe going deep cover somewhere else, or just retiring and being put out to pasture. Tell me to walk away right now and we'll finish breakfast and turn into strangers. I already have a *lot* of experience at quietly slinking out the side door in the morning."

Okay, maybe a little harsher than she deserved. But deadly honest, every word of it. And Oluchi had learned a long time ago that honesty with a woman is far better than flattery.

He reached for his juice glass and caught the waiter's eye with a quick nod.

That worthy disappeared into the kitchen immediately, so the food was probably sitting on the counter under the heater, waiting for this little snit to unravel itself however it was going to.

Anya grabbed her water and downed half of it in a single gulp, it seemed. Set the glass down a little harder than she intended with a sheepish "Sorry," as he jumped.

He watched her. She watched him.

Food arrived like battlements between them on some new field.

She had not spoken. Might not speak.

Oluchi attacked his eggs and steak like a condemned man's last meal before the hanging. Somewhere, a clock was ticking.

No, more like a fuse burning down.

Anya ate mechanically, but her eyes never once focused on anything within one thousand light-years of this table.

She buttered her toast and he watched her hands for signs of an impending assassination. She chewed and he studied the line of her jaw for clues to the moron who had hurt her before.

At one point, her eyes finally softened, about the moment when fresh coffee got topped up.

"Oluchi…" she started to say, but a squad of Council Guards led by a senior officer appeared at the door of the restaurant and stomped over to the table as loudly as their boots would allow on the nice, thick carpet.

Everyone stopped what they were doing and turned to

watch. Oluchi took a sip of coffee, utterly imperturbable now. Anya fell silent, a sudden bystander from the way the man subtly ignored her.

Was he in on the secret? Or utterly ignorant of her role?

Neither was obvious.

"Where are they?" the man demanded in a voice loud enough that the chefs might have heard it back in their kitchen.

Oluchi smiled. He could string this out for a while if he wanted, just to stick burning slivers under the man's fingernails, but it wouldn't gain him anything and just piss off the people who would probably be responsible for his well-being in a little while.

"Gone," he answered with a bright, innocent smile. "Off-planet by now and not to return for a month, if I understand the timeline correctly. Until then, she has designated me as her Ambassadorial representative, with authority to negotiate deals, pending her final approval on her return."

Stick it in, twist it, break it off.

Oh, and smile.

The man scowled like he wanted to knock down the walls of Jericho.

"Oluchi Pryce, you are under arrest," the man announced, still in that parade ground voice that would echo down the halls to any reporter that happened to be in the building right now to get an exclusive. "Get up."

Oluchi set the coffee down carefully and rose, winking at Anya as if they were on a different stage. She didn't react, but he didn't expect her to.

The stakes had just gone all the way up.

"That's *Ambassador* Pryce," he corrected the man as he stepped away from the table.

The officer grabbed his arm and shoved him into the

midst of the other troopers, who wrenched his arms behind him and added shackles as they frog marched him out of the dining hall to whispers and titters.

At least he looked good doing it.

FORTY-SIX

LAZARUS

LAZARUS CONSIDERED the sailors assembled to hear from their new commander. Not him. Wybert. These were the gunners he had asked Santos and da Silva to send with him.

Or rather, Gun Geams, since it took time to bring such a key unit together. Battery Commander, Gunner, Loader—dating back to when they still used projectiles in space instead of beams—and Swab. Three senior teams for the Star Lances. More than three dozen other teams for various Star Spears and Powerbolt turrets mostly used as defensive weapons against small ships.

There were two Senior Chiefs and a Master Chief in the group. Sailors with thirty or more years in service. Plus an astonishing number of senior sailors in the other ranks.

Lazarus had asked, but hadn't really believed that either Admiral would come through like that.

Beware what you wish for.

But it was not his meeting. He was merely attending, along with his command staff.

Wybert was running things, standing at the center of the

stage, while Lazarus, Addison, and Aileen were seated off to one side watching.

What was even more frightening, at least to Lazarus, was how well Wybert was handling things.

Just how many videos and correspondence-style classes had that lunatic Ilount completed while Lazarus had been off having his various adventures?

"Sir, respectfully begging your pardon," the Master Chief spoke up now in a voice that was neither begging nor particularly respectful. "But I've served in this navy for thirty-four years, a good chunk of that on Heavy Starcruisers and Battlestations. You've worn the uniform for what, six months?"

Lazarus was just sorry that Chief Garcia was an engineer, rather than a gunner. He'd have liked to see her here, snapping the whip on these folks. That woman took no shit. These troops were grumbling. Not bad, but headed that way.

"That's right," Wybert replied in a voice that even sounded like a proper officer. Instead of the bird-like chirping you occasionally got when he was excited.

"So why are you qualified to use the big gun, sir?" the Master Chief asked, getting a lot of hooting and foot stomping from the sailors around him.

Lazarus wondered when he would need to step in, if good order was going to be maintained. He only needed these men for a short period of time. Vilga's Stand and back. Then he could hopefully spend the time to get the crew he'd originally planned for.

These bastards in the audience were feeling their oats this morning.

Wybert watched them for a time. He was standing at the front of the room on a platform, while the men and women were in rows of chairs like a movie theater, so everyone had a good view.

Lazarus and the others were off to one side, mostly as a reminder.

Wybert literally held center stage alone.

Lieutenant Wybert of Capantzina let the men and women carry on with their noise and crap for about ten seconds without answering. At some point, they started to fall silent, since the officer hadn't taken the obvious bait.

Nervousness began to settle in on the audience like a cold fog that brushes your neck.

Rather than speak, Wybert slammed the end cap of his powerspear once onto the deck hard enough that it might have left a dent. Then he snapped it around his upper torso once, shifting all four arms into the process as he crossed it behind his head, then around his lower arms, across the top of his abdomen and caught it again in his right hands and twirled it several times.

Lazarus was reminded of a Drum Major in a marching band, except that Wybert didn't do any of the fancy high stepping.

Instead, he slammed the end down again and speared the Master Chief with all five eyes.

"Because I've killed one hundred and seventy-three Humans in the last two months, Master Chief," Wybert said in a voice that had Lazarus doing a double take. "About the population in this room. How many people have you killed with ship's cannon in those thirty-four years?"

The room fell to such utter silence that Lazarus was pretty sure he could hear all the hearts out there in the audience beating. Rapidly.

Wybert snapped all four mandibles as far open as they would go and then clacked them back together. Someone must have told him how frightening that would be, because the entire audience recoiled in their seats.

Chief Garcia would have started laughing now.

Hopefully, the engineering staff wasn't as fractious as gunners could be.

"One hundred and seventy-three?" the Master Chief gasped.

"The first shot with Kirov's Lance broke that destroyer into four significant pieces," Wybert explained. "We left those to de-orbit because they had lost their engines and weren't going anywhere, and I still had two assault pinckes in the air with combat troops. Except that they decided to run instead of fighting me."

Again, dead silence.

Lazarus leaned over to Addison.

"What have you been feeding him?" he asked the Churquen in a whisper.

Addison turned and gave a frightened smile.

"I'm not sure, but maybe we all need to be eating it," Addison whispered back. "Remind me to have a chat with Khyaa'sha."

Lazarus grinned.

"My second shot dead centered the pincke at higher altitude," Wybert continued. "They were only about fifteen miles up and close to horizon at that point, so maximum deflection through the atmosphere, as fast as their little biped legs could pedal."

For emphasis, Wybert did a thing like a Human drumming their fingers on a desk, except it was all ten of his feet in sequence. Right rear to right front. Left front to left rear.

Must have been practicing, because the Wybert Lazarus had met when Addison first took him aboard *Shiva Zephyr Glaive* would have fallen over, trying that.

Lazarus smiled, and then let it expand out so all his new sailors could see.

Let them be a little more nervous about their new commander.

"Number three chose to ground and abandon, so those forty-seven got taken prisoner by the colonial authorities," Wybert said. "Or I'd be well over two hundred. I don't count the ones taken prisoner after I was done shooting, either from the pincke or lifepods on the destroyer."

He paused and eyed the entire crowd with all five eyes.

"I only needed gunners so we could fire more weapons than just the Kirov Lance," Wybert explained. "You people are there to kill the Gun Wall for me, while I go after the Heavy Starcruiser, then kill the station. That's not too much to ask, is it?"

Lazarus kept the grin. He recognized the phrase right out of a leadership course, except that it was one for Lieutenant Commanders hoping to be promoted. One he had taken, way back when.

But who was he to doubt where Wybert of Capantzina's heart was today? Or that he was dedicated to being the kind of warrior who would mate with a queen?

You just never expected someone like Wybert to really have it in him.

"Is it?" Wybert snapped now, a harder voice he must have been practicing in the shower, or some abandoned bay.

"No, sir," a few voices called back half-heartedly.

Wybert turned just his head to his right, almost theatrically. All five eyes blinked at him and Addison.

"Captain, I thought you were bringing me warriors," Wybert cat-called the room, lower left arm gesturing to the crowd. "Folks worthy of mating with a queen. Are you sure these aren't engineers?"

He turned back to the room again and scowled with all five eyes, four mandibles, four arms, and ten feet. And a powerspear he slammed once more for emphasis.

"Is it?"

"SIR, NO SIR!" the room challenged back, finally understanding that the weird-looking alien at the front of the room might be an officer after all.

And a killer, like them.

Lazarus nodded.

He would need killers.

FORTY-SEVEN
ADDISON

THEY WERE IN HIS OFFICE. Addison was surprised that Lazarus had dragged in a Human chair and set it on the front side of the desk, leaving Addison's coiling chair behind it. It was technically Lazarus's office.

Eha was on the other coiling chair. The three of them were alone in the office.

"Admiral Santos has put you in for a medal," Lazarus began in an off-hand way. "You've impressed the Chief of Staff with your behavior. That's a large part of the reason we have the size and quality of the crew we have."

"Do we trust them?" Eha asked, before he could get the words entirely out of his mouth.

"That depends," Lazarus shrugged back at them. "I was largely held out of contact, except to be regularly debriefed on everything that had happened since *Ajax* first went into jump. I didn't tell them where or who, but was happy to describe as many of the species as I've encountered. That tea shop owner at Zhoonarrim, the Kdari, probably fascinated them the most."

"What if there are spies in this group?" Addison asked.

"We've wiped all the planetary coordinates from the system," Lazarus replied. "They probably suspect the Phraettis Nebula, but that's a solid wall across a good chunk of sky to most people, so they can't easily get around it and then find Innruld Space. Even a thousand worlds don't cover that much volume."

"What happens after the battle?" Addison asked.

"My parole, if you wish to call it that, involves returning to Brasilia," Eha said. "All of their delicate plans might have been disrupted by Oluchi choosing to remain behind, since the Human woman they had inserted as something of a spy was forced to remain behind with him."

"Is he safe?" Lazarus asked.

Eha shrugged.

"You know the man better than I do, I suspect." She turned to Lazarus now. "I left him there in my stead, so hopefully his combination of greed and personal self-interest will align with his ethics and he will continue negotiating trade and cultural deals. Is Yisan a good center point for trade?"

"It should be," Lazarus nodded. "Right now, a lot of trade flows through there because Westphalian hulls can land next to Rio ones and everyone largely behaves. Where it gets complicated is when Westphalia knows how to get to Innruld Space. Will they send fleets over to attack? Nothing the Innruld have can stop them."

Addison shuddered at the thought. There had been a small concern that the Rio Alliance might just displace the Innruld. With Westphalia, it would become a certainty.

"We need your technology," Addison said simply. "We can overthrow the Innruld with it. With *Ajax*. But we have to be able to build a fleet capable of defending our worlds. I would like the Rio Alliance's help doing that, but we must be prepared to step out on our own."

He liked the smile that came over Lazarus's face.

"I might know a design engineer with experience and expertise in warships," he laughed casaully. "Willing to work pretty cheap, too, since he'll be with friends."

"What do we do with the rest of the crew, though?" Eha asked. "Would they be willing to go to Innruld Space with us, instead of just returning home in a month?"

"Technically, as their captain, I make those decisions, but I agree, Eha," Lazarus said. "They have to want to come with us. Otherwise, they might mutiny, even if the Admiralty Staff wouldn't see it that way if I was in active rebellion to their orders."

"Caught between the rapids and the depths?" Eha asked.

Addison smiled. It was a Churquen thing he didn't think Lazarus knew. Humans could swim. Hells, some of them actively strapped themselves into small boats for the express purpose of paddling through whitewater rapids and diving into large pools of water.

But Humans were completely insane and everyone knew that.

"Caught somewhere," Lazarus agreed. "We can none of us be in two places at once, regardless of the need. Brasilia and Zhoonarrim both have their attractions, but we have a significant problem first."

"6357 Wei Xiu IV," Addison noted. "The system known as Vilga's Stand. Can *Ajax* really take on two GunWalls and a Heavy Starcruiser? One GunWall nearly destroyed you the first time."

"They had surprise and were waiting for me," Lazarus nodded. "This time, we will have three escorts joining us in a few days, and I plan on trying something evil and sneaky a certain Churquen taught me."

"Oh?" Addison asked, intrigued.

"Can Churquen slither retrograde?" Lazarus asked.

"Slowly," Eha spoke up. "We look heavily medicated when we do, as well. Why?"

"Addison reminded me that since our engines use gravlines to push instead of reaction mass, they will work just as well going backwards. In fact, next time I design a ship, I plan to put guns at both ends, just so they can come and go equally well."

"What will that mean to Westphalia?" Addison pressed.

"We will land and start shooting," Lazarus replied. "Normally, the GunWall swarms us and we have to maneuver wildly, losing the ability of the Kirov Lance to be used effectively."

"Will three Escorts be sufficient?" Addison asked.

"Not if I was planning to stay and fight," Lazarus smiled. "One Escort is a little tougher than a Phalanx, to say nothing of an Archer. But if they have to chase me, us, then we have an advantage and I plan to use it. I'll fight like a scorpion."

Addison had never heard of such a creature, so he made Lazarus explain it. They didn't sound like they moved backwards, but he supposed anything with a poison stinger like that would learn to skitter in reverse if it was surrounded by lots of other creatures wanting to fight.

"Can we do this thing?" Addison finally asked.

"That's my plan," Lazarus nodded. "I have Humans along to help us. And to witness everything and report back that you folks are at least as competent as their other officers. That will go a long ways towards hopefully convincing them to help."

"And if they don't?" Addison asked.

"Then we add a whole other block of stars with warrants out for my arrest."

FORTY-EIGHT

OLUCHI

OLUCHI HAD BEEN ARRESTED a few times. Mostly either soliciting or trespassing, depending on who it was that ended up pressing charges when things had gotten a little sticky.

He was quite familiar with the standard interrogation room, like the one he found himself confined to now. At times, he wondered if that was the only thing cop shows ever actually got right about the setup.

Ugly, industrial gray room, ten feet deep by fifteen wide. Overhead vaulted enough that he couldn't jump up and touch it. Gray tiles on the floor, speckled in a way that made dirt and grime invisible.

Or blood, he supposed, once it dried.

Oluchi tried not to look too closely.

Gray walls. Off-white, hanging ceiling panels.

A box designed to degrade your soul. If you were of the sort of folk who took that shit seriously.

Table welded from heavy steel tubes sealed up against rust and crap. Top was cheap plastic laminated down, probably glued onto another steel sheet.

Heavy. Didn't need to be bolted to the floor. Oluchi would need the rage of the heavens to overturn it.

Lazarus could probably flip the damned thing quite theatrically, if he was of a mind. Apparently he'd done something similar at Zhoonarrim, from the stories the others told.

Three chairs, identical in form, weight, and age. Grimy. Steel. Hints of rust. Past their prime and then some.

Two of them on the far side. One where he was seated, hands in front of him on the table, still shackled together but at least not attached to the table.

At least the tabletop was clean enough that he wasn't going to ruin his nice shirt, depending on how recently the Council Guards had cleaned their shackles.

They had looked like the sorts of folks who got a lot of use out of such equipment, rather than just leaving them to wither and rust in their carriers. Whatever that might say about men and women like that.

Oluchi studied his reflection in the two-way mirror that took up the short wall, facing the next room up the hallway. At least he was still in the palace, and hadn't been carted off somewhere to disappear and maybe be sweated a little harder than expected for information.

His hair definitely needed a decision soon. Should he go professionally short, like Lazarus? Shave it close like Xiuying and Lucas? Or return to his decadent youth and spend three years growing it down to his waist again?

That internal monologue kept him from fidgeting as he waited. Hopefully those bastards on the other side of the dirty glass were twitching instead.

Gone. Maybe she'll come back in a month. Maybe not. What will I need to tell her when I see her?

Or will some dreadfully terrible accident have occurred before then and oh, we're so sorry to report…

Oluchi kept the snarl off his face. Most of his face. He let it come into his eyes, in case anyone was looking closely.

The door opened suddenly and that same senior peon who had arrested him walked into the room, followed a moment later by His Pompousness, the High Council Chair Roald Cavalcanti.

The man was still tall, thin, gray, and dangerous. He wore a simple business suit today, similar to Oluchi's, rather than the formal robes for public events. Cavalcanti was in gray, while Oluchi had gone for a sedate green.

Death and Life, as it were, if you wanted to get pissy and symbolic.

Oluchi refrained from commenting out loud.

Cavalcanti sat in one of the chairs. The goon closed the door and took up a spot behind Oluchi, in a corner where he could practice his glower in the mirror.

He needed the practice. Looked like a bout of gas, rather than intimidation.

Nothing a good, long rip of a fart couldn't fix, though.

Oluchi studied the Chair. Smiled, even.

"Something has gone wrong with palace security," Cavalcanti began abruptly, as though this was maybe their second or fourth meeting. "All the tapes from the last twenty-seven hours have somehow gotten erased in a terrible accident."

"Terrible," Oluchi agreed. "I'm sure the cameras in here have all been fixed by now, though."

As threats went, it was subtle enough. Anything you say or do will be admissible later, if only in a court of public opinion.

"Indeed," the man said in a calm baritone that could probably wind a stadium up pretty good if he was of a mind. "Right now, we have groups out tracking what happened to the Ambassador, but you could save us a great deal of time."

Oluchi did the math in his head. The Humanist Block on the nine-member Council was generally three, and the Alliance Block four, with the Chair and another as swing votes.

Oluchi would be willing to call and raise on the thought that those two had swung to the side of the Humanists at the present moment. Or were getting there. And so the Alliance folks had gone and done something extravagant to counter them.

"We were contacted last night on the comm in the suite," Oluchi lied as facilely as he would to any husband who suddenly came home and found a stranger seated in the kitchen with his wife. Fully clothed and enjoying dinner, perhaps.

At least on paper.

"And?"

"And they offered the Ambassador an opportunity to depart the palace grounds," Oluchi continued. "I'm not really sure after that, because the conversation didn't include me. Madam Ambassador did leave me behind specifically to continue negotiations with the Rio Alliance High Council in her absence. I don't know any planetary coordinates, but we can certainly make other progress in the meantime. I'm expecting her back in a month, give or take."

"That's all you're going to offer, isn't it?" Cavalcanti's eyes bored in now.

"For now," Oluchi nodded, hanging it out there that maybe he'd give them more.

Later.

If they were nice.

About the time *Ajax* was safely off to wherever they were going. He hadn't looked too closely.

"And your relationship with Anya Persaud?" the man pressed.

"Entirely sexual," Oluchi smiled in that way that hid as much as it told. "A man needs a good release from time to time. She seems to be the kind of woman most people overlook, which is a shame, considering some of her appetites and proclivities."

Oluchi wondered if Cavalcanti had been the one she'd caught coming out of someone else's room in the dead of night. He hadn't asked and she had not named names.

Cavalcanti leaned back now and studied him. Oluchi smiled. Roald Cavalcanti was a pale shadow of a man like Eduardo Martìnez, and Oluchi played poker with that worthy on even terms.

"So you'll play me for a fool?" the Chair suddenly turned harsh without moving.

"Eha and the others need help," Oluchi snapped back, finding some spark of anger beneath all the usual *bonhomie*. He leaned forward just enough to make the punk in the corner stir uneasily. "They need someone to break the Innruld, as I understand it, and not just come in like Dorian barbarians from the north and change ruling classes. That's what Westphalia would do, which is why they came to Rio Space first. Nothing I've heard so far about you engenders in me a great belief that you'll save them. Why is that?"

The flinch never made it past the man's eyes, but Oluchi played high-stakes poker for a living, as frequently as anything else. That look was as good as a nervous tic when you had Jacks showing.

Fear that the other guy was sitting on Queens. Eha and Aileen, for instance. Maybe Kuei and Khyaa'sha to make it four of a kind?

"And you take responsibility for the negotiations in her stead?" Cavalcanti countered.

"Give me a pocket warfleet for a year and that's probably all the negotiation necessary," Oluchi smiled. "I get the impression that the Innruld are broadly powerful but fragile. Rigid and tottering, although I've never been there myself. A good stiff push might end them as a sovereign power."

"Or bring a flood of refugees into Human Space," the Chair growled.

Ah. The Humanist Block argument. Can we keep them *from overwhelming* **us**?

Oluchi smiled.

"How many worlds are there to be had?" he asked. "How many systems that could be terraformed into new homes for Churquen or Vaadwig? How big is this galaxy, Mister Chairman?"

"Sufficiently huge," the man allowed. "But I'm facing Westphalia. Did she mention that *Ajax* had arrived in system with news of an imminent Westphalian invasion?"

There is a particular flinch a professional card player masters. The one that conveys utter shock, but does so at such a quiet level that the other player might miss it.

Except those players never miss anything at the table. Done right, you convince them that the bluff you've been running has just paid off as you've drawn an inside straight on the last card.

It is the opposite of that little slump that you use occasionally to get them to call and raise a weak hand, convinced you've missed it and they can rake in the pot.

It must be used rarely, as you don't want them realizing that you can do it on demand.

Then they might not fall for it again.

Oluchi let hope blink once through his system. Like he didn't know about the craziness Addison Wolcott had apparently gotten into.

Cavalcanti took the bait.

"We think that's where she's gone," the Chair said. "To join Oliveira."

"Wait, you're sending Lazarus and *Ajax* to stop an invasion?" Oluchi let raw confusion play across his face now.

Never let a sucker have an even break.

"That's right," Cavalcanti said. "Which presents me with a serious problem."

"How so?"

"If something happens and they get captured or killed, nobody but you know where Innruld Space is, when we finally do decide to go help them," the Chair said. "And if they get captured, then Westphalia discovers all the faster than they would anyway."

Oluchi finally felt a hint of remorse at the game. He could see where the man was possibly maneuvering the Humanist Block into backing off to let the Rio Alliance return to its founding. To be a multispecies polity opposed to places like Westphalia or Innruld.

But they would need time to wrap their heads around all the changes that were coming.

And Addison plus whoever was behind Anya might have just run the clock out on them.

"Well then, hopefully you've sent a big enough fleet with Lazarus," he smiled cruelly at the man. "Or you might have a serious problem on your hands."

FORTY-NINE

LAZARUS

LAZARUS SIGHED HAPPILY, not caring who might hear it. He was home.

The bridge of *Ajax* hadn't changed one bit since he'd been gone, but he didn't care. He had designed this exact space with his idea of perfection. Of Heaven.

And he was back.

He studied the stars on the screen. And the three ships that he had been training with for the last two days.

The Margar system was a sparsely inhabited colony that just happened to be on the way to Vilga, so it had been perfect to use to maneuver. And to teach the three escorts how to sail with *Ajax*.

It had gone well, but now the final act was upon them. Lazarus was looking forward to it, and yet not, at the same time.

He was pretty sure he'd just have to retire when he could no longer command *Ajax*. No other vessel would fit him as well.

Well, unless Addison had him building stuff at Aceanx or Dormell. That might make up for it.

He studied the people around him, found them all smiling back. Even Cormac seemed to have a smile going from the way his optical sensors were tilted.

Kuei grinned with her ears straight up. Wybert was in his nest with his back two feet quietly tapping in anticipation. Someone, probably Kuei, had added a pad so he didn't click loudly.

Lazarus looked down at his control screens and confirmed that the channel aft to Addison and Eha was open. They were in the Emergency Bridge, safely at the other end of the ship in case anything happened.

On another screen, Ereshkiki Nisab had put H'Brige Slani in charge of Auxiliary Control, handling all the reactor and engine controls forward while he was aft, tending things with Thadrakho and Chief Garcia, among others.

Aileen was working on a small console in her office with Remahle close by. She found it amusing that he referred to the space as the flag bridge, since it wasn't much larger than her bathtub.

Everyone was present in person or on screen except Khyaa'sha, who was down in her kitchen suffering occasional paroxysm of joy at having so many people to feed; and Lenox, in the sickbay waiting for customers.

Even the light in here was giving Lazarus a smile.

"Comm, open a channel to the Escort Squadron," he said to Cormac.

Two Protector/Escorts and a Protector/Leader. Not enough to take on even a patrol of Four-and-One, but more than enough to keep them off his back if he was in the process of pulling a fast one.

"*Communications established,*" Cormac answered a moment later. "*Commander Rodriguez speaking.*"

Three faces appeared on the screen, the commanding officers of his escort team.

"*PL-371*, *P-4491*, and *P-4502*, this is Captain Oliveira, aboard *Ajax*," Lazarus spoke the words with a formal lilt. Around them the stars waited poised. "Stand by for the first transit. We will arrive in formation, make sure everyone is ready, and then make our jump to the vicinity of 6357 Wei Xiu VII. Not all that far from Vilga's Stand itself. From there, we will have just enough time to ascertain the current deployments of the Westphalian Fleet, and then we will jump directly into combat. Are there any questions?"

"Negative, sir," Commander Rodriguez replied immediately, smiling grimly. "It's a novel way to fight, but we've got it down at this point. We'll do you right."

"Of that I have no doubts, Commander," Lazarus smiled back at them. "All vessels on my mark. Three. Two. One. Jump."

And the Margar system was again empty.

FIFTY

EHA

SHE WOULD NOT LET her concerns show, but Eha was uncertain that this was the best course of action. Still, it had gotten her a break from the Humans for a time. Nights spent coiled with Addison, making up for a decade of neither of them being willing to make the first move.

But they had fallen into a Human war.

Innruld Space did not have such a thing as war.

Smuggling, yes. Occasional piracy.

But nothing like dedicated warships sailing at each other with the express purpose of blowing the other up. It was a Human thing, except that the new crew also included Moah, Gnashiiley, and Atomarsk like H'Brige Slani.

And that would be her future, if they were successful.

"Top three?" Addison asked as a way to break the tension.

They were alone in this space. Addison could fly the ship from here if he needed to, although not as well as Kuei Akeley. And fire that fearsome Lance if he had to.

But that would suggest that the bridge had been damaged enough to render it inoperable.

Or destroyed, leaving Addison in command. But he had already fought a battle with this ship, hadn't he?

"Worrying about the future," Eha finally managed to corral her thoughts. "About wars, both intra-Human and galactic in scale. About finding us a place to leave Innruld Space behind, if we have to."

"Both of the systems I scouted would be delightful as Churquen colonies," Addison replied. "Vilga would be exceptional for just about all the species, with a little work. Especially as it has two worlds where folks could immigrate. Will they allow it?"

Eha shrugged and adjusted herself a little more comfortably on her coil.

"They have all the obvious reservations," she said. "We dared not tell them how few we were in comparison to Humans. At least not yet. Nor how weak technologically. They might have imagined Innruld Space as a greater hazard than it really is."

"How do we convince them?" Addison asked.

"I fear that we will have to throw ourselves on their supposed mercy and hope for the best at some point," she sighed again. "But we knew at Zhoonarrim that we would be gambling with the future of the entire Species Underground."

"We have Lazarus on our side," Addison reminded her. "And I suspect that a great many of the Humans and others on his crew will want to see Innruld Space, especially if you remind them that they will get to be heroes by liberating everyone from the Masters of the Galaxy. They would belong to Westphalia if that sort of thing didn't appeal to them."

"I hope you are right," she said.

Any other words were interrupted as the ship blinked across space a second time. If everything was correct, they would be in close vicinity of the planet known to Human history as Vilga's Stand from yet another insane conflagration of violence a century ago.

But what was she, except a revolutionary getting ready to ignite an even greater fire?

"All ships, we confirm 6357 Wei Xiu VII," Lazarus's voice suddenly came across the line. "You have thirty minutes to prepare and handle any last minute issues before we jump directly into combat, so keep this line open for orders. Stand by."

She watched Addison hit a switch on his console, but wasn't paying attention to which until he turned and smiled at her.

"That's the mute button," he said slyly. "We can hear them, but they cannot hear us."

Eha perked up as he slid off his coil and smiled at her.

"We have a few minutes," he offered, sliding close. "I would like to use them for personal business."

He reached a hand and she took it, remembering why she had fallen in love with the man in the first place.

FIFTY-ONE

AILEEN

AILEEN LOOKED up from her screen as Remahle harrumphed.

"So when do I get to go have some adventures?" he pleaded with her.

Aileen caught herself up short of snapping. He'd been her assistant for years until Lazarus came along and did things nobody else could do. Like lifting a fifty pound box over his head and stacking it fourth tall, without using a crane.

She studied the Kr'Mari with a much more jaundiced eye than a year ago. Before Humans. Before Lazarus. Before Yisan. Before Brasilia. Before Vilga's Stand.

"What kind of adventures were you looking for, Remahle?" she asked carefully, unwilling to poke at him. He was older than her. Not more mature. Less, if anything. Kind of middle-aged-go-along-with-things more than anything.

Not as focused as she was.

Lazarus had needed her expertise as Loadmaster, both times he had left the ship. Trade and warships were both all about tonnage logistics. Remahle had been left behind as a minor player both times, just filling in for her until she returned. He had the skill, but not that unmeasurable thing that made her *her*.

"I dunno," Remahle replied. "I just want to go see some of the places we go. The others are up on the bridge. Khyaa'sha is cooking. I don't have anyone to talk to."

"That'll change if this all works, you know," she reminded him. "We'll have a full crew and you can be an officer if you want."

"Not sure that's a bright idea, ya know," he offered defensively.

"Maybe, but you have to tell me what you want before I can go find it for you," Aileen said in a tart voice.

Not like this was the first time they'd had this discussion over the years. Probably not the last.

It was one of the things that marked them as different. Aileen had known early on that she could solve a three dimensional packing problem better than anyone she encountered. Got her a job on a cargo runner. That got her to *Shiva Zephyr Glaive* when Addison needed a new Loadmaster.

"I don't know," Remahle was almost pleading with her. "I'm just always left behind."

Aileen didn't bother saying anything about the Kr'Mari's inability to have a useful opinion. Hard to guess when he didn't even know.

But she supposed that was why Lazarus had set her up as Second Officer behind Addison. She did know. Could articulate her dreams and needs.

Could organize people and get them to do things.

Aileen wasn't sure Remahle could organize an orgy in a multi-species whorehouse, to use an old joke. Sure, he'd go along when one started, but it wouldn't have been his idea. Maybe something he said as a crude joke, because he didn't always say appropriate things, but it would be nothing more than that.

Still, she considered it. Khyaa'sha could probably handle everything for a few days without her or Remahle, if she spent a little time up front and got all the supplies organized. And the chances of Lazarus and Addison both going somewhere were low, so there would at least be a command officer around.

Wow. When had she become one of *those people*? In charge? Her?

Crap.

At some point, her sister Noreen would hear about it and the teasing would never cease after that.

"If Lazarus allows it, I'll see if you can come with us next time," Aileen temporized for now.

Remahle lit up like a kid with ten credits in a candy store, so she let it go with a smile.

She could always have a private word with Lazarus later, if she didn't think the Kr'Mari had earned it, and the Human could play bad cop.

But Remahle might also earn it. They were about to go fight a war with a bunch of crazy Humans.

Who knew what might happen?

FIFTY-TWO

LAZARUS

LAZARUS SUPPRESSED THE GROWL, lest it carry over to the entire bridge around him. This was supposed to be a calm place. Rational. Logical. Professional.

Not the sort of room where you went to plan and exact a bloody vengeance on folks who didn't even rate names.

Just hull numbers.

"Cormac, confirm your scans," Lazarus said aloud instead, falling into the old patterns.

"*Station in orbit of the fourth planet, Captain,*" the NavCrawler replied immediately. "*Operational status unknown. By the number of pods and such in close proximity, perhaps half the weapons are in a position to fire, but we do not have an answer as to their status until they do.*"

Lazarus nodded to the camera pointed this way. Cormac was plugged directly into the ship, so most of the data flowed into his brain and he didn't need to read it off a screen. Made him an excellent sensors officer as a result, once he understood what information you were needing.

"*The Heavy Starcruiser is located in the same orbit as the station, but trailing it by a sufficient amount that the two could*" *be engaged separately if desired. One GunWall remains in close proximity to each of the capital targets.*"

Lazarus felt his face pull into a rictus that might charitably be called a smile. By a stranger who was more than a little drunk at the time.

Others would mutter and slowly begin sidling away without ever turning their backs on that kind of face. But Lazarus didn't really care.

"Squadron Operations, this is *Ajax*," he said after opening the general channel. "Stand by to jump and then begin retrograde engagement. We are going after the Starcruiser first, because the station cannot run from us later. Show green lights on my board now."

He paused and waited for all four ships to acknowledge. This was the hardest, weirdest part.

Traditionally, two hostile squadrons sailed roughly at each other, firing until one broke off. Evenly matched heavy forces might broadside each other for a time first, hammering shots off hulls.

Ajax was going to do something *completely crazy*.

He let his smile turn fierce and maybe a little less bloodthirsty.

The next ship he designed was going to have to be able to handle this insanity. Possibly with all the guns such that they could turn fully sideways and engage on a single side, like the ancient maritime battleships of the industrial age.

Something.

Pancho Oliveira was about to launch a naval revolution. Again. Tomorrow he would need to counter it when they figured out what he had done this time.

"All Helm Officers, on my mark," Lazarus said, raising his voice a notch. "Three. Two. One. Jump."

The universe blinked.

Four ships hopped across roughly three light-hours with

enough combined blueshift that every sensor in the Westphalian force was probably screaming bloody murder right now.

"Cormac, are the escorts in place?" Lazarus asked first. That would be the most critical part.

"*Affirmative, Captain.*"

"Helm, all aft, maximum acceleration," he called to Kuei next.

"Aye, sir," she called back. "Full aft, nose locking center forward."

"Fusilier, you are cleared to engage," Lazarus said.

Deep in his soul, he heard an echo of trepidation. That panic about an Ilount warrior about to start slaughtering Humans on industrial scales. Even as Westphalians it would be ugly.

But at this point, they probably deserved their time in hell.

"Gun crews, this is the Fusilier," Wybert's voice sounded solid enough to carve into statues of war gods. "Engage as you bear. Engineering, stand by for the Kirov Lance."

Wybert had actually done something Lazarus had only dreamed about. Used the Kirov Lance in battle. Lazarus had only blown up moons and asteroids. Even that first mission wouldn't have gotten to battle. Only tested the weapons with maneuver, to make sure everything worked before declaring it operational and moving forward.

But Wybert of Capantzina assured him that the pirate encounter had verified everything Lazarus and Kirov had theorized.

On his screens, Lazarus watched the trio of Star Lances lash out and slam into the Westphalian Heavy Starcruiser *Gotland*. Hopefully, they had achieved surprise and caught the vessel with ray shielding down at merely navigational levels.

Sufficient for orbital debris, but not enough to stop heavy beams, even if they were at the outer edge of useful range when firing.

Two solid hits, one fore and one aft. After this, it would probably be like trying to stab someone to death with an icepick. You had to get lucky, or rely on forcing them to bleed out from a myriad of wounds.

And then Wybert pressed his firing stud.

All of the gases between *Ajax* and *Gotland* fluoresced at the same wavelength, causing everything to flash brilliant white for an instant that stayed in his eyes as an afterimage.

Gotland staggered like a horse that had just been shot.

"First shot home," Wybert called in a calm, casual voice that sounded like Addison was seated there, instead of the goofball Ilount they had all come to know and love.

The one Lazarus had accurately described as a little soft in the head, once upon a time.

"Helm, continue evasion aft," Lazarus called, more out of habit than anything.

Wybert and Kuei would fight most of this battle. He would need to step in and remind them of the rest of the Westphalian fleet.

Speaking of which.

"All Gun Teams on Pylon Two," Lazarus overrode Wybert now, as was necessary for the Captain. "CommandWall One has been caught out of position. Bring all your guns to bear on him now, before he can spin his Gunshield over to protect himself. Escort Team, also engage as you can."

Damned things were built like mushrooms with a hinged leg. That Gunshield contained weapon turrets and a solid mass of armor to protect everything behind it.

Assuming you were pointed the right way when trouble broke out…

Ajax had caught the commander of this GunWall facing almost exactly away from them.

"Two, acknowledged," one of Wybert's Chiefs replied a moment later.

"*PL-371*," Rodriguez came over the line. "We're on it, Captain."

Sixteen Phalanxes. Four Archers. Only one CommandWall. And everybody firing that way as fast as things would recharge.

Lazarus kept his attention on that force as *Ajax* started to slide backwards past it, skirting them like a wolf moving along the edge of the meadow in the shadows, where the sheep might not see him.

Except that they knew he was there. *Ajax* had already drawn blood.

Lazarus looked at *Gotland.*

Oh, that's bad. Caught you asleep, didn't we?

The Heavy Starcruiser had apparently been at minimal shielding. Kirov's Lance had hit low and a little aft. The vessel was slowly rolling, like a log in a storm.

"Stand by for second volley," Wybert called calmly over the line. "*4502*, shift your fire onto *Gotland* with us this time, and then ignore him until I say otherwise and hit GunWall vessels."

Lazarus was simply amazed at Wybert. If everything else in his life failed, *Pancho* Oliveira would still be able to stand in front of St. Peter and point to that Ilount Warrior as one measure of the success in his life.

"Firing," Wybert announced as he pressed the button again.

A beam of bluish eternity connected the two vessels.

Gotland had finally woken up, getting some ray shielding in place to deflect a chunk of that energy, but the beam still created serious local overloads. Wybert's gunners had paused a half-beat to fire this time instead of anticipating.

One of them hit bare metal with a look like a nuclear bomb going off, a ball of plasma suddenly appearing on the scanners.

"Cormac, scan *Gotland* for changing movement vectors," Lazarus called.

None of his bridge crew would understand the phrase, but Cormac thought fast enough to translate it and figure out the meaning.

Sure enough. Rolling over onto his left originally. Now *Gotland* was now also running a hard yaw as his ass end got pushed away, pulling the bow towards *Ajax* like a stick flying through the air.

They'd probably be twenty minutes getting all of that stabilized enough to get back into battle.

If they ever did.

Lazarus considered overriding Wybert right now. Telling him to ignore *Gotland* and start hammering the swarm of wasps about to become dangerous.

"Helm, up three and yaw six," Wybert called as Lazarus took a breath. "All Gun Teams engage GunWall One at maximum rate of fire until I order otherwise."

Up three and yaw six?

Lazarus looked at his screens frantically, trying to figure out what Wybert was up to but nothing was obvious.

What had he seen?

The three Star Lances and the three escorts began to hammer on GunWall ships now, as Phalanxes and Archers started to come around so that they could interpose their shields. The CommandWall looked like a sheep that had been mauled. Lazarus wondered if it was still on line.

"Engineering, stand by for Kirov's Lance," Wybert called out.

Lazarus gave up looking at his screens and echoed Wybert's targeting optics instead.

Really? From here? Hell of a shot, Wybert.

Good luck.

There were two CommandWalls present. One for each of their combined GunWalls. One of them was already heavily damaged. Kirov's Lance was going to be at the immense, outermost range of attenuation, going after the other one, clear the hell over there.

But it might break the Westphalian force entirely if Wybert succeeded.

Then *Ajax* would be hunting, instead of running, whatever the Westphalians thought on the matter.

"Firing now," Wybert said unnecessarily. The whole hull rang with a harmonic as everything dumped into the beam array.

Maximum range shot. Small target already shifting to get his field in the way.

Impact.

Wow.

Theory had suggested it, but Lazarus had only dreamed until now.

It looked like someone had taken a bite out of the ship's shield. The galaxy's biggest, meanest shark having a quick snack as it swam by.

A cloud of white-hot vapor was slowly turning red as it expanded and cooled. From the scans, it looked like some of the energy of the bolt had gotten through and been liberated on the bare metal of the hinged engine section.

Like kicking a boomerang across the floor as the other CommandWall spun away from them.

Lazarus wondered if the ship would actually de-orbit from damage, assuming that they survived.

"Engineering, I am done with Kirov's Lance for now,"

Wybert announced with a hint of triumph in his voice. "Route all available energy into ray shielding."

Lazarus smiled.

Doing so in that first battle had held Lazarus in place long enough that *Ajax* could run. Propped up the shields just enough that his crew could get into their escape pods and *Pancho* Oliveira could consign himself to hell.

Lazarus wasn't going to be running today.

FIFTY-THREE

ADDISON

THE HUMANS HAD a term Addison had learned from studying a little of their literature in his spare time. Any way to get a better handle on the species to which he was likely to consign his fate.

Hell on Earth.

An ancient, religious reference from one or more of the major sects from Human history. The normal, day-to-day goings-on upended by the sudden arrival of inimical creatures from some magical abyss.

Random, chaotic death.

Over there, it had to feel that way for the sailors suddenly being attacked by a force that had managed to sneak up on them and unleash a terrible fury.

This was exactly what he wished to visit on the Innruld, at least once, since he doubted that there was any other way to make the so-called Masters of the Galaxy give way and learn to share power with the rest.

To break Innruld Space and give the Churquen and others the opportunity to live their own lives, free from bondage.

He watched Wybert attack the enemy warship with as much clinical disconnection as he could manage. Those flashes of light from explosions were deaths on a magnitude Addison found frightening.

Worse, they were literally in a day's work for Lazarus and the Humans he had brought with him from Brasilia.

And this was what he wanted to take with him to Zhoonarrim.

Ajax could kill Zhoonarrim station. Addison had not truly internalized that concept when Lazarus had first mentioned it. Marked it down as hyperbole.

But no.

That pirate vessel had opened fire on *Ajax* at 9087 Geminorum IV. Wybert had fired back and killed it. Simple as that.

A gasp caused Addison to look up from his screen. He had forgotten that Eha was here in the room with him, even though the smells lingering in the air would let any Churquen know what they'd been up to.

Hopefully Human olfactory senses really were as weak as the records suggested. Addison didn't feel like putting himself on report for fooling around on duty.

Even it had calmed him tremendously.

"That's what you did?" Eha asked when their eyes made contact.

She had moved around the desk to coil next to him, and could see the screens.

He had gotten so wrapped up that he had even forgotten the rest of the room existed until she made a sound.

"It is," Addison acknowledged simply.

On the screen, the enormous vessel known as *Gotland* was tumbling like a drunk Churquen on ice. Smaller vessels were taking and giving fire around them, but *Ajax* had apparently been successful enough in their initial surge.

Or those two CommandWall vessels were more important to the Westphalian fleet than Addison had understood yesterday.

"Dare we…?" Eha asked, but choked off the rest of the sentence before she could get it out.

Still, Addison understood the genesis of the question.

"We dare," he replied. "We will take this Human technology back to Innruld Space with us and use it on the Innruld themselves, and all who would support them."

"We'll bring down civilization," she whispered.

"Perhaps," Addison agreed.

He paused to consider his next words, aware that somehow the two of them had reached one of those strange moments that historians would write about in uncounted future centuries.

If *Ajax* won, the war to free the Churquen and Yithadreph and others would begin here. Possibly in this very cabin.

If they lost, whoever won the war would record this as one of those moments when history could have been changed.

But…

"We must bring down the Innruld," Addison continued, focusing on Eha's eyes as he spoke. "They will not surrender willingly, like any recalcitrant pup who has never been properly disciplined, so the pain will be magnified. It is my hope that a few examples will be sufficient to our cause."

"What's the alternative?" she asked in a hollow, dry voice out of a desert wind.

"When we met Lazarus initially, there in the nebula, *Shiva Zephyr Glaive* had just taken on a cargo designed for Dormell, Aceanx, and Zhoonarrim, Eha," he replied, reminding her that none of them had clean hands. "We were already killing the Innruld, since those narcotics did not affect any other species. Ending them, because eventually they would have hopefully stopped breeding in meaningful numbers."

"But this…"

"This is the same, Eha Dunham," Addison said. "Killing them. But there are some in the Underground who will not stop at the moment when the Innruld have been broken. They will not choose to stop until the Innruld themselves are ended. All of them, everywhere."

"Can you envision such a massacre?" Eha asked, her voice finding strength now. "Killing them all? Xenocide?"

"I am one," Addison said. "I have killed hundreds of Humans in this quest. Probably thousands of Innruld. Among Lazarus's kind, I am a sailor of no great note, save for being the first Churquen to command a warship in Rio Alliance service. In Innruld Space, I am already one of the greatest mass murderers in history. Do not forget that part."

"Will you break them, or end them?" she asked.

"Break them, be it sufficient," he replied. "End them, if it is not. That is what *Ajax* means. We, you and I, can encompass the end of Innruld Space, or we can become the end of the Innruld. Never forget that part."

On the screen, he watched a long-range shot from Kirov's invention shatter that second CommandWall.

How many lives was Addison Wolcott responsible for now? How many had he ended by bringing a Rio warfleet to this place?

Eha seemed to understand. A hand found his and gripped it tightly as he shuddered. Every shot that slammed home on one of his screens was that many more Humans he had killed.

How they managed to survive with their sanity intact he did not know.

Perhaps that was their secret? Humans were simply

insane, and thus capable of acts so outrageous that normal species quailed away from them?

"What will we do?" Eha asked as all the screens lit up, registering hits and damage as *Ajax* began mercilessly pounding away at a GunWall that was only now beginning to come around and engage them.

"We will free the Churquen," Addison said. "And all the other species. Even if that means we must fight the Humans for our liberty. That is not too great a price to pay."

There, he had said it. All those morbid thoughts that had crowded around his mind since that first moment he laid eyes on *Ajax* in the nebula.

He would take that power, and Addison Wolcott would be free.

And he would bring Hell on Earth with him.

FIFTY-FOUR
OLUCHI

OLUCHI DIDN'T LIKE to think of it as a last meal for the condemned man, but the thought niggled at the back of his mind unbidden.

They had put him in a suite that lacked being a cell only in that there were no literal bars between him and the outside world. But the windows would not open. Nor did the hallway door. He had a small front room he could use as a meeting space, presumably with an attorney if he rated one. A sleeping chamber not much larger than the double bed it contained. A bathroom at the high end of middle class, with tiled floors and walls rather than linoleum, and the nicer towels you got at the expensive hotels.

He was still a prisoner.

At least he had rated the prime rib for dinner. Medium rare and a good cut of meat. Steamed vegetables out of someone's garden instead of an industrial greenhouse. Mashed cauliflower with real butter and all the fixings on top and mixed in. Half a loaf of sourdough bread and enough garlic butter to actually enjoy it.

Enough red wine in a decanter for two glasses, if he was careful with his pour.

Oluchi ate alone after the guard closed the door and made a point of locking it as loudly as the key in the door would allow.

None of the guards had faces, all hidden away behind helmet screens even indoors, but he had learned to tell them apart by height, weight, and gender.

The one who had been his minder when Anya was busy seducing him had vanished.

Probably gone to a reeducation camp or something. Oluchi didn't ask, assuming that all the ugly truth of the situation would either come out relatively soon, or never, depending on the tradecraft of Anya's people.

So he ate, not fearing poisoning. They could just shoot him if they were really that irate. And they wouldn't waste the good cut of meat on him, so he savored his day and wondered at the many currents flowing quietly under the still waters.

Oluchi reached for the sourdough as the door unlocked. Whoever it was better damned well know what time it was and when his food had been delivered, so they could wait, or sit and watch him eat.

He didn't bother rising as Erlyn Teixeira, High Councilor generally associated with the Alliance Block, entered.

She still reminded him of Fernanda Flores, back on Yisan. That rich vibrancy of a woman that hadn't dimmed much with age. The curves that were perhaps ten pounds heavier than she'd been at twenty-five, but that just dragged your eyes down to her hips to appreciate things.

Gray hair verging on white, but shoulder length to frame sharp, green eyes. Sparkling with mischief, if he had to give them a purpose.

Oluchi wondered if someone had realized what his type

was in older women and recruited a dangerously-perfect example of what a woman could aspire to as a way of seducing him.

Not that Anya had done a bad job. Far from it. But this one might be Fernanda's long-lost sister. With all that implied.

She smiled as she entered and someone locked the door behind her.

Oluchi studied her, standing just inside the door. Translucent sea green skirt in gauze over slate gray leggings that just emphasized those calves. Thighs. Hips. White silk blouse over a chemise that promised to be a little too thin on a cold day. And she could pull off the look with nothing else underneath.

Squarish jaw and big eyes managed to complement each other in a way that made her look even more impressive, without detracting from her femininity.

But the sourdough was still warm, and he didn't feel like fencing with a beautiful pixie right now.

"There's wine," he said as he offered her his glass, setting it on the other side of the table and pulling the half-carafe closer to his plate.

He'd drunk straight from a bottle more than once when a beautiful woman was involved. Cut glass carafes almost made it feel erudite.

She smiled and stepped two feet closer to stand behind the chair as he stared at her face and chewed. Something met her satisfaction because she pulled the chair and sat.

If she had any true understanding of Oluchi Pryce's background, this woman would probably be desperately offended right now. It had been years since another woman had pulled her own chair out from the table.

But he was still a bird in a gilded cage.

Teixeira watched him chew. After a moment, she reached out for the wine and had a sip.

So if they were planning to poison him, they hadn't told her. Not that that meant much.

Oluchi still hadn't figured out sides on this one.

He had about four bites of steak left, so he went to work with a knife. Again, if they considered him dangerous, he wouldn't have anything sharp when a Councilor appeared.

Of course, if they didn't consider him occasionally dangerous, they might not respect him. Oluchi wondered if he needed to cause a scene, just to ram home a few things, in case these folks had forgotten.

Teixeira reached for the bread basket with a questioning face. And dimples.

Oluchi nodded and watched the woman butter herself a piece while he went for meat and mash.

She was wearing a subtle perfume with all the right floral hints. Naturally made, instead of industrially produced.

Usually the most expensive kind.

He wondered what he might have done to rate this level of seduction. Unless Anya had set them a high bar and they needed to surpass it.

She hadn't yet, but Teixeira looked like the kind of woman that might be willing to bid.

Oluchi might be the kind of man to let her, if she wanted something *bad enough*.

White teeth took a delicate bite of white bread and chewed. Oluchi dabbed some horseradish root in cream on his steak and played along.

They both reached for wine at the same time, so he silently toasted her, wondering how long it would be before her patience ran out and conversation interrupted the quiet.

She sipped. Oluchi found it to be a little generic. One of those red blends that were made up by an expert vintner working with second tier grapes. The leftovers from a place with inferior *terroir*, as it were.

A middle class wine.

He was not impressed.

But he was still a prisoner.

Steak done, he finished his veggies as Teixeira finished her bread.

Oluchi grabbed the last slice and used it to mop up the juices from his plate, still studying this strange creature across the table from him.

They sat and stared at each other for a moment.

"Someone forgot dessert," he said mildly, wondering if she was meant to fulfill that role.

Or had chosen to.

What are you about, madam?

She shrugged and sipped. Oluchi did the same, wondering what it was he was supposed to say to this woman. She wasn't any different than Cavalcanti, save that she arrived in a much more interesting shell. Still a Rio politician at the top of a most dangerous field.

And he was still a prisoner.

Wine done, she rose. Oluchi insulted her profusely by watching instead of rising, although he doubted she would grasp that fine of a detail.

Erlyn Teixeira didn't look like a woman who expected the world to pull out her chair from the table. And if you rose when she entered or left the room, it was a mark of her power, not her gender.

Oluchi smiled.

She returned it.

Teixeira moved to the door and knocked three times in rapid sequence. It opened immediately from the outside.

She paused, looking back over a shoulder in such a way as to show off her bottom. It was a bottom worthy of notice.

"Thank you," she said as the first words out of her mouth. She had a pleasant alto speaking voice. "You've been most helpful."

"You didn't ask anything," he replied.

"Not verbally," Teixeira grinned and slipped out.

Oluchi wondered if she was truly sharp enough to see all the things Cavalcanti had missed earlier. Or misidentified.

Whether she had sent Anya originally. Or decided to offer the other woman competition.

At least Oluchi had known what he was in for, in volunteering to stay behind.

Now he just had to see if he could pull it off.

FIFTY-FIVE

LAZARUS

LAZARUS STUDIED THE GAME BOARD, a three-dimensional assembly of vectors and curves in the orbit of IV.

Gotland was still tumbling. Lazarus wondered if that second shot had broken something significant, deep in the bowels of engineering where they couldn't patch it in the middle of a battle.

Both CommandWalls had been bashed over their heads with a frying pan.

A number of remaining vessels were in pursuit of *Ajax* right now, but they had to constantly maneuver evasively. Any time the bow got close to coming on line with them, a Phalanx or Archer would hinge their engines sideways to dodge.

"What are they doing?" Wybert's voice was suddenly less professional and more frantic, but he'd gone far further than Lazarus had expected.

"Which ones?" Lazarus asked, unsure what Wybert was looking at with those five eyes.

"This group," he said, circling a pair of Patrols that were suddenly turning tail and running.

Except that a patrol of four Phalanxes and an Archer didn't run as a group. Two of them even less so.

But Wybert had never fought a major fleet action. His only experience to date was with the guns on *Shiva Zephyr Glaive*, which were enough to chase off low-end pirates, and blowing up those pirates at 9087 Geminorum IV.

Lazarus nodded, but kept the smile inside. Four years of war college would have shown Wybert, but the Ilount wasn't panicked. Just confused.

"It might be time for me to take over, Wybert," Lazarus said quietly. "You've done one hell of a job here, but this will be something new."

The Ilount's head rotated enough for one of the side eyes to glance back, so Lazarus highlighted the fleeing group and marked what he suspected was their new vector.

Like many young officers, Wybert had mostly ignored that the battle was being fought more or less in orbit of a planet. Ships were maneuvering wildly, but still riding that gravity in such a way that they stayed more or less at the same altitude above the surface.

"They look like they're running," Lazarus told his Fusilier. "If I was in charge over there, I'd send them looping around the planet, maybe dropped down to a much lower elevation in the process, so that maybe we forget about them until they sneak up on us."

"Oh," Wybert replied. "Huh."

"So Lieutenant, your job is to watch and learn," Lazarus continued. "And perhaps snipe occasionally with Kirov, just to keep everyone honest."

"Don't we want the front shields reinforced as much as possible?" he asked.

"Yes, but this is where you have to take risks," Lazarus

said. "If they stop worrying about Kirov, they'll decide to charge us. Just moving the bow around has caused them to shy away."

"I saw that," Wybert nodded.

"Excellent," Lazarus noted. "We'll make a fleet officer out of you yet."

Wybert's whole head rotated this time, all five eyes wide with fear and consternation.

"Helm, it's time to get mean," Lazarus announced, opening the microphone to include the squadron. "Squadron, bring your bows down fifteen degrees and yaw three-five-zero. Increase speed by point six. Engineering, begin trickle-charging Kirov."

"I beg your pardon?" Ereshkiki Nisab came over the line, but H'Brige Slani was there a moment later.

"Understood, Captain," she said simply. "Proceeding to trickle charge. Ninety seconds to load."

"That will be acceptable," Lazarus said. "All vessels cycle your fire to a lull in eighty seconds and stand by. I will provide a sequence of targets for you to engage."

Kuei looked like she was playing a symphony on her keyboard now, furry hands flashing hither and yon like a hummingbird getting territorial with an intruding eagle.

Lazarus watched the ragged GunWall in pursuit suddenly have to come about as *Ajax* began to back out of orbit.

He had started with two GunWalls in the wide vicinity. Half of the closer one had been hammered mercilessly at the same time *Gotland* had been bushwhacked, and were mostly out of the battle.

Half of the more distant one had just turned tail and seemed to be fleeing, but now they would be even further out of position, if they were trying to sneak around behind him.

That left two patrols in medium range, and two more trailing in ragtag lines, trying to maintain their diamond-

and-one formation as Star Lances lashed out in both directions.

The GunWalls had a physical shield that could protect them at longer ranges as well as energy shielding. That design let them get close enough for a Phalanx to use their Star Spears to soften up a target while the Archers used their Star Lances to probe.

A Rio Alliance squadron either had to pound on the escorts to keep them at bay, or strike the Archer to keep him from sniping.

But Addison had suggested a retrograde engagement. Tempt them from too close and then taunt them by withdrawing.

And it was working. Enemy patrols had to either fire, reinforce their shields, or put extra power to the engines, but they couldn't do all three. And their flag officers had been aboard the first three vessels knocked out of the game.

Still, *Ajax* was getting hammered. And it would get a little worse as he pulled power from reinforcement for Kirov and maneuvering.

Hopefully, the senior commander over there wasn't that good.

Or that lucky.

"Helm, yaw just a little less," Lazarus called to Kuei, drawing a line on his screen and sending it to her. "Get me this shot in seventy seconds."

Kuei was just as raw and green as Wybert at pitched battled, but she'd been flying starships for decades. Even if her ears were pointed almost completely backwards right now, her hands moved smoothly.

"Aye, sir," she called faintly a moment later, remembering that she was official now, and not just another smuggler.

Lazarus watched the ships come. He'd leapt a little ahead of the pursuit with the sudden shift in tactics, and now two of the patrols were closing and two were falling further behind as they tried to fire more desperately.

Ajax's forward ray shielding was leaking like a sieve at this point, but all of the damage was on the forward hull, and *Ajax* had been designed for it.

Plus, all the forward sections were intended to be empty in battle, specifically because Lazarus had been expecting all the damage to come at them bow-on.

And you had to hit a narrow cross-section when he had his bow pointed at you. Grappling hook with three tines.

It would have been different had they reacted faster when they could just turn and rake his broadside.

But then *Ajax* had fled. Just fast enough that you had to go in headlong pursuit, instead of maneuvering wide enough to hit more hull.

Tomorrow, they would figure out better tactics, but that was tomorrow. Right now, he was a fox baiting the hounds into the swamp while he ran across tree branches.

"Engineering, what is your status?" Lazarus asked as the timer in his head counted down.

"You are fully charged, Bridge," H'Brige replied a moment later.

Lazarus checked his alignment. Prayed for all the lives he had ended today. And all those he might yet shed in this quest.

But Westphalia had invaded the Rio Alliance. There was a generally recognized border, and this fleet was on the wrong side of it, so they were in the wrong.

"Firing," Lazarus said, pressing the virtual button on his screen.

In a stern chase, you can't always keep your bow where you want it to be, in order to fire.

And maneuvering physics were brutally simple.

Kirov's Lance caught the closest Archer almost dead

center. As he had suspected, the lack of heavy fire from the biggest gun had lulled them to sleep a little. Added to that the sudden deke up and out that had forced all those ships to maneuver to stay in contact, rather than letting him flee.

They had lost track of the big gun in their excitement.

An Archer was smaller than that vessel that Wybert had engaged. And all the ruggedness was in the shield itself.

Kuei had let him bullseye that ship from far closer than was safe.

It exploded.

Worse, the beam was not a single flicker in time, but a burst of energy lasting nearly a second as all the capacitor systems dumped in sequence.

The Archer shattered, but the beam cohered.

Then it found another target, farther back and still in the chase.

Another Archer that had been taking more frequent potshots because he thought he was safe, out at the far end of Star Lance range, where the blows were softer, like being hit with a pillow rather than a fist frequently.

Lazarus still had a fist, even after it went through the first target.

The second Archer didn't shatter like the first, but it was definitely out of the battle. Maybe scrap just waiting to be hauled off by a tug.

"Wow," Wybert squeaked nervously. "I never thought about doing that."

"Advanced tactics, Wybert," Lazarus said approvingly. "And I designed this ship to do that. Kirov's Lance is a deadly innovation that will take Westphalia time to develop and steal, assuming they don't already have the plans from their spies."

"*Captain, I am receiving a number of signals from the enemy forces,*" Cormac suddenly spoke up. "*Traffic has jumped three hundred and twenty percent. Pursuing vessels have slowed down."*

Lazarus studied the survivors. Everyone had grown more distant, but that was them shutting down as hard as they could on their engines, while *Ajax* continued to accelerate.

"Kuei, slow us down, but not enough that anyone catches us," Lazarus said. "It's probably time to chase them. Coordinate with the escorts. Cormac, put me on an unencrypted channel that they have been using."

"Channel connected, Captain."

"Westphalian forces, this is Rio Alliance command vessel *Ajax*, Captain Oliveira commanding," he began in as stern a voice as he could manage. "You will surrender to my authority right now, or I will destroy all of you. Respond on this channel."

He waited, but not as long as he might have expected.

"This is Governor MacArthur, aboard the station," a man's voice came back. "What are your conditions?"

Calm. Rational. Professional. Without more than a hint of fear that *Ajax* really could annihilate the squadron. But a broken Heavy Starcruiser, two dead CommandWalls, and the other casualties that they faced would be sufficient to convince even the most stubborn that maybe they had bitten off more than they could chew.

"This is Rio Alliance Space, intruder," Lazarus announced. "You are trespassing. I will not order the station destroyed in place with you aboard, but your entire crew will transfer immediately to other vessels and then your force will retreat from this system. Failure to comply forfeits your ransom and your lives."

Lazarus figured he was probably pushing his luck and *Ajax*'s capabilities.

Maybe not. He could still stand off at a greater range

than they could shoot back. Then it would be like gaffing fish in a bucket.

On another screen, he watched as all of the remaining pursuers came to rest briefly and then backed away.

Interestingly, to keep your shield pointed this way, a GunWall ship looked like it had tucked tail when the engines shifted to maximum reverse deflection.

Nothing more maneuverable in the galaxy than a GunWall, which was why they were so dangerous. At least as long as their shields protected them from ruin.

PL-371, *P-4491*, and *P-4502* couldn't take on an Archer and expect to win, but the Phalanx was a much more balanced fight.

Plus *Ajax*.

Without a Command Admiral over there issuing orders, nobody had fired much at the Protectors, so they were largely unharmed at present. And nothing that had penetrated *Ajax*'s ray shielding had been all that hurtful. Rooms designed to be destroyed to protect frames deeper in. Hull that would actually regrow itself once shattered plates were replaced from specially-treated stores.

"We cannot allow the station to be captured," MacArthur finally replied, with about a one second light-speed lag.

"If you destroy that station, I will destroy you," Lazarus promised. "Neither you nor *Gotland* will ever make it home, although I suppose a few of your escorts might manage to evade my wrath if they can run fast enough. What is your decision, Governor?"

Longer pause this time. Thinking. Considering the value of his career against his life. For most men, that was not a particularly hard choice, but there were always fanatics that you simply could not reason with.

Do you want to die today?

Lazarus knew he had to hammer on the man's psyche

while it was still fragile from the battle just at a lull, rather than giving him time to plan and consider. *Gotland* could limp close to the station, if they had enough guns. With a staggered defensive array of GunWall vessels, they would be safe for now.

Safe for long enough.

Lazarus needed them gone before they figured that out.

"You promise safe passage?" MacArthur asked, his strong voice suddenly a little more tentative.

"If you are gone within an hour," Lazarus said. "I will not grant you time for shenanigans and booby traps. If you kill any of my sailors with such things, I will hunt you down personally, MacArthur. I will come into your bedroom in the dead of night and make sure you are awake to know who killed you. That is a promise if you wish to try me. I used to do such things in my terrible youth."

"We will withdraw," he said after a long breath, almost a sigh that the microphones still picked up.

"You have sixty minutes from now," Lazarus said. "At that moment, I will open fire on any Westphalian vessel still in system. Use them well."

Lazarus cut the line and let go his own breath as both Kuei and Wybert turned back to look at him. Cormac, not to be left out, lifted another camera from his hull just so he could make the same motion.

"Yes, I know," he said in a softer, less violent voice. "Most of that was a bluff, but hopefully they will believe it."

"What if they don't?" Wybert asked in a small squeak.

"Then they'll find out how little of it wasn't, Lieutenant."

FIFTY-SIX

LAZARUS

LAZARUS HAD NOT MOVED from his command chair. Coffee would be necessary at some point, but then he'd have to pee, and most of this situation hung on his ability to out-bluff everyone over there.

He could wait.

"Cormac, what is the status of that cargo ship?" Lazarus asked calmly.

Once things had settled down, *Ajax* had done another hard scan of the station and discovered that there was a cargo transport tucked up against it. Presumably it had been delivering supplies, and nobody had noticed it in the heat of battle.

The ship had not moved once during the shooting, so presumably it had been caught as off-guard as everyone else.

Now, it would provide an easy way for the construction crew to depart. Lazarus wondered if that was where they had been sleeping, and the ship was configured as a passenger liner or something.

He'd never worked on designing or upgrading stations to know those little details.

"*Engines are coming on line,*" Cormac replied coldly, even for a NavCrawler. "*Escorts have taken up a double ring around where it will detach, also enclosing* Gotland. *Stand by. Vessel has detached and has begun a slow redshift away from us.*"

"Maintain our current distance, but keep the bow centered on *Gotland* until they jump," Lazarus ordered.

He watched the badly mauled formation limp up out of orbit and point themselves in the general direction of Earth.

Good riddance.

"*All enemy vessels have jumped, Captain,*" Cormac announced unnecessarily as the screens went clear, leaving the four Rio warships in command of the system.

"Scan the station and begin closing slowly," Lazarus ordered. "All extra energy to the forward shields until we know nothing is going to shoot at us or explode."

"Would they do such a dishonorable thing?" Wybert cranked his head all the way around to look.

"That was why I threatened to kill the man personally," Lazarus said in a cold voice.

"Have you ever done something like that?" Kuei asked, also looking back now.

"You do not have a sufficiently-high security clearance to know that answer, Lieutenant Commander," he snapped.

Hopefully, he would never need to do something like that again.

Kuei's ears flickered back hard once and then came to rest forward again, so hopefully she had figured out the non-answer and would leave it be.

He opened the intercom and took a deep breath.

"Lt. Commander Slani to the bridge," he said simply. "H'Brige Slani to the bridge, please."

Then he poked at various menus until he located the rest of what he thought of as the Important Players for what was coming next. Addison. Aileen. Eha. Grace.

Xiuying. Even Lucas, as he would be critical for the next step.

Ereshkiki Nisab would remain with *Ajax*. As would Kuei and Wybert, but they were already present on the bridge with him.

He opened the new line.

"Could all of you come forward to the bridge for a chat?" Lazarus asked and cut the line.

He returned to the squadron channel and took a breath.

"*PL-371*," he said. "Commander Rodriguez, we're going to drop into planetary orbit and have a personal conference, outside the range of the guns on the station. You have command of the area while *Ajax* is distracted."

"Aye, sir," the man said. "We've got your back."

Lazarus waited until everyone had arrived. H'Brige had the furthest to come, and was last. She blinked a little in surprise when she saw everyone waiting for her.

She took a seat like the others when gestured and Lazarus noted all the bright smiles and nervousness around him.

The newcomers had never seen Human violence on fleet scales, so Addison, Eha, and Aileen were a little frazzled from their body language. Wybert and Kuei were less so, but they'd been in the thick of it.

Grace took his breath away still, but he had to put that aside to concentrate on matters at hand.

"H'Brige, I'm going to work on the presumption that there are no bombs left behind, or reactors set to overload, but we're still going to wait an entire day before we board," Lazarus focused his attention on her. "That's where you come in."

"Me?"

Her tail fluttered just a bit at the very tips. You had to be paying attention to see it. And then not blink.

"This station is only partly complete, but most of the

materials are probably on hand in shipping containers over there," Lazarus said. "Certainly, I didn't give them time to do much in terms of removing anything. And I expect someone to come back eventually, either to destroy it or try to capture the station again, so it needs to be completed as soon as possible. I want you to take command over there and oversee the completion of the station."

She gasped, but that was fine. H'Brige Slani was a Lieutenant Commander, and he had just offered her a slot that would normally be filled by a Captain in Rio Alliance service. That would look excellent on her record in the future, but she'd already impressed him with her ability to get things done.

She fell into thought.

"Permission to speak freely, sir?" H'Brige said in a guarded voice after a moment.

"Granted."

"You aren't staying, are you, Captain?" she asked as the others stirred uncomfortably. "*Ajax* will deposit a repair crew, wait a few days, and then you are heading to Innruld Space, unless I miss my guess."

"What makes you think that, H'Brige?" Lazarus asked.

"You could take command of the station, sir," she grinned. "And leave Commander Wolcott here. Or vice versa. Thus, you're both unavailable. That does not suggest that *Ajax* is immediately returning to Brasilia."

"And?" he asked.

"And I would like to go with you, Captain," she turned serious. "Atomarsk are, as everyone here has said, just a legend in those systems. I want to see what that means, much more than a gold star on my record for overseeing the construction. Thank you for thinking of me, by the way, and the vote of confidence."

"You could handle it, H'Brige," Lazarus nodded. "But I

also understand your concerns. And you are right, but I hereby order you not to tell anyone until I do."

"Understood, sir."

Lazarus let his eyes unfocus for a moment and then keyed the comm again.

"Chief Garcia to the bridge," he called. "Chief Elena Garcia to the bridge."

Lazarus watched the confusion percolate around him. Everyone except Xiuying and Grace, which he found informative. Even Lucas Lam was lost right now.

The Chief arrived a few minutes later, messy with something that had splattered her left side with some black lubricating oil. Hopefully none of it had been hot, but Lazarus didn't think that even that would slow the woman down.

"Sir?" she came to rigid attention as she saw everyone seated around her.

"At ease, Chief."

Lazarus studied her in turn.

Gruff, loud, tough, competent. Everything you wanted in an Engineering Chief.

Shorter than average but broad, like a normal-sized woman squished some. Darker than many in the Rio Alliance, but still *Sud American*, rather than African origin like Grace. Smarter than the average bear, though.

"Chief, I have a problem," Lazarus said in a light voice. "I need you to solve it for me."

"Sir?" she echoed in an unsure voice now.

"Lieutenant Commander Slani has turned me down, Chief Garcia." Lazarus smiled at both women now to put them at ease. "I need someone to go over to the station tomorrow and take command of it while also completing construction. That is, as Slani has noted, normally a Captain's slot, rather than a Chief's, but I'm remarkably short of staff right now. Can I entice you into a brevet, field promotion to Commander, subject to approval by the Admiralty Staff at a later date? I honestly don't know if Admiral Santos would uphold it, but he might, after what we've accomplished here. Doubly so after you finish things off over there and he can route proper forces over to relieve you later. You will be in command of the station until such relief arrives."

Lazarus had expected her to turn white at his words, not blush.

But she went umber now, her skin suffusing with blood.

Then—and only then—she paled.

"Where are you going, sir?" Garcia asked. "That you won't be here in command?"

"Innruld Space, Garcia," he replied. "That will remain your secret. I'll leave you all three of the escorts and most of the gunnery crews and engineers as well, because I won't need them as much as you will."

"Won't you be violating your orders, sir?" she asked carefully.

"Most likely, but you don't worry about that, Garcia," Lazarus said. "You have a job to do entirely separate from mine. If I have to go into open rebellion against the Admiralty Staff and Admiral Santos, that happens after you accept this job, so it will not reflect on you."

"If you say so, sir," she seemed uncertain.

Lazarus turned to the marine next.

"Now, Lucas, I know you'd like to join us, but I need you to handle security on the station," Lazarus turned to the marine.

"Begging pardon, Lazarus," Xiuying spoke up suddenly. "But if it's okay with you, I'll swap billets with Lucas and take that gig. Closer to what I was doing on Yisan, and all that."

Both men smiled, so Lazarus wondered if they had had this conversation yesterday.

"You're sure?" he asked. "Both of you?"

Both men nodded.

"Time in grade, sir," Xiuying said. "I need a couple more months to step up a notch on my retirement pay."

"This is nominally a Lieutenant Commander's slot, Bălan," Lazarus pointed out.

"And if I had all that service time and ended with extra promotion on top of it, sir, it's just about double my current retirement pay, too."

Lazarus shared his grin.

"All right, Xiuying," Lazarus said. "You're her First Officer. Assuming you'll take the gig, Garcia?"

"Sir, absolutely, sir," she smiled now.

"Lucas, you just became my Security Marine aboard *Ajax*, subject to the Fusilier's orders," Lazarus turned to the newest member of his crazy force. "Recruitment will include almost exclusively non-Humans, so start familiarizing yourself with the current crew and prepare for your first Kreeghal."

"Kreeghal, sir?" Lam asked.

Aileen laughed.

"Don't wrestle one, whatever you do, Lucas," she said, snorting and shivering with laughter.

He nodded, a little lost, but that was fine.

Eha leaned forward now, catching his eye.

"I promised those people on Brasilia that I would return shortly," she said simply.

"Yes, but I need you in Innruld Space, Eha," Lazarus said. "I need you to connect me, us, with the Species Underground, if I'm going to be a revolutionary, and not just another pirate. Nobody else here has the connections I need to pull this off in any sort of time. And I will not trust strangers with this level of firepower."

He gestured to the monument to war around them.

"The Innruld must be broken before Westphalia figures out what they could do over there," Addison spoke up now. "And before the Rio Alliance finally gets off their coil and decides to do the right thing."

"You are sure that they will?" Eha turned to her mate.

"They sent Lazarus and *Ajax*," he nodded. "Protector/Escorts and crews. The internal arguments on Brasilia might be ugly and loud, but at the end of the day they made the right choice, as Lazarus has always told us they will."

"I made a promise," she said curtly, as if that was the end of it.

In a way, it was. Lazarus understood that. But to free the Species Underground, he needed to become a rebel in Rio Space, just as he was in the Innruld sectors. Eha Dunham already was there as well, so she could join him.

"This will not work without you, Eha," Addison said with a hint of a shrug around the shoulders and in the scales on his jaw. "But I have a suggestion."

"What?" she demanded, maybe a little louder than she was expecting, to watch her pupils slit open.

"You go with Lazarus to Zhoonarrim," Addison said. "Or Aceanx. Wherever your connections can get you the crew and support you need."

He turned this way and Lazarus saw all the pain in his eyes.

"I will return to Brasilia with one of the escorts, bearing news," Addison continued. "And as the Species Underground representative here, assuming that Oluchi is not already doing a better job than I ever could. That puts us at opposite ends of the galaxy, but it will be necessary for a short time yet."

His eyes slid back to Eha with infinite sadness in them now.

"We have waited a decade," Addison said. "And had a moment of triumphant glory. I can wait another year."

Lazarus watched her lungs fill to argue with the man, but she subsided like a pricked balloon. Studied Addison. Turned his way and let Lazarus see her own level of pain.

They were both older than he was, relative life span, but it had been something of a teen romance ignited on his deck, to watch the two of them fall in love.

She snapped her jaw now, in a moment when a Human with molars would have been grinding them.

Duty was a complete and utter bitch, and only Lazarus was going to be able to defy his. Or rather, both of them were now answering to a higher calling. One that did not rely on the old laws of the Innruld or the Rio Alliance.

"Yes," she said, defeated.

Addison reached out a hand to squeeze hers. Everyone felt a moment of sorrow on their behalf.

"You should take Remahle with you," Aileen spoke up, drawing all heads around in surprise.

"What?" Addison stammered.

"He was complaining earlier that he never gets to go have adventures with the rest of us," Aileen said. "Either Yisan or Brasilia or anywhere else. Just has to stay here and count boxes with me gone. Since I'm back, maybe it's his turn."

Addison turned and Lazarus nodded.

It made a certain bit of sense. Aileen was better at logistics than *anyone* he was likely to find. And Addison would do well to have someone along that he could talk to. Oluchi was still Human, and didn't have the depth of Innruld culture to draw on. Not like a Kr'Mari.

Plus a species Lazarus might compare to a glider squirrel was likely to be hauled planetside and given a tall building to jump off of, just to demonstrate.

He suspected that Remahle would enjoy that part, too.

"Very well," Lazarus announced. "It is decided and I will draw up orders for everyone tonight after Khyaa'sha makes us a final dinner together."

He reached out and keyed the squadron comm line open again.

"*PL-371*," the voice replied instantly. "Rodriguez here."

"Commander, I'm going to need you to fly yourself and two pinckes over here in a few hours so you can join us for dinner and a planning session," Lazarus said. "Then I'm going to requisition one of the shuttles for *Ajax* for the long term, and you're going to send the second one back to Brasilia with messages and a request for squadron reinforcements, crew for the station, and supplies."

"I see, sir," Rodriguez said in a sinking voice, like he had already figured out where all this was going. "Is this a wise course of action, Captain?"

"It is necessary, Commander," Lazarus replied. "Some things are bigger than any of us. Keep that in mind."

"Aye, sir," the man said. "Best of luck on your mission, Captain Oliveira."

"And you," Lazarus said, cutting the line.

"Necessary?" Grace asked him. Of all of the people present in the room, she was the one he least expected to speak now.

"Necessary," Lazarus answered with a nod.

FIFTY-SEVEN
OLUCHI

OLUCHI WAS late into his evening, reading a paper book that he had found on a shelf when nobody would allow him any sort of electronics. Not that they should have known what he might be able to do. As far as Oluchi knew, his previous proclivities were unknown on Brasilia, so he supposed just a modicum of acute paranoia on their part.

That or they really wanted to torture him with literature, not understanding his love for the ancients. Oluchi considered stealing this worn and well-thumbed copy of *The Prophet* when he was let out of here, assuming that it wasn't a real jail cell.

And even then he might request that they let him take Kahlil Gibran into solitary confinement with him.

Oluchi sat in his semi-comfortable chair and let the words wash over him like the evening tide coming in.

> *And others came also and entreated*
> *him.* (he said) *But he answered*
> *them not. He only bent his head;*

*and those who stood near saw his
    tears falling on his breast.
And he and the people proceeded
    towards the great square before the
    temple.*

*And there came out of the sanctuary a
    woman whose name was Almitra.
And she was a seeress.
And he looked upon her with exceeding
    tenderness, for it was she who had
    first sought and believed in him
    when he had been but a day in
    their city.*

A knock at the door seemed to echo down from heaven, dragging Oluchi up from the depths of night.

He was amazed that the door wasn't just thrust open by someone large and imposing who wanted to stomp in and scowl at the furniture.

The furnishings would probably care more than Oluchi would, after all.

He marked his page with a finger and rose, stepping close to the door and putting a hand on the cold, chrome handle.

Oluchi turned it and stepped back, surprised that it opened to his wishes.

Anya stepped into the room and closed the door behind her softly.

Her scent marked him from a step away. Stronger than Teixeira's had been earlier. Bolder, perhaps. More certain.

She grinned and leaned forward for a kiss, so he obliged.

Anya looked down at the book in his hands and pulled at it, slipping her own finger in to mark his spot as she turned and looked at the spine. Her eyes twinkled mischievously.

"*And one of the elders of the city said Speak to us of Good and Evil,*" she quoted at him, still a stride apart.

Oluchi smiled. At least he understood who had placed the book here for him to find.

> *Of the good in you I can speak, but not*
> *of the evil. (he said)*
> *For what is evil but good tortured by its*
> *own hunger and thirst?*
> *Verily when good is hungry it seeks food*
> *even in dark caves, and when it*
> *thirsts it drinks even of dead waters.*
>
> *You are good when you are one with*
> *yourself.*
> *Yet when you are not one with yourself*
> *you are not evil.*
> *For a divided house is not a den of*
> *thieves; it is merely a divided house.*
> *And a ship without rudder may wander*
> *aimlessly among perilous isles yet*
> *sink not to the bottom.*

Her smile expanded to encompass the entire room. She held the book to one side and kissed him fully now, her other arm sliding around his side to pull him against her hungrily.

Oluchi wondered if someone had miscalculated again with their preferred methods of torture. After all, he wasn't sure he could suffer such ministrations from this woman for more than a month or six before she broke him.

Not that he was opposed to such a contest of wills.

"You won me twenty cruzeiros," she whispered in his ear as she continued to hold him.

Oluchi wrapped both hands around her and let them

wander free.

Condemned men and final suppers, as it were.

"Did I now?" he murmured.

"Erlyn Teixeira expected you to make a pass at her over dinner," Anya giggled quietly. "To turn the charm up to eleven to see if you could fast talk your way out of this situation, or somehow arrange an escape from captivity. Or just invite her to bed because you could."

"I've spent enough years running from responsibility," he countered. "And she'll need to come to Yisan sometime to compare herself directly with Fernanda if she's serious about seducing me."

"You'd prefer that?" she asked, pouting, but it was an act. The grin in her eyes said that.

"Smart, powerful, confident, sexy women throwing themselves at me?" he grinned back. "Perish the thought. She'd only be competing with Fernanda for second place anyway."

"I got interrupted at breakfast," Anya snuggled up close, still holding the book but entirely focused on him.

"Were you going to say something bad?" he asked into her hair.

"No," she leaned back enough to study his face. "My cover isn't completely blown yet, but only because I have powerful personages like Erlyn protecting me while others will be magnificently compromised and embarrassed if the story does come out."

"But you will be unemployed at some point in the near future?" he asked, adding a lascivious grin. "Available for recruitment?"

"Worse," she said, grinning. "Attached to some weird-ass foreign embassy as bureaucratic make-weight. Transferred out of Planning and I probably won't even get to count that time against future promotions and retirement benefits."

"The horrors," he whispered back, sneaking a kiss because she seemed to be inviting it.

She spoke now in a faint but firm voice.

> *When love beckons to you, follow him,*
> > *(Anya quoted as he listened*
> > *to her)*
> *Though his ways are hard and steep.*
> *And when his wings enfold you yield*
> > *to him,*
> *Though the sword hidden among his*
> > *pinions may wound you.*
> *And when he speaks to you believe*
> > *in him,*
> *Though his voice may shatter your*
> > *dreams as the north wind lays waste*
> > *the garden.*
>
> *For even as love crowns you so shall he*
> > *crucify you. Even as he is for your*
> > *growth so is he for our pruning.*
> *Even as he ascends to your height and*
> > *caresses your tenderest branches that*
> > *quiver in the sun,*
> *So shall he descend to your roots and*
> > *shake them in their clinging to the*
> > *earth.*

"So what can I do for you, Anya Persaud?" Oluchi asked, turning serious now.

"Take me to bed and make love to me," she replied, equally seriously. "Tomorrow morning they are going to take you up on the offer to become Eha Dunham's deputy."

READ MORE

Be sure to read all the books in the Lazarus Alliance series!

Escape
Return
Rebellion
Revolution
Liberation
Retribution
Alliance

Available at your favorite retailers!

ABOUT THE AUTHOR

Blaze Ward writes science fiction in the Alexandria Station universe (Jessica Keller, The Science Officer, The Story Road, etc.) as well as several other science fiction universes, such as Star Dragon, the Dominion, and more. He also writes odd bits of high fantasy with swords and orcs. In addition, he is the Editor and Publisher of *Boundary Shock Quarterly Magazine.* You can find out more at his website www.blazeward.com, as well as Facebook, Goodreads, and other places.

Blaze's works are available as ebooks, paper, and audio, and can be found at a variety of online vendors. His newsletter comes out regularly, and you can also follow his blog on his website. He really enjoys interacting with fans, and looks forward to any and all questions—even ones about his books!

Never miss a release!
If you'd like to be notified of new releases, sign up for my newsletter.

http://www.blazeward.com/newsletter/

Buy More!
Did you know that you can buy directly from my website?

https://www.blazeward.com/shop/

Connect with Blaze!

Web: www.blazeward.com
Boundary Shock Quarterly (BSQ):
https://www.boundaryshockquarterly.com/

ABOUT KNOTTED ROAD PRESS

Knotted Road Press fiction specializes in dynamic writing set in mysterious, exotic locations.

Knotted Road Press non–fiction publishes autobiographies, business books, cookbooks, and how–to books with unique voices.

Knotted Road Press creates DRM–free ebooks as well as high–quality print books for readers around the world.

With authors in a variety of genres including literary, poetry, mystery, fantasy, and science fiction, Knotted Road Press has something for everyone.

Knotted Road Press
www.KnottedRoadPress.com

www.ingramcontent.com/pod-product-compliance
Lightning Source LLC
Chambersburg PA
CBHW060237100726
47907CB00003B/665